Praise for

Tamed

"An endearing, laugh-out-loud, funny read. If you loved Drew, you'll love Matthew. Once again, Emma Chase doesn't disappoint."
—K. Bromberg, bestselling author of *Driven*, *Fueled*, and *Crashed*

Fans are talking, texting, and blogging about Emma Chase and her *New York Times* and *USA Today* bestselling series

"Emma Chase will keep you enthralled and captivated. A brilliant 5-star read!!!!" (Neda, *The Subclub Books*) • "A brilliant, out-of-this-world hysterical, swoon-worthy five stars. Emma Chase's unforgettable characters are absolutely beyond compare. One of the best reads of 2013." (Tessa, *Books Wine Food*) • "It was absolutely amazing! Drew Evans is hands down my favorite leading man." (Liz, *Romance Addiction*) • "A 5-heart read. It's perfection in a book. RΛWR hot, hilariously funny, and a romance so good you won't want it to end." (Tamie & Elena, *Bookish Temptations*) • "*Tangled* is panty-dropping, outrageously funny, and overwhelmingly lovely. I finished it in nearly one sitting because I had to know more of Drew and Kate." (Angie, *Smut Book Club*) • "Witty and hilarious insight into a man's head. I fell in love with Drew Evans's playful and cocky attitude and I will never forget him. . . . A sexy hero." (Lucia, *Reading is My Breathing*) • "The characters are insanely hilarious! Drew had my sides splitting and in stitches with his witty and undeniably competitive personality! The funniest and most creative book told by the male point-of-view. You will not be able to put this book down!" (Stephanie, *Romance Addict Book Blog*)

ALSO BY EMMA CHASE

Tangled

Twisted

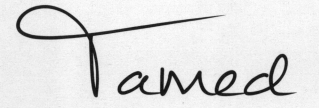

Tamed

Emma Chase

GALLERY BOOKS

New York   London   Toronto   Sydney   New Delhi

G

Gallery Books
A Division of Simon & Schuster, Inc.
1230 Avenue of the Americas
New York, NY 10020

First Gallery Books trade paperback edition July 2014

GALLERY BOOKS and colophon are registered trademarks of Simon & Schuster, Inc.

For information about special discounts for bulk purchases, please contact Simon & Schuster Special Sales at 1-866-506-1949 or business@simonandschuster.com.

The Simon & Schuster Speakers Bureau can bring authors to your live event. For more information or to book an event, contact the Simon & Schuster Speakers Bureau at 1-866-248-3049 or visit our website at www.simonspeakers.com.

Manufactured in the United States of America

10 9 8 7 6 5 4 3 2 1

Library of Congress Cataloging-in-Publication Data is available.

ISBN 978-1-4767-6360-6
ISBN 978-1-4767-6361-3 (ebook)

This one is for all the "nice" guys and "crazy" girls in the world. May you find each other and enjoy the roller coaster ride of life together.

Acknowledgments

By the time *Tamed* is released it will have been one year since *Tangled,* book #1 in the Tangled Series, was published. What an amazing, beautiful year it's been! I'm tremendously grateful to be able to work with so many talented and dedicated individuals, who believe in me, my writing, and these fun, heartfelt stories.

Thanks to my super-agent, Amy Tannenbaum, and everyone at the Jane Rotrosen Agency for your wonderful guidance, encouragement, and support. Thanks to my editor, Micki Nuding, publicists Juliana and Kristen, and the entire Gallery Books family for all you've done to make these books more than they ever would've been without you. I'm always grateful for Nina Bocci of Bocci PR for your superb advisement and enthusiasm. Thanks to the tireless online bloggers for helping so many readers discover and fall in love with these characters—please never stop doing what you do!

I am so grateful for my readers—the best in the world. Thank you for each online post, email, and message—I read every one!

Your excitement is humbling and inspiring. Thank you for loving these characters every bit as much as I do.

Finally, to my husband, my children, and my whole family: I love you. Thank you for your unending patience and encouragement—and for giving me a lifetime of golden comedic material.

Tamed

Chapter 1

During the last few weeks, it's been brought to my attention that sometimes women actually like to cry. They cry over books, TV shows, those awful abused-animal commercials, and movies—especially movies. Sitting down to purposely watch something you know will make you unhappy? It makes no frigging sense.

But that's okay; I'm just going to chalk it up to another thing I will never understand about my girlfriend. Yes—I said girlfriend. Dee Warren is officially my girlfriend.

One more time for those in the back—girlfriend—Delores—*mine*.

Repeating it might make me sound like a Harry Styles–obsessed prepubescent girl, but I don't give a damn. Because it was a hard-won victory—if you knew what I had to go through to make her mine, you'd understand.

Anyway, back to what I was saying. Chicks like to cry—but this isn't one of those stories. There's no dying best friends, no dark tortured pasts, no hidden secrets, no sparkly vampire break-ups, and no kinky fuckery.

Well . . . okay . . . there's some kinky fuckery—but it's the happy kind.

This is a story about a player, who meets a slightly crazy girl. They fall in love and the player changes his ways forever. It's a story you've probably heard before, maybe even from my buddy, Drew Evans. But the thing is, while he and Kate were figuring their shit out? There was this whole alternate universe going on with Delores and me that you don't know about. So stick around, even if you think you already know the ending. Because the great-est part of a road trip isn't arriving at your destination. It's all the wild stuff that happens along the way.

Before we start, there's some background info you may need to know. First off—Drew's a great guy, a true best friend. If we were the Rat Pack, he'd be Frank Sinatra, I'd be Dean Martin. Although Drew and I are tight, we differ in our opinions about women. At this point in our tale, he sees himself as a bachelor for life. He's got all these rules about never bringing a chick to his apartment, never dating someone he works with, and the Cardi-nal Rule: Never hook up with the same woman twice.

I, on the other hand, don't care where I get laid—my place, her place, the observation deck of the Empire State Building.

That was a great night.

I'm also not opposed to seeing someone from the office—though most of the girls in my line of work are stressed out, chain smoking, coffee-obsessed women with an unpleasant chip on their shoulders. I have no problem hanging out with the same woman on multiple occasions, as long as the good times keep rolling. And someday, I imagine myself settling down—marriage, kids, the whole deal.

But while I'm looking for Mrs. Right? I'm having a blast with all the Ms. Wrongs.

Secondly, I'm a real glass-half-full kind of person. Nothing gets me down. I have a great life—a good career that lets me enjoy the best man-toys on the market, awesome friends, a weird but loving family. "Emo" doesn't exist in my vocabulary, but YOLO should've been my middle name.

Next up is Delores Warren—Dee, if you want to stay on her good side. By today's standards it's an unusual name, but for her it's a perfect fit. She's unusual—different—in all the best kinds of ways. She's brutally honest, emphasis on "brutal." She's strong and doesn't give a rat's ass what people think of her. She's true to herself and makes no apologies for what she wants or who she is. She's wild and beautiful—like an undomesticated thoroughbred that runs best without a saddle.

And that was where I almost went wrong. I wanted to tame her. I thought I had the patience for it, but I pushed too hard and pulled too much on the reins. So she broke them.

Are you offended that I compared the woman I love to a horse? Get the fuck over it—this is not a tale the PC police will enjoy.

But I'm getting ahead of myself. Just know that Kate Brooks is our coworker and Delores's best friend—the Shirley to Dee's Laverne. And in all the years I've known Drew—which is every one of them—I've never seen him react to a woman like he reacted to Kate. Their attraction, even though it was mostly antagonistic in the beginning, was palpable. Anybody with eyes could see they had it bad for each other.

Well . . . anybody but them.

Kate, like Delores, is a great girl. The type of woman who, in the immortal words of Eddie Murphy in *Coming to America,* could arouse a man's intellect as well as his loins.

You got all that? Great. Let's get this party started.

My life changed about four weeks ago. On a normal, average day—when I met a girl who was anything but average.

Four weeks earlier

"Matthew Fisher, Jack O'Shay, Drew Evans, this is Dee-Dee Warren."

There's no such thing as love at first sight. It's just not possible. Sorry to ruin your fantasy, but that's how it is. Ignorance might feel like bliss, but when you peel away the happy layer, it's still just a lack of information.

To really love another person, you have to know them—their quirks, their dreams, what pisses them off and makes them smile, their strengths, weaknesses, and flaws. Have you heard that quote from the Bible—the one they always read at weddings: "Love is patient, love is kind . . ."? I have my own version: Love is missing the taste of someone's morning breath. Thinking they're beautiful, even when their nose is Rudolph-red and their hair is bird's nest crazy. Love isn't putting up with someone in spite of their faults—it's adoring them because of them.

Now lust at first sight, that's very real. And much more common. In fact, when most guys meet a woman, they know within the first five minutes which category of "fuck, kill, marry" they fall into. For guys, the fuck category has a pretty low bar.

I'd like to tell you the first thing I noticed about Delores was something romantic, like her eyes, or her smile, or the sound of her voice—but it wasn't. It was her tits. I've always been a boob man, and Dee's set was fantastic. Slightly overflowing in a tight, hot-pink top, pressed together just right to create an enticing cleft of cleavage, beautifully framed by a gray knit sweater.

Before she uttered her first word to me, I was in lust with Delores Warren's rack.

After she banters with Drew for a minute, I steer her attention my way. "So, Dee-Dee . . . is that short for something? Donna, Deborah?"

Warm, honey-colored eyes turn my way. But before she can answer, Kate lets the cat out of the bag, "Delores. It's a family name—her grandmother's. She hates it."

Delores glares playfully at Kate.

If you want to make an impression on a girl, humor is always a safe bet. It shows a woman you're clever, smart, confident. If you've got balls? Flaunt them.

Which is why I tell Kate's friend, "Delores is a gorgeous name, for a gorgeous girl. Plus, it rhymes with *clitoris* . . . and I really know my way around them. Big fan."

As planned, my line gets an instant reaction. She smiles slowly and runs one finger across her lower lip, suggestively. Any time a woman touches her body in response to something a guy's said? It's a good sign.

Then, she breaks our gaze and says to us all, "Anyhoo. I have to jet, gotta get to work. Nice meeting you, boys." Dee-Dee hugs Kate and winks at me. *Also a good sign.*

I watch her as she walks out and can't help but notice the rear view is almost as awesome as the front.

Drew asks Kate, "She's got to get to work? I thought the strip clubs didn't open until four."

I have to agree with him on that one. When you've been to as many strip clubs as we have, you start to see a pattern. The clothes the women wear—though minimal—are similar. Like they all shop at the same store. And Dee is definitely rocking the Strippers "R" Us vibe.

Though it may just be wishful thinking on my part. It would be awesome if she were a dancer. Not only are they limber—they party hard. Totally uninhibited. The fact that they generally have a low opinion of the male species is a plus too. Because it means the simplest act of chivalry is returned with extreme gratitude. And a grateful stripper is a blow-job giving stripper.

But Kate dashes my hopes. "Dee's not a stripper. She just dresses like that to throw people off. So they're shocked when they find out what she really does."

"What does she do?" I ask.

"She's a rocket scientist."

Jack reads my mind. "You're fucking with us."

"Afraid not. Delores is a chemist. One of her clients is NASA. Her lab works on improving the efficiency of the fuel they use on the space shuttles." She shivers. "Dee-Dee Warren with access to highly explosive substances . . . it's something I try to not think about."

And now my curiosity is almost as strong as my lust. I've always had a taste for the unusual—the exotic—in women, music, books. And unlike Drew, whose apartment is meticulously decorated, I tend to gravitate toward pieces with a history. Even if they don't match, nontraditional is always interesting.

"Brooks, you've got to hook me up. I'm a nice guy. Let me take your friend out. She won't regret it."

Kate thinks about it. Then she says, "Okay. Sure. You seem like Dee's type." She hands me a neon-green business card. "But I have to warn you. She's the love-'em-and-leave-'em-with-bruises type of girl. If you're looking for a good time for a night or two, then definitely call her. If you're looking for anything deeper than that, I'd stay away."

And now I know how Charlie felt when he was handed the last golden ticket to Wonka's Chocolate Factory.

I stand up from the table and kiss Kate on the cheek. "You . . . are my new best friend."

I consider hugging her too—just to fuck with my scowling buddy—but I don't want to risk getting nut-punched. I have plans for my nuts. They need to be in top form.

Kate tells Drew not to pout, and he makes a comment about her boobs, but I'm only half listening. Because I'm too busy thinking about where I'll be meeting Delores Warren for a drink—or several. And all the fantastically lascivious activities that are sure to follow.

So that's how it started. It wasn't supposed to be complicated—no love at first sight, no grand gestures, no hard feelings. A sure thing, a good time, a one-night stand with an option for a second. That's what Kate told me Dee was into, and that's all I was looking for. All I thought it would ever be.

Elvis Presley was right. Fools really do rush in. And if you haven't figured it out yet, I'm a major fucking fool.

Chapter 2

A lot of people live for their job. Not because they're forced to financially, but because what they do for a living is who they are—their profession gives them confidence, purpose, maybe even an adrenaline rush. It's not always a bad thing. The office is a businessman's playground, a courtroom to a lawyer feels like home. And if I ever need a surgeon? Only a full-blown workaholic is getting near me.

That being said, I'm an investment banker at one of the most respected and prestigious firms in the city. I'm good at my job, the paycheck is nice, I serve my clients well—keep them happy and keep new ones coming in. But I wouldn't say I love it. It's not a passion. When I die, I'm not going to go out wishing I had spent more time at the office.

I'm similar to my father in that respect. He's committed to the firm he, John, and George founded, but he doesn't let the obligations interfere with his golf game. And he's an old-fashioned family man—he always was. Growing up, dinner was served at six o'clock sharp. Every night. If my ass wasn't in that dining room chair, I'd better have been in the Emergency Room, or there was hell to pay. Dinnertime discussion focused heavily on "What did you do today?" and "Nothing" was never an acceptable response. Being an only child, there weren't any siblings to distract my parents from keeping tabs on me. My old man was well aware of the potential pitfalls of growing up privileged in New York City, so he made damn sure I stayed out of trouble.

Well . . . most of the time, anyway.

Every kid deserves to get into a little trouble. It helps them learn to be resourceful, think on their feet. And if a teenager isn't allowed to have some kind of life, they'll go totally ape-shit when they get to college. Which could end badly.

My father's three basic rules were: Keep your grades up, keep your criminal record clean, and keep your pants zipped.

Two out of three ain't bad, right?

Even though my dad knows the importance of family and separating business from pleasure, that doesn't mean I get a free pass at the firm because I'm his son. Actually, I think he rides my ass a lot harder than the other employees', just to avoid any claims of favoritism. Impropriety at the office is something he would never tolerate. He'd come down on it like Gallagher's sledgehammer on a watermelon.

Which is another reason my dad and his partners were able to build such a successful business—because each of them brings their own unique talents to the team. John Evans, Drew and Alexandra's father, is like Face from the A-Team. He's the charmer, the convincer—he makes sure the clients are happy and the employees are not only content, but enthusiastic. Then there's George Reinhart—Steven's dad. George is the brains of the operation. My dad and John aren't exactly lacking in that department, but

George is like Stephen Hawking without the ALS. He's the only guy I know who actually enjoys the technical, number-punching aspect of investment banking.

Then there's my father, Frank—he's the muscle. The intimidator. He's a man of few words, which means when he speaks, your ears better fucking be listening, because he's saying something worth hearing. And he has no problem firing people. My dad makes Donald Trump look like a pussy. Doesn't matter if you're the sole family breadwinner or a pregnant woman in her last trimester—if you're not getting the job done, you're out on your ass. Tears don't move him, and second chances are rare. Ever since I was a kid, he'd say, "Matthew, family is family, friends are friends, and business is business. Don't confuse them."

Even though he's a hard-ass, he's always fair. Honest. Keep your i's dotted and your t's crossed and there won't be a problem. I always make sure my i's are dotted and my t's are crossed. Not just because I prefer to keep my job, but because . . . I'd never want to disappoint my old man. Sadly, that attitude's become scarce. So many little assholes running around today give no thought to making their parents proud—but it's what Drew, Alexandra, Steven, and I were raised on.

Anyway, back to the real story.

After lunch with the guys, I spend the rest of the afternoon at my desk, drafting a contract and making nice with clients on the telephone. Around six o'clock, I'm packing up when Steven comes breezing through my door.

"Guess who spent their lunch break surrounded by rabid gamers in line for the latest fix?"

I slip a folder into my briefcase for some non-enjoyable reading before bed. If you don't want to live life chained to a desk? Time management is crucial.

I answer, "That would be you?"

He smiles and nods. "Damn straight, brother. And look what I scored."

He holds up a square cellophane-wrapped package.

Back in my father's day, guys would occasionally get together for a fishing trip or drinks at the local pub to unwind after a long day's work. But what Steven holds in his hands is more addictive than alcohol and a hell of a lot more fun that baiting a hook.

It's the latest edition of *Call of Duty.*

"Sweet." I take the disk from his hand and flip it over, checking out the updated real-to-life graphics.

"You up for a mission tonight? Around nine?"

In case you don't already know—Steven is married. And he's not just married—he's married to Alexandra-formerly-Evans, also known as The Bitch. But you didn't hear that last part from me.

If a regular wife is a ball at the end of a chain? Alexandra's a Sherman tank. She keeps Steven on a short leash—doesn't let him come out to the bars on Saturday night, only allows him one poker game a month. Even though Steven's not the straying kind, Alexandra thinks hanging out with us carefree, single friends would be a bad influence on her husband. And . . . she's probably right.

But, like any good warden knows, you can only restrict the inmates so much. You can lock them in a cage ten hours a day, ban yard time—but try and take away their cigarettes? You've got a major revolt on your hands.

Xbox is Steven's one permissible vice. As long as his playtime doesn't disturb their daughter, Mackenzie, after she's down for the night. One time, Steven got a little too loud during an ambush and woke Mackenzie up. He was on lockdown for a week. Lesson learned.

"Yeah, dude, count me in."

I hand him the game back and he says, "Cool. See you at twenty-one hundred." Then he salutes me and heads out the door.

I pick up my briefcase and gym bag and walk out a few minutes later. On the way to the elevator, I swing by Drew's office.

He's bent over his paper-covered desk, making notes with a red pen on a document.

"Hey."

He glances up, "Hey."

"Xbox tonight, nine o'clock. Steven's got the new *Call of Duty.*"

With his attention back on the paper, Drew says, "Can't. I'm gonna be here until ten, at least."

The people I mentioned who live for the job? Drew Evans is that kind of people.

But it works for him. He's not a bedraggled, stressed-out clock puncher—he's the exact opposite. Drew genuinely enjoys the grind; he gets a rush out of negotiating a deal, even if it's a hard sell. Because he knows he can close it, that he's probably the only one who can.

Well . . . at least until a certain dark-haired woman joined our ranks.

I look across the hall to Kate's office. She's at her desk, the mirror image of Drew—but way hotter.

Leaning against the chair, I say, "Did you hear Kate's close to signing the Pharamatab account?"

Still not looking up, he mutters grumpily, "Yeah, I heard."

I smirk. "You better step it up, man. If she makes that deal, your old man's gonna be so psyched I wouldn't be surprised if he wants to adopt her. And incest—even between adopted siblings—is illegal in New York."

Busting balls is what friends do. It's the equivalent of women giving those half-cheek half-air kisses to each other. A sign of affection.

"But I guess incest wouldn't be an option anyway, with the way she keeps shooting you down."

"Blow me."

I chuckle. "Not tonight, dear. I have a headache." Then I walk toward the door. "Have a good one."

"Later."

After leaving the office I hop on the subway, like I do every day after work, to go to the gym. It's in Brooklyn, a real bare bones kind of place. Some would call it a dump, but to me it's a diamond in the rough. The floor is hard and dirty and worn red punching bags line the back wall. There are weights stacked in front of a cracked mirror, a milk crate filled with jump ropes beside the lone rowing machine. There aren't any spandex-wearing, bored housewives looking to hook up or show off their latest cosmetic enhancement. There are no elliptical machines or high-tech treadmills like the ones that can be found in the workout room of my building. I come here to sweat and strain my muscles to their limit with time-tested calisthenics. And most of all, I come for the boxing ring in the center of the gym.

I was twelve the first time I watched *Rocky*. It takes place in Philly, but it could've been in New York. I've been a fan of boxing ever since. I'm not going to quit the day job to train for the heavyweight title or anything, but there's no better workout than a few rounds in the ring against a decent opponent.

Ronny Butler—the fiftyish, stubbly chinned guy in the gray sweatshirt with the thick gold crucifix around his neck who's in the ring's corner, yelling out critiques to the two sparring partners dancing around each other—he's the owner. Ronny's no Mickey, but he's a good man, and an even better trainer.

Through the years, I've pieced together bits of information he's let slip when I've been the last one here at closing. In the late eighties, Ronny was a Wall Street big shot, living the dream. Then, on a Friday night, he and his family were driving out to the Hamptons for the weekend. Because he'd gotten jammed up at work, they'd had a late start, and a drowsy truck driver nodded off at the wheel, flew across the median into oncoming traffic—and smacked headfirst into Ronny's BMW. He made it out of the accident with a concussion and a shattered femur. His wife and daughter didn't make it out at all.

He spent a few years drowning in a bottle, a few more sobering up. Then he used the settlement money to buy this place. He doesn't come off as bitter or sad, but I wouldn't say he's happy either. I think the gym keeps him going, gives him a reason to get up in the morning.

"Back up, Shawnasee!" Ronny yells at the fighter who's got his sparring partner pinned against the ropes, pummeling his ribs. "This isn't Vegas, for fuck's sake, let the guy breathe."

That Shawnasee kid's an asshole. You know the type—young, hot-headed, the kind of prick who would get out of his car to beat down some poor schmuck for cutting him off on the freeway. Which is another reason I like boxing—it's the perfect opportunity to put idiots in their places without being charged with assault. Shawnasee's been trying to goad me into the ring for a few months now, but it's no fun fighting someone with piss-poor technique. No matter how hard they hit, they've got no shot at winning. I'm waiting until he gets better—then I'll kick his ass.

I catch Ronny's eye as he breaks up the fighters and greet him with a nod. Then I head back to the locker room, change out of my suit, and hit the bag for half an hour. Next, I use the rowing machine until my biceps are screaming and my legs feel like Jell-O. I finish off with ten minutes of speed jump roping, which might sound easy, but it's not. You try jumping rope for half that time and I'll bet you feel like you're going into cardiac arrest.

When the ring is empty, I climb in and go three rounds against Joe Wilson, an uptown lawyer I've sparred with before. Joe puts up a good fight, but the session clearly goes my way. Afterward, we tap gloves affably, and I go back into the locker room and grab my stuff. I smack Ronny's back on the way out, jog to the subway, and catch my train home.

I'm not ashamed to say my parents hooked me up with my apartment after college—in those days, this place was slightly above my pay grade. The location is great—walking distance to the office and a killer view of Central Park. Because I've lived here since college, it lacks the stylish consistency you'd typically expect in the home of a successful businessman. Take a look around.

Black leather sofas face a big-screen television with a top-of-the-line sound and gaming system sitting on the glass shelves below it. The coffee table is also glass, but it's chipped around the edges from years of contact with reclining feet and glass bottles.

A shadowy painting of a mountaintop by a renowned Japanese artist hangs on one wall, and my prized collection of vintage base-ball caps hangs from hooks opposite it. A lighted display case is perched in the corner, showing off the crystal etched EXCELLENCE IN INVESTMENT MANAGEMENT award I received last year . . . and the authentic Boba Fett helmet that was worn during the filming of *The Empire Strikes Back*. Built in, dark-wood bookshelves are lined with collectible sports memorabilia, books on art, photography, and banking, and about a dozen mismatched frames with photographs of family and friends from the best times in my life. Photographs I took myself.

Photography is a hobby of mine. You'll hear more about that later.

In the dining room, instead of a totally useless formal set of table and chairs, there's a pool table and a *Space Invaders* arcade game. But my kitchen is fully set up—black granite counters, Italian marble floors, stainless steel appliances, and cookware that Emeril would be honored to own. I like to cook, and I do it well.

The way to a man's heart may be through his stomach—but it's also the most direct route down a girl's pants. For women, a guy who knows his way around a kitchen is a big selling point. Tell me I'm wrong.

Anyway, my apartment is kick-ass. It's large, but comfortable, impressive without being intimidating. After hosing down in the glass-enclosed, triple-headed shower, I towel off and spend a minute looking at my reflection in the full-length mirror. My normally light brown hair is dark from being wet and sticks up at odd angles from the towel. I could use a cut—it gets pretty-boy curly if I let it grow too long. I rub the stubble along my squared jaw, but I don't feel like shaving. I turn to the side and flex my bicep, proud of the muscle that bulges. I'm not bulky like a meathead, but I'm tight, lean, and powerful, without a centimeter to pinch from my six pack, let alone an inch.

Checking myself out in a mirror might seem douchey to you, but, trust me—all guys do it. We just don't like to be caught doing it. But when you put as much time into your body as I do, the payoff makes it worth it.

I pull on a pair of silk boxers then heat up a bowl of leftover pasta and chicken. I'm not Italian, but I'd eat this every day of the week if I could. It's about eight thirty by the time I finish washing the dishes. Yes, I am a man who washes his own dishes.

Be jealous, ladies—I'm a rare breed.

Then I flop back on my awesome, king-size bed and grab the golden ticket from the pocket of my discarded pants.

I finger the letters on the bright green cardstock.

DEE WARREN

CHEMIST

LINTRUM FUELS

And I remember the soft, smooth flesh that swelled from the confines of her tight, pink shirt. My dick twitches—guess he remembers it too.

Normally I'd wait a day or two to call a girl like Delores. Timing is everything. Looking too eager is a rookie mistake—women enjoy being panted after by puppies, not men.

But it's already Wednesday night, and I'm hoping to meet up with Dee on Friday. The twenty-first century is the age of "Maybe He's Just Not That Into You" and "Dating for Dummies" and "The Girlfriends' Guide to Dating," which means calling a chick for a random hookup isn't as easy as it used to be. There are all these frigging *rules* now—I found that out the hard way.

Like if a guy wants to meet up with you the same night that he calls, you're supposed to say "no," because that means he doesn't respect you. And, if he wants to take you out on a Tuesday, that's a sign he's got better plans for Saturday night.

Trying to keep up with the changing edicts is tougher than keeping track of the goddamn health care debate in Congress. It's like a minefield—one wrong step and your cock won't be getting any action for a long time. But, if getting laid were easy, everyone would be doing it. It . . . and pretty much nothing else.

Which brings me to my next thought: I know feminists always complain about how men have all the power. But when it comes to dating—in America, at least? That's not really the case. In the bars, on the weekends, it's ladies' choice 24/7. They have their pick of the litter because single men will never reject a come-on.

Picture it: The music's pumping, bodies are grinding, and a non-hideous female approaches a dude having a drink at the bar. She says, "I want to fuck your brains out." He replies, "Nah, I'm not really in the mood for sex tonight." SAID NO MAN *EVER*.

Chicks never have to worry about getting shot down—as long as they're not shooting too far above their pay grade. They never have to stress about when they're going to get lucky. For women, sex is an all-you-can-eat buffet—they just have to choose a dish. God created men with a strong sex drive to ensure the survival of the species. Be fruitful and multiply and all that. For guys like me, who know what the fuck they're doing, it's not exactly difficult. But for my not-as-skilled brethren, getting some can be a daunting task.

A slight buzz of adrenaline rushes through me as I pick up the phone to dial the cell number on the business card. It's not that I feel nervous, more like . . . cautious anticipation. My hand taps my leg in time to *Enter Sandman* by Metallica, and my stomach tightens as her phone rings.

I imagine she'll remember me—I did make quite the impression after all, and I assume she'll be receptive to a meeting up— maybe even eager. What I don't expect is for her voice to slam into my eardrum as she yells: "No, jackass, I don't want to hear the song again! Frigging call Kate if you need an audience!"

I pull the phone a little ways away from my ear. And I check the number to make sure it's the right one. It is.

Then I say, "Uh . . . hello? Is this Dee?"

There's a pause as she realizes I'm not jackass.

Then she replies, "Yes, this is Dee. Who's this?"

"Hey, it's Matthew Fisher. I work with Kate—we met at the diner this afternoon?"

Another brief pause, and then her voice lightens, "Oh yeah. Clit-boy, right?"

I chuckle deeply, not entirely sure I like that nickname, but at least I made my mark. Note to self: Use that line again.

"That's me."

"Sorry about yelling. My cousin's been up my ass all day."

My cock stirs from the ass talk, and I have to stop myself from offering to trade places with this cousin.

"What can I do for you, Matthew Fisher?"

My imagination gets crazy. And detailed. *Oh, the things she could do . . .*

For a moment I wonder if she's talking like this on purpose or if I'm just a horny mess.

I play it safe. "I was wondering if you wanted to get together sometime? For a drink?"

Let's pause right here. Because, despite my earlier complaints about the modern complexities men face when trying to hook up, I feel it's my duty to educate others, get the word out, about how to decode guy-speak. Think of me as a studlier version of Edward Snowden or Julian Assange. Maybe I should start my own website—I'd call it DickiLeaks. On second thought, that's a shitty name. Sounds like an STD symptom.

Remember the mental game of "fuck, kill, marry" I mentioned earlier? If a man asks you to get a drink or hang out, you are squarely in the "fuck" category. Nope, don't argue—it's true. If a guy asks you for a date or dinner, maybe even a movie, you're probably in the "fuck" category, but you have potential for upward mobility.

You don't have to base your response to a dude's proposition on this information; I just thought you'd want to know.

Now, back to the phone conversation.

I can hear a smile in her voice as she accepts my invite. "I'm always up for a drink."

Up. More sexual innuendo. Definitely not my imagination. I am *so* getting laid.

"Cool. You free on Friday?"

Silence meets my ears for a beat, until she suggests, "How about tonight?"

Wow. Guess Delores Warren missed the chapter requiring two days' advance notice for all screwing offers.

Lucky me.

And then she elaborates. "I mean, there could be a blackout, a water shortage, aliens could finally decide to invade and enslave the entire human race . . ."

There's one I haven't heard before.

"Then we'd be shit out of luck. Why wait for Friday?"

I like the way this girl thinks. As the saying goes, "Don't put off till tomorrow anyone you could be doing today." Or . . . close enough.

"Tonight works for me," I readily agree. "What time?"

Some girls take forever and a day to get ready. It's fucking annoying. Going to the gym or the beach? Shouldn't require prep time, ladies.

"How about an hour?"

Two points for Dee—great tits *and* low maintenance. I think I'm in love.

"Sounds good," I tell her. "What's your address? I'll swing by and pick you up."

My building has private parking for tenants. Lots of New Yorkers spend thousands of dollars a month for parking spaces—only to *not* drive their cars because of city traffic. Auto congestion doesn't bug me; I always leave myself extra time. Like I said before—time management is key.

And another thing: I don't have a car. I drive a custom-built Ducati Monster 1100 S. I'm not looking to put on a cut and join an outlaw MC or anything, but riding is another hobby of mine. Few things in life feel as great as cruising down an open highway on a blue-skied, crisp fall day when the leaves are just starting to change. It's as close to flying as a human being can get.

I take the bike out at every available opportunity. Sometimes a girl will bitch about being cold or messing up her hair—but when all is said and done: Chicks dig motorcycles.

Delores responds, "Um . . . how about I just meet you?"

This is a smart move for a single woman. Just like you wouldn't give out your social security number online, you don't give out your address to some guy you barely know. The world is a fucked-up place, and women especially need to do everything they can to make sure the fucked up doesn't find its way to their front door.

But, unfortunately, it also means the hog is staying home tonight. I'm a little sad about that.

"Meeting up sounds good."

Before I can suggest a place, Dee takes charge. "You know Stitch's, on West Thirty-seventh?"

I do know it. It's low-key with good drinks, live music, and a comfortable lounge. Because it's a Wednesday night, it won't be packed, but no bar in New York is ever empty.

"Yeah, I'm familiar with it."

"Great. I'll see you in an hour or so."

"Awesome."

After we hang up, I don't get dressed right away. I'm not picky about my clothes, like some young semi-asexual professionals, but I'm not a slob either. I can be ready to walk out the door in seven minutes flat. So I grab the folder from my briefcase and use the extra time to finish the work reading I planned to do before bed. Because it looks like I won't be hitting the sheets any time soon—and when I do, I'm definitely not going to be alone.

Chapter 3

I get to Stitch's early. I drink a beer at the bar, then step outside for a cigarette. Yes—I'm a smoker. Break out the hammer and nails and commence with the crucifixion.

I'm aware it's unhealthy. I don't need to see the internal organs of deceased cancer patients on those creepy-ass commercials to understand it's a bad habit—*thank you, Mayor Bloomberg*. Making me go outside doesn't stop me from lighting up—it just pisses me off. It's an inconvenience, not a deterrent.

But I'm considerate about it. I don't toss my butts on the street, I don't blow smoke in the faces of the elderly or children. Alexandra would literally slit my throat if I ever lit up anywhere near Mackenzie. Literally.

I do plan on quitting . . . eventually.

But for now, the long-term damage I might be doing to my lungs falls second to the fact that I like to smoke. It feels good. It's really just that simple. And you can keep your bar pretzels to yourself, because nothing goes better with a cold beer than a cigarette. It's as good as a mom's old-fashioned PB&J.

I snuff out my cigarette on the wall of the building and throw it into the trash can on the street. Then I pop an Altoids in my mouth. Because—like I said—I'm considerate. I don't know if Dee is a fellow smoker or not, but nobody wants to slide their tongue into another person's mouth and taste ashtray. And getting Dee's tongue in my mouth . . . among other places . . . is definitely on the schedule for tonight's festivities.

I head back in the bar and order a second beer. I take a swig and notice the front door opening. I watch as she walks in.

Did I think Delores was a hottie when I met her this afternoon? I need to get my vision checked. Because she's so much more.

Her strawberry blond hair is down, curled under at the ends, pulled back from her face with a thick black hair band. A black, tuxedo-like jacket covers her torso, with a low-cut white tube top underneath. Short, white shorts barely peek out from the bottom of the jacket, revealing long, creamy, toned legs. She finishes the look with white sky-high heels. Red lipstick accentuates her mouth.

She's gorgeous—shockingly stunning. Put her in a black-and-white photo and she could easily be in a Calvin Klein campaign. Her business card isn't Charlie's Golden Ticket—it's the lottery kind—and I just hit the jackpot.

She scans the room and spots me from the doorway. I wave, coolly. She smiles back, revealing straight, shiny teeth.

"Hi," she says as she approaches.

"Hello—that jacket looks great on you." You can't go wrong by starting off with a compliment. Girls love them.

Her smile turns into a smirk as she teases, "Let me guess—'But I'd look better out of it'?"

I chuckle. "I wasn't going to say that. I would never give a line that cheesy." Then I shrug. "I was going to say, 'It'd look even better on my bedroom floor.'"

A rich, deep laugh escapes her throat. "Yeah—'cause there's nothing cheesy about that."

I pull out a bar stool and she sits.

"What's your poison?" I ask.

Without a pause she answers, "Martini."

"Dirty?"

"I like my martinis just like my sex." She winks flirtatiously. "Dirty is always better."

Yes—I'm definitely in love.

The bartender comes to us, but before I can order for her, Dee starts giving specific instructions on how she wants her drink made.

"Two ounces of gin, heavy on the vermouth, just a dash of olive juice . . ."

The babyfaced, plaid-shirted bartender, who barely looks twenty-one, seems lost. Dee notices and stands up. "You know, I'll just demonstrate—it'll be easier." She turns, hops backwards onto the bar, and swings her legs over the top—while I discreetly try to get a peek up her shorts. If she's wearing underwear, it's gotta be a thong.

My cock processes this information by straining against my jeans, hoping for a peek of his own.

Dee stands up on the business side of the bar and quickly mixes her drink, explaining every move to the unperturbed bartender. She tosses an olive into the air and catches it expertly with her mouth, before sinking the two-olived toothpick into the clear-liquid-filled glass.

She places it on the bar and motions to it with an open palm. "And there you have it—the perfect Dirty Martini."

I've always believed you can tell a lot about a person by what they drink. Beer is laid back, easy-going, or cheap, depending on the brand. Wine coolers tend to be immature or nostalgic. Cristal and Dom Pérignon imbibers are flashy and try too hard to impress—there are many champagnes that are just as expensive and exquisite, but lesser known.

What does Dee's choice of beverage tell me about her? She's complicated, with very specific, but refined, tastes. And she's outspoken, bold without being bitchy. The kind of girl who can send back her steak to the kitchen if it's cooked wrong, in a way that doesn't make the waiter want to spit in her food.

The bartender raises his brows and gives me a friendly look. "You got a live one here, buddy."

Dee swings back over the bar as I say, "So it seems."

Once Delores is seated back on the stool, I comment, "That was impressive. So, I guess you're big on the micromanaging, huh?"

She sips her drink. "I bartended through college—it made me very particular about my poison."

I take a drag off my beer and move into the small talk portion of the evening. "Kate tells me you're a chemist. What's that like?"

She nods. "It's like playing with a chemistry set every day and getting paid to do it. I enjoy analyzing things—breaking them down to their smallest components—then fucking with them a little. Seeing what other substances they play nice with . . . or don't. The don't part can get pretty exciting. Sort of makes me feel like I'm on a bomb squad."

She stirs her olives in the glass. "And you're a banker?"

I nod. "More or less."

"That sounds very unexciting."

My head tilts left to right as I consider her comment.

"Depends on your outlook. Some deals are a high-stakes gamble. Making money is never boring."

Dee turns in her chair, facing me.

Body language is important. Typically, a person's movements are subconscious, but understanding the feelings behind them can either guide you to the Promised Land or get your ass locked outside heaven's door. If a girl folds her arms or leans back, that generally means you're coming on too strong or she's just not interested in what you're selling. Eye contact, open arms, full frontal attention are all sure signs she's feeling you—and is hungry for more.

Her eyes quickly trail my body, head to toe. "You don't look like a banker."

I grin. "What does a banker look like?"

She scans the other patrons at the bar and in the lounge. Her gaze settles on a middle-aged, balding dude in a cheap suit, hunkered down over a double scotch, whose expression implies he's lost his life savings in a stock market crash.

Dee points at him with her crimson-nail-painted pinkie finger. "Him."

"He looks like a mortician. Or a pedophile."

She giggles and downs the rest of her martini.

Leaning close to her, I ask, "If not a banker, what do I look like?"

She smiles slowly and scrapes the olives off the toothpick with her teeth.

"You look like a Chippendales dancer."

Fabulous answer. I don't really need to explain to you why, do I?

In a low, seductive voice I say, "I do have some great moves. If banking doesn't work out, Chippendales is Plan B."

I motion to the bartender for another round. Delores watches him work closely, and he must not screw it up too badly, because she smiles when he places the drink before her.

Then, she says to me, "So . . . your buddy Drew—he's been giving my girl a hard time. Not a smart thing to do."

"Drew has a weird relationship with competition. He thrives on it, but it also pisses him off. Kate hasn't exactly been taking it easy on him, either. She brings her A-game to the office—I think she can hold her own."

"Well, you feel free to let him know he should watch his step. I'm very protective of Katie—we Ohioans stick together."

"But you're in New York now. We're 'Every Man for His-Fucking-Self.' It's the second state motto—right after 'The City That Never Sleeps.'"

Her eyes shine as she laughs. And I think the first drink might be hitting her hard.

"You're cute," she tells me.

My head leans back in exasperation. "Great. *Cute.* The adjective every man wants to hear."

She laughs again, and I'm struck by how much I'm enjoying myself. Dee Warren is a cool girl—unreserved, quick-witted, funny. Even if I don't end up nailing her, the night won't be a total loss.

That's not to say I'm not dying to get her out of here and see what's—or, preferably, what's not—under those tiny shorts. But, it'd be like rich icing on an already fuck-awesome cake.

I veer back toward small talk. "You're from Ohio?"

She tastes her drink and nods. "Yes, the original Podunk, USA."

"Mmm, no love for the hometown?"

"No, Greenville was a great town to grow up in, but it's sort of like the Hotel California. People check in, but they almost never leave. If all you want out of life is to get married and have babies, it's the place to be. But . . . that wasn't what I was looking for."

"What are you looking for, Dee?"

She thinks for a moment before she answers. "I want . . . life. Newness. Discovery. Change. It's why I like the city so much. It's alive—never stagnant. You can walk down a block and go down that same block a week later and it'll be totally different. New people, new sights and smells—the smells aren't always good, but that's a small price to pay."

I chuckle.

Then she goes on. "My mom used to say I reminded her of a dog on a leash that never learned how to heel. Always pulling on the chain, raring to go. There's a country song with lyrics I like: 'I don't want easy, I want crazy.'" She shrugs, a little shyly. "That's me."

Everything she said—they're my favorite parts about the city I grew up in too. Life is too damn short to stay safe, to stay the same.

My cell phone buzzes, but I ignore it. Checking your phone in the middle of a conversation, even if it's with a one-nighter, is just rude. Low class.

Dee asks me what my Zodiac sign is, but I make her tell me hers first. Some people are really into signs—I've been ditched on more than one occasion by a horrified Leo or Aquarius when they found out I'm a Capricorn. Since then, I'm not above fudging my birth date if needed.

In this case, I didn't have to. Dee's a Scorpio, which is supposed to be super hot with Capricorns in the sack. Personally, I think the whole thing is a crock of shit. But, if you want to play, you've got to know the rules of the game. Including potential fouls.

Dee nurses her second drink as the conversation turns toward family and friends. Without getting too deep, she tells me about Billy, her more-like-a-brother cousin, and her single mother who raised them both. She touches on her lifelong friendship with Kate Brooks and a few surprising wild-child incidents during their teen years that are just too embarrassing *not* to mention to Kate at the office tomorrow.

I fill her in on Drew and Steven and Alexandra and how growing up with them saved me from ever feeling like an only child. I tell her about the coolest four-year-old I know, Macken-zie, and that I would hang with that kid every day of the week if I could.

By the time I finish my fourth beer, two and a half hours have flown by. When Dee hits the bathroom, I whip out my phone.

I have six texts. They're all from Steven.

Shit. Call of Duty. I forgot.

They vary in their degrees of panic. Wanna see?

Dude ur late—starting without you
**

Come on, man, I'm in the shit and outnumbered. Where the hell r u?
**

Where's the goddamn aerial support? My men are dying out there!
**

Not going out like this—taking as many of them with me as I can. Ahhhhhhhh!
**

Thanks a lot, dumbass. I'm dead. If you make a move on my widow I'll haunt you.

And finally, the last one just says:

Fucker.

I laugh out loud and send him an apologetic text, telling him something suddenly came up. Steven's great at reading between the lines:

You mean your dick suddenly came up. What happened to bros before hoes? You owe me. I expect payment in the form of babysitting hours so I can take my wife out . . . or stay in. ;)

Personally, I think he spends too much time with his wife as it is—as demonstrated by the winky face in his text.

Dee comes back from the bathroom and stands close to my chair. "You want to get out of here?"

Yes, please.

With a devastating grin, I answer, "Absolutely. You want to go to my place? I'd love to show you the view."

She glances at my crotch. "What view would that be?"

"The kind you'll never want to stop looking at, baby."

She chuckles. "I was thinking more along the lines of dancing?"

"Then we're thinking alike. Horizontal is my favorite dance."

She runs her hand up the sleeve of my black button-down shirt. "The vertical kind is a nice prelude—gets me in the mood. There's a club around the corner from my apartment. Their Wednesday night DJ is the shit. You want to come with me, Clitboy?"

I put my hand over hers and rub my thumb slowly against it. "I don't think I like that nickname."

She shrugs unapologetically. "Too bad. You never get a second chance to make a first impression. You're Clit-boy until you give me a reason to think of you as something else."

I lean in closer. Goose bumps rise on the flesh of her chest as my breath tickles her ear. "By the end of this night, I'll have you calling me 'God.'"

Her breathing picks up slightly, and the pulse point at her neck thumps faster. I want to put my mouth on it, suck on the skin and experience her taste.

But I don't get the chance.

Delores steps back, her amber eyes practically glowing with anticipation. And she commands, "You pay the tab, I'll get the taxi."

Independence in a woman is damn sexy. Only insecure losers get turned on by a chick who clings like you're the oxygen she needs to survive. Although it's obvious Delores is the stand-on-her-own-two-feet kind of girl, I like that she lets me pay the tab. I would've insisted on it anyway. Opening a door, paying a bill: These are not digs against a lady's capabilities. Sometimes a guy just wants to do the old-fashioned thing.

Let us.

Think of it as considerate prepayment against our future screwups, which are pretty much guaranteed to occur.

I take care of the bartender and join Dee on the sidewalk, where she stands next to an awaiting cab. And—get this—Delores reaches out and opens the door to the taxi for me. There's a playful gleam in her eye that makes me suspect she can read my mind. I just smile, say thanks, and get in.

The club Delores suggested is called Greenhouse, in SoHo. Although I've heard of it, this is the first time I've walked through its doors. It's surprisingly crowded. The bar area walls and ceiling are coated with moss and lit up with blue, red, and green spotlights. The dance floor has a cave motif, with long jagged crystals hanging from the ceiling in hues of blue, purple, and pink. It's dimly lit—shadowy—perfect for some up against the wall action. That'll come in handy later on.

The music is loud, too noisy for any kind of conversation, but that's fine with me. Talking is nice—action is better. We get our drinks and grab a table near the dance floor. Dee takes a sip from her glass, puts it down on the table, and gives me a sexy, "watch this" kind of smile before making a beeline for the dance floor.

I sit down at the table, lean comfortably back in the chair, knees spread, content to caress her with my eyes for now. She closes her eyes and rocks her head in time with the beat of the music. Her hips sway, and her arms rise over her head. The blue and pink lights dance over her hair—lighting her up—making her seem magical. The music gets faster, louder, and Dee keeps up. Shaking her shoulders and her ass, bending her knees and sinking toward the floor, before swirling back upward.

She knows how to move, and it makes me want her more. I glance around and notice Delores has gained the attention of several guys—make that every guy—in the club. They watch her dance with appreciative, slimy smiles on their faces and hoping-to-tap-that gleams in their eyes.

I'm not usually a possessive person. I've gone to clubs with girls before and ended the evening with both of us leaving with someone else. It's par for the course.

But at the moment, my fists are clenching, ready to shove

the first fucker who tries to approach Delores through the wall and out to the street. It pisses me off that they're even looking at her—that she's fodder for their wishful thinking and deviant desires.

Maybe I feel like this because I haven't screwed her yet. Maybe I don't want to share a dessert I haven't gotten to taste.

Or maybe, it's because Delores Warren is just . . . different . . . in a way I can't yet explain. What I know about her, I like—a lot—and there's a part of me I haven't consciously acknowledged with a deep craving to know more.

The music changes as I stand. "Wake Me Up" by Avicii pours out of the speakers and washes over the room. The crowd hums their approval. I walk onto the dance floor, straight to Delores.

The beginning of the song is slow, heavy with acoustic guitar. Dee's body sways side to side in time, her long hair swinging out behind her, baring her neck. I step up behind her and wrap one arm around her waist, resting my palm on her stomach, over her jacket—pulling her gently back against me.

She tenses for a split second, opens her eyes and turns her head to the side. Then she sees that it's me. And she smiles.

She relaxes against me, her back to my chest, and I lean forward, pressing us together. Her ass nestles perfectly against my dick, which hardened the moment she started dancing.

I think she feels it—she must.

She leans forward, bending a little at her waist, and moves her hips in tight circles, rubbing right against where my body is screaming for contact.

If feels fan-fucking-tastic.

I bend my knees and move with the music, even though my focus is solely on Dee.

I don't mean to brag . . . well, okay . . . I'll brag. I'm a good dancer. It's a lot like screwing, finding the right rhythm, staying attuned to your partner's moves and responding accordingly.

I'll rip the tongue out of anyone who'd let this get out, but when I was a kid, my mother made me take lessons. Drew, Steven, and I all did. Not the flashy, sequined costume kind—*thank Christ*—but the ballroom kind. It was a year or two before Alexandra's cotillion. Yes—in our social circle, girls have cotillions, and knowing how to dance like a gentleman is a must. We all hated it. Drew and I had a detailed plan to run away and live in the Museum of Natural History until the danger passed, but it didn't work out.

Still, as miserable as I was, I'm grateful for those lessons now. Because a kid who can dance is a fucking pansy, but a man who can dance is smooth—sophisticated.

For hip-hop club dancing, you need some natural rhythm, something that poor son of a bitch Steven is sorely lacking. But for a guy like me, with some inherent ability and former training? I kill it on the dance floor.

The synthesized portion of the song takes over—faster, more primal, with a strong bass. Dee straightens up and wraps her arms around my neck, behind her. I have one hand on her hip, holding her steady as I thrust against her. My other hand creeps under her jacket, to the taught, warm skin of her stomach.

I feel the vibration of her moan as my hand strokes and climbs higher.

When the music slows down once more, Dee turns in my arms, facing me. With her heels, we're almost nose-to-nose. I'm caught in the dark gaze of her eyes as the singer croons about traveling around the world, staying young, and winning love.

The beat picks up again, but our eyes hold. Our bodies move

against each other, hot and needy. My fingers dig into the flesh of Dee's ass, pushing her harder against me.

To the lyrics of a man not knowing how lost he was until he found what was missing, Dee's palm caresses my face. And it feels tender and intimate.

Meaningful.

I lower my head and press my lips to hers. And she's right there with me, opening for me—warm and wet—taking everything I have to give and kissing me back with equal ardor. Both my arms wrap around her, the dancing forgotten. One hand stays on her lower back, while the other buries in the softness of her hair as our mouths move together. Her hands cling to my shoulders, kneading the muscles, pulling me to her.

Have you ever had a moment when you think to yourself, this is going to change everything? From this point on, there will be a before, an after, and this event will forever divide the two?

Most people don't. They're too caught up at the time to recognize the significance of what's happening.

That's how I was.

But looking back now—this was it. That first, scorching, perfect kiss. This was the moment that would determine the rest of my life. And nothing after it would ever be the same.

Chapter 4

We walk back to Dee's apartment. Stumble might be a more appropriate word.

Dry-hump would fit too.

I have the overwhelming need to kiss her every few steps—to pull her to me, or press her against the wall of a building to gain the necessary friction. And she's in no way passive—dragging her fingernails along the bare skin of my abs, dipping her hands into my pants to squeeze my ass. We're like two hormone-driven teenagers, making out in the school hallway, who don't give a shit if they get caught.

We eventually arrive outside her apartment door. I stand behind her as she fiddles with the double locks—grinding my pelvis against her ass, cupping both tits in my hands, massaging and teasing those beautiful attributes. Once we're inside, Dee crashes against me, standing on her toes to give me an intense, wet, tongue-tangling kiss. Her hands are all over my hair, pausing in their exploration just long enough for me to rip the jacket off her body. Then I bend low and make quick work of those minuscule shorts, leaving Dee wearing the white tube top and a string thong, with a scarce lace triangle.

I thought Delores was beautiful clothed, but naked—she's breathtaking. Long, lean legs, narrow hips, a tight stomach with skin so soft it feels like a caress. She's not overly sculpted; she has a yoga body—slim with the suggestion of firm muscles just below the surface. On my knees, I unbutton my shirt. Dee bends at the waist and pushes it off me, her hands grazing my back's physique appreciatively.

"God, you're so fucking hot." She sighs.

Already using the new nickname, and I haven't even made her come yet. *I'm good.*

Without pause, I spread her knees wide enough to fit between them. Her upper body uses the wall behind her for support. And I place a long, openmouthed kiss against her cloth-covered cunt. Delores's chin rises and she keens. Her scent is sweet, fruity, with a hint of spice—like a ripe apple with a touch of cinnamon. I drag her thong from her body, craving full contact. With my moist, heated tongue, I trace her cropped, flaxen landing strip, then I move lower to lick and nibble the rim of her pussy. Done with the warm-up, I sink into her, laving and sucking, making her whimper and buck.

I wasn't talking shit when I said I know my way around a clit. Most guys think heading straight for the hot-button is the way to go—but they're wrong. Too much pressure, applied too fast, isn't enjoyable, might even be uncomfortable for a woman. You have to tease it, gradually stimulate it, until it's stiff and reaching and pleading to be fondled. Once Dee is at that breaking point, I open her lips with my fingers and dance over her knotted bud with my tongue.

She screams—in relief and decadent bliss. I lick her with more force, up and down, without ever losing contact, then I slide two fingers into her sodden, clenching pussy. Her hips thrust against my face and her hands hold me in place as she comes with an openmouthed moan.

With the sound of Dee's heavy breaths still in my ears, I stand up and wrap an arm around her waist. She sags against me, pleasure spent and wobbly. I lift her feet from the floor, but she doesn't seem to have the strength to wrap her legs around me. Her lips seek mine, and her arms cling to my shoulders.

"Bedroom?" I ask between kisses.

"Last door on the left."

My tense legs carry both of us to the room. When I step in, I don't take in my surroundings or notice the décor—my senses are solely attuned to Dee and my own raging desire. Slightly recovered from her come-coma, Delores sits on the edge of the bed and beckons me forward with entreating amber eyes. Holding my gaze, she unbuckles my pants—the hiss of the zipper and our labored breathing making the only sounds. She pushes the clothing down, and I step out of them. She eyes me eagerly, like a treasure hunter seeking a fervently sought bounty.

My cock is at his best—long, thick, painfully willing. Delores licks her palm.

And it's the sexiest fucking thing I have ever seen. Bold and brazen.

Then she encases my dick in her slippery, searing hand, gripping it firmly, jerking tenderly. I move closer, without really thinking, and Dee takes it as a sign to bring her mouth into play. I watch as she licks me from base to tip, swirling around the foreskin, before taking me fully into her mouth—so deep I feel the back of her throat.

My eyes roll closed. I grunt and I curse and I beg for more. Dee doesn't disappoint—plunging me in and out of her heavenly fucking mouth over and over. But when she takes my balls in her hand—rolling, rubbing them, tugging in the most delectable way—I have to put the brakes on. I'm afraid I may blow my load—and I've got way too many ideas for that to happen now.

I grasp a handful of her hair and ease her off. Then I lean down and kiss her as blood pounds in my eardrums. She lays back and takes me with her until we're stomach-to-stomach, thigh-to-thigh. I rip at the remaining fabric of her tube top and yank it down, revealing two plump, gorgeously full tits.

And on one, is a winking diamond piercing.

Holy mother of fuck.

My cock grows harder, weeping at the sight. I attack her breasts like a gluttonous animal—sucking and biting, grasping and tugging with my hands. My mouth covers her pierced nipple, tasting cold metal and warm flesh. I pull at it with my teeth and lap it with my tongue. Dee writhes and whimpers below me, scratching my back with her nails, leaving scalding, sensuous gouges in their wake.

"Fuck me, Matthew," Dee wails. "I need you to fuck me, now."

In a flash, I retrieve a condom from my wallet and roll it on in record time. Holding her ankles, I pull her to me, so her ass is at the edge of the bed. I drag the head of my dick over her needy pussy, teasing at the opening.

Then I look her in the eyes and ask, "How . . . how do you want it?"

"Hard," she moans. "Hard and deep. I want to feel every fucking inch of you inside me."

I thrust inside harshly, as deep as I can. Dee's back bows off the bed and she screams, "Yes! Please . . . yes."

I pull out slowly, until just the head remains in her, then I push back in, circling my hips, rubbing against her clit when I'm buried balls-deep.

This is lust at its finest—primal passion, visceral hunger.

I keep the pace Dee craves, fucking the breath out of her with every thrust. Until she's reaching for me, begging for *faster*. I cover her with my body, and she wraps her arms around my neck, tasting my mouth as I drive into her furiously.

Her cheek is pressed against mine when she comes—eyes closed, crying my name over and over, a phenomenal sound that I'll never forget. And as her orgasm clenches my cock, I come too—so exquisitely long and hard, I'm pretty sure I blacked the hell out.

It's amazing. Groundbreaking. Easily the greatest sex of my life. And while I'm still inside her, before my heartbeat is able to relax, I know that Dee Warren is like no other woman who has ever come before.

After we get our breaths back, Delores gets up and disappears into the bathroom then exits a few minutes later wearing a multicolored, paisley, silk robe. I grab my pants off the floor, fish out the pack of cigarettes from my pocket, and ask her, "Do you mind?"

She opens a window, then retrieves a half-smoked joint from the wooden jewelry box on her dresser. She holds it up. "Smoke 'em if you got 'em."

I lay my head back on one bent arm and light up. Dee slides into the bed beside me, putting an ashtray on my chest as she tokes up. Her robe falls open, exposing her magnificently pierced breast. I blow out a line of smoke and run my finger around the ring.

"What's the story behind this?"

She inhales deeply, smoke escaping her lips as she tells me, "Remember how I told you Billy, Kate, and I grew up together?"

I nod.

"Billy's the youngest, only by a few months. When he turned twenty-one, we all got trashed celebrating. Kate and Billy had tattoos done. I got pierced."

I tug gently on the ring, touching and testing it out like a kid with a new toy on Christmas morning. "It's sexy as hell. But I'm curious, why didn't you get a tattoo?"

She snuffs out the dead bud in the ashtray. "Tattoos are too much of a commitment. I don't like having anything on—or in—my body that I can't get rid of."

I put out my smoke and move the ashtray to the bedside table. Then I turn on my side to face Dee.

Her hand trails down my stomach and wraps around my cock, brushing her thumb across the foreskin. "What's the story behind this? I thought all Catholics had to be cut?"

"I think that's Judaism." Then I explain, "I was a sickly newborn—nothing major, but enough for my mother to be wary of anything that might've caused an unnecessary complication."

For some insane reason, my parents assumed I'd have a circumcision performed when I was a strong, healthy adult. Like I would ever—*ever*—let a scalpel anywhere near my dick unless my life depended on it.

And maybe not even then.

Yes, in case you're wondering, there were a few girls in high school who were slightly . . . unsure about how to proceed with a non–cookie cutter cock. But once they took it for a test ride and realized it works the same as all the other models, it was in high demand.

She continues to stroke me until I'm hard and hot in her hand. Then she looks down and says, "I like it. It's pretty."

I grip Delores's hips, roll onto my back, and lift her over me so she's straddling my waist. "Okay, you officially suck with adjectives. Pussies are pretty, not dicks."

Her robe falls fully open and I lick my thumb then press it to her clit to show her just how pretty I think her pussy is. *Fucking gorgeous*.

Dee starts with a giggle but ends with a breathy moan. "Enlighten me. What adjective is suitably masculine for a mighty dick?"

Her hips mimic my thumb's movements, rotating in tight circles.

"Mighty is a good start. Scary works. Powerful, impressive are always winners."

I rub with more pressure. Her hips move faster and in ever-widening circles. She pants. "I'll keep those in mind for next time." Then she bites her lip and looks me in the eyes. "I love to fuck when I'm high."

She rises higher on her knees, lining us up.

"I have a feeling I'm going to love it too."

❦

"Shit, that was awesome," Dee exclaims into the pillow, where she's just planted her face.

On my knees behind her, I remove condom number two with a tissue and collapse next to her. "It really fucking was."

Doggy style never disappoints.

She lifts her head and looks at the bedside clock. "Damn. I have to get up for work in four hours."

Just to clarify—this is my cue to leave. It's the nice way of saying, *Thanks for the sex. Good-bye.* Most of my one-night stands aren't sleepovers. Unless I'm completely wiped out, I prefer to sleep in my own bed.

I stand up and start to get dressed. I zip my pants, but still shirtless, I tell Dee, "I had a great time tonight."

She rolls over to her back, making no attempt to hide her naked glory. "Me too."

My eyes trail over her lustrous, after-sex-sheen-covered skin, settling on the nipple piercing that begs for more playtime. "I want to see you again."

Dee smirks. "You mean you want to screw me again."

I slip my arms into the sleeves of my shirt and admit, "Baby, that goes without saying." I pick my pack of cigarettes off the floor and put them in my pocket. "I'll call you."

She responds with a short bark of laughter and an eye roll. She grabs the silk robe and stands beside me.

"What?" I ask, slightly confused.

She shakes her head condescendingly. "You don't have to do that. I'm not the kind of woman you have to make promises to, that you have no intention of keeping. It was fun, let's just leave it at that. If I never hear from you again, that's okay too."

This isn't the reaction I expect from a chick I spent the last hours giving multiple orgasms to. Most of the time, they're asking to check my phone to make sure their digits are in my contact list. Demanding specifics—dates and times when their phone will be ringing.

Dee's attitude is refreshing. And intriguing. And definitely challenging.

As we walk down her hallway, I insist, "That'd be terrific . . . except, you *will* be hearing from me again."

She pats my shoulder. "Sure I will. But, if it's all the same to you, I won't hold my breath."

I take her hand from my shoulder and kiss her knuckles. She watches. And the smirk falls from her face and is replaced with . . . surprise. Yearning.

"Don't hold your breath"—I wink—"just make sure you're waiting by the phone."

Then she's smiling again. She holds the door open, but before I step through it, I lean in close and kiss her cheek. "Good night Dee."

Her hand covers the spot my lips just touched. And her honey-colored eyes meet mine. With a trace of sadness in her voice she says, "Good-bye Matthew."

When she closes the door behind me, I stick around until I hear all the locks click into place. Then I head home for some well-deserved shut-eye.

Chapter 5

On Thursday night, there's a Columbia University fund-raising dinner at the Waldorf Astoria hotel. Normally, I'd send a check and skip the dinner. But Alexandra is one of the organizers, so attendance is mandatory. Although raising Mackenzie is a full-time job, Alexandra's always been an overachiever and a multitasker. Like many of the women in her station—stay-at-home Manhattanite moms with money to spare—she wants to give back to the community. Plus, I think philanthropic activities help her feel connected to the outside world when her everyday life has fallen into a black hole of Barney episodes, macaroni necklaces, and playdates that could easily turn her brilliant brain to mush. Steven says she's a lot more agreeable when she's planning an event—but, when D-Day actually arrives, she has a tendency to get stressed out. Bitchy . . . if you will.

You've been warned.

I'm standing with Drew and Lexi, overlooking the elegantly

decorated room filled with tuxedo- and cocktail-dress wearing Columbia alums. Seems like a success to me—hors d'oeuvres are being passed, drinks are flowing, chatter and laughter abound. Though her expression is serene, Alexandra's eyes dart around the room with the exactitude of a long-range sniper, scanning for potential targets.

"Can I leave yet?" Drew asks his sister.

"No," Alexandra spits out in a way that tells me this isn't the first time Drew's submitted this request. "It's a party—eat, drink, mingle."

Drew scowls. "You've obviously been away from the party scene for far too long. This isn't a party. This is an excuse for old biddies to whip out their beaded dresses and compare the carats in their diamond rings." He takes a sip of wine. "Although, the wine is excellent. Good choice."

Lexi takes a drink from her own glass. "Wine loosens lips . . . and wallets."

"And tequila makes the clothes fall off," I offer with an eyebrow wiggle.

Just then an extra-large woman with dark, beehive-styled hair and heavy makeup, wearing a pool-table-green gown, approaches us.

Under his breath, Drew quips, "Let's hope the tequila is locked up nice and tight."

"Alexandra, my dear," she cackles. "You've outdone yourself! This soiree will be the talk of the town for days to come."

Lexi's hand presses humbly against the chest of her white gown. "You're too kind, Mrs. Sinclair."

Sinclair. I know that name. She's old money—her grandfather made a fortune in steel during the turn of the century construction boon. And her nephew, the heir apparent, is a piss-poor

CEO with a legendary coke habit. Here's a lesson for you: Money can't buy class, but it *can* buy a boatload of calamity.

Alexandra turns Mrs. Sinclair's attention to me. "You're acquainted with our dear friend Matthew Fisher?"

New York society is a lot like the mob—if you're not a friend of *ours* or part of *our thing*, they want nothing to do with you.

"Ah, yes," she says, "you're Estelle's boy."

I nod my head respectfully. "Lovely to see you, Mrs. Sinclair."

Alexandra continues with, "And have you met my brother, Andrew?"

Drew, ever the gentleman, greets her with a smile. "It's a pleasure."

Mrs. Sinclair's eyes sparkle as she regards him. And she fans herself with one pudgy hand. "No, we haven't met . . . but I've heard such stories about you."

"Vicious rumors." Drew winks. "That just happen to be true."

Judging by her quick breaths and the flush of her cheeks, I'd say there's a high probability Mrs. Sinclair may actually pass out. It'd certainly add some excitement to the evening. But—she doesn't. An old friend that hasn't seen her in years hobbles by and drags Mrs. Sinclair away.

Alone once more, Drew tries again. "*Now,* can I leave?"

"Stop asking me that. We haven't even sat down to dinner yet," Alexandra hisses.

Drew doesn't whine . . . but he's close. And he speaks for both of us as he says, "But I don't want to *be* here. I came, I smiled, I wrote you a check. Unlike some people, I actually have better things to do with my time."

Before the squabble gets too heated, someone across the room catches Alexandra's attention. Her eyes widen, but her face falls . . . with disappointment. She ignores her brother and gawks. Drew and I follow her line of vision.

And that's when I see her.

Almost every guy has a woman like her in his past. For some sad sons of bitches, there's more than one. The girl who fucked him over, broke his heart, shattered his self respect. They say the first cut is the deepest . . . and she cut me straight to the bone.

Shakespeare wrote, "O serpent heart, hid with a flowering face . . ." And if I didn't know better, I'd swear he composed it with Rosaline Nicolette Du Bois Carrington in mind.

We met during our second year at Columbia, and we dated seriously for two years. Rosaline is intelligent, charming, an expert equestrian. She wasn't interested in frat parties or the bar scene, preferring instead to spend her time engaging in highbrow discussions about art and travel. I thought she was perfect: the woman I'd marry, have children with—the girl I'd love when she was wrinkled and gray, and who would love me in return.

Sally Jansen may have been the first girl I ever loved, but Rosaline . . . she was the last.

I haven't seen her since graduation. Six years. But she looks exactly the same—a heart-shaped face; classic but full cheekbones that make her appear both sophisticated and innocent; crystal blue eyes with an exotic slant; plump, smiling lips; thick, dark-brown tresses; and a long, lean body that would bring any man straight to his knees. I watch her move across the room, her cotton-candy-pink dress swaying with every step.

"Why the fuck would you invite her?" Drew asks.

"I didn't invite her—Julian's on the board. I didn't think they'd show up."

Julian is Rosaline's husband. He's ten years older and about ten times wealthier than any of us.

"I thought they were in Europe."

"They came back to the city last week."

As Rosaline reaches our trio, Drew and Alexandra move in front of me—like bodyguards. Rosaline flashes a captivating smile—one that I used to know well. "Alexandra, Drew, it's so nice to see you. How long has it been?"

"Not nearly long enough," Alexandra replies with a deceptive smile.

This is The Bitch, in full force. To the outside world, Alexandra is a refined lady—but simmering below the surface is a ferocious, protective person who'll pull her hair back, take her earrings off, and open up a major can of whoop-ass on anyone she perceives as a threat to the people she loves. And she has a special kind of hate for my ex.

I didn't find out Rosaline was screwing around until after she dumped me. Getting kicked to the curb was rough, but discovering she'd been fucking someone else the entire time . . . that was utterly crushing. In the days that followed, Drew was the one who took me out, got me drunk, made sure I got laid. But Lexi . . . she was the one I cried to. It's not pussy to admit I cried—shedding a few tears is perfectly acceptable after your chest is ripped open and your heart is peeled like a potato.

Following in his sister's footsteps, Drew says, "I read there was a Listeria outbreak in Europe. You seem to have escaped unscathed. Pity."

Rosaline's smile stays in place as she ignores the barely veiled insults. "Yes, we enjoyed our European travels—the culture, the history. But Julian missed New York. We'll be here until the spring."

Separately, the Evans siblings are capable of throwing some deadly verbal daggers—you've seen them in action. But together? They're a tag team that would put professional wrestlers to shame.

Alexandra's voice lowers to a whisper. "I hate to be the one to tell you this, Rosaline . . . well, actually . . . I don't mind telling you at all. I've heard your Julian is having a torrid affair with his secretary." She touches a thoughtful finger to her lips. "Or was it the nanny?"

Drew adds, "I've heard he's screwing them both."

Again, Rosaline's composure doesn't waver. I used to think her poise was an asset—a sign of sophistication and maturity. But looking at her now, she just seems . . . unfeeling. Distant. Annoyingly passive.

She sighs sweetly. "Men do so love their variety."

"I wouldn't know," Alexandra counters.

"I would," Drew admits. "But, then again, I haven't vowed to forsake all others."

She folds her hands demurely. "I've resigned myself to Julian's dalliances. As long as I'm the woman he comes home to, it's not a problem."

Drew was always annoyed by his inability to goad a reaction out of Rosaline, no matter how crude he was. He gets a sick sense of amusement out of being able to drive people to the brink of assault. Which is why he digs deep and says, "Until he realizes the icebox you call a twat just isn't worth the price of admission anymore. *That* could be a problem."

Rosaline chuckles softly. "You always did have a colorful way with words, Drew."

And another round goes to the Stepford Wife.

"It was nice to see you both again. If you'll excuse me." Just like that, they've been dismissed. Rosaline steps around Alexandra and Drew and approaches me from the rear.

I run a hand through my hair and turn to face my heart-breaker. She looks at me kindly, sympathetically, the way a nurse would behold a patient who's recovering from a life-threatening sickness. "Hello, Matthew."

I'm determined to show her that my recuperation is complete. "Rosaline."

"You look wonderful."

"Thank you," I reply coolly. "And you . . . haven't changed a bit."

It's weird talking to her again, even after all these years—especially after all these years. There's no attraction, no hatred, no strong emotion at all. There's some regret—a part of me wishes I could reach back in time and beat the shit out of my younger self for being so stupid. And blind. But that's more about me. As for Rosaline? She's just someone who I used to know . . . that I never really knew at all. Even though I'm intimately acquainted with every swell and crevice of her body, she's still a stranger.

I clear my throat. "So . . . you have a son?"

Did I forget to mention that? Yeah—Rosaline didn't only screw around on me, she got knocked up. I'm fairly certain that was her plan all along. Like with the royal family, the heir and the spare? I was the spare, just in case things didn't work out with Julian. Luckily for me, his dart hit the bull's-eye first.

She smiles. "Yes, Conrad." *Poor kid.* "He's at boarding school in Switzerland."

I do the math in my head. "Boarding school? Isn't he, like, six years old?"

"He'll be six next month." I must look dumbfounded, because she adds, "It's crucial that he have the right start in life. His school will provide that for him."

I nod. Pointing out the extreme fucked-upness of this philosophy really isn't worth my time. "Right. Of course it will."

And I'm just about to extract myself from the conversation when Julian Wolfe comes striding on over. He's decent looking for a guy, tall but thin, with white-blond hair and a pale complexion. Kind of reminds me of a high-ranking Nazi officer.

"Rosaline, there are some important individuals I need you to meet." Then he notices me. "Hello, Fisher." He doesn't extend his hand, and I sure as hell don't offer mine.

I just nod my head. "Julian."

Rosaline and Julian are prime examples of why people need a hobby. If money is your only passion, you're going to be a miserable human being. And eventually, your hobby will be spreading that misery and being a general douche to everyone you meet.

"Sorry to steal her away. Again." He chuckles, because that's his idea of a joke.

And although it's more of a woman's game, if he wants to play with words, I'm up for the challenge. "No, take her off my hands, please. You're doing me a favor."

Julian sobers. And Rosaline touches my arm. "It was good to see you, Matthew."

"Take care," I tell them both.

Once they walk away, Drew comes up next to me. "Bet you're glad you dodged that bullet."

"You have no idea."

He nudges me with his elbow. "You okay?"

Take a good look—this is as close to "a moment" as guys like Drew and I will ever get. We could hang out all day and not utter a single word about anything important going on in our lives. Words aren't necessary—'cause when the chips are down, we'll be in each other's corner.

I assure him, "Yeah, man, I'm top-notch. Like you said, dodged a bullet."

We return to Alexandra's side, and I can tell by his expression that he's going to ask to be excused again. But then, Drew seems to decide on a different strategy. He smiles deviously. "Hey look—Squeaky's here."

"Who?" Alexandra inquires.

Drew gestures with his wineglass. "Curly haired brunette, in the blue dress near the bar."

Lexi's head bobs until she spots the lady in question. "That's . . . Alyson Bradford."

Drew shrugs. "She'll always be Squeaky to me."

"Why do you call her Squeaky?"

Mentally I shake my head. Because Alexandra should've known better.

"She squeaks when she comes."

"What?"

Casually, Drew explains, "Like a dog's chew toy." He holds up his hand, opening and closing it. "Squeak, squeak, squeak, squeeeeeak. At least she did when we were seventeen, but I don't think that's a condition she'd outgrow."

"How do you know that?" Alexandra asks, expectedly grossed out. "When did you have sex with Alyson Bradford?"

Drew looks to the ceiling, recalling the event. "Um . . . junior year. It was in the dark days following our loss to St. Bartholomew's in the playoffs. I wouldn't say she was my rock bottom, but she was close."

Lexi turns away. "Eck . . . forget it, I don't want to know."

If it's one thing The Bitch can't stomach, it's detailed stories of her brother's sex-capades.

Which is precisely why Drew says, "She also does this nasty thing with her tongue . . ."

Alexandra clasps her eyes shut. "All right! You know what?

Fine—if you want to go that badly, then go. If you want to leave me in my hour of need . . ."

She never should have given him an out.

Drew smiles brightly, puts his glass on the tray of a passing waiter, and kisses her cheek. "You're the best sister ever. Bye." Then he asks me, "Are you coming or what?"

I've never been one to look a gift horse in the mouth, or in this case, an escape route. "Super party, Lex. See ya." Then I follow Drew to the door. And if you look to the far side of the ballroom, you'll see Rosaline—following me with her eyes.

Chapter 6

After leaving the fund-raiser, Drew and I head out to a bar. He ends up going home with a leggy, black-haired lawyer looking for some sexual healing to ease the pain of a courtroom defeat. I nurse a beer and spot a few prospects, but none that motivate me to make an effort. On the walk home, I'm tempted to break the Three-Day Rule and call Delores.

What's that? You don't know what the Three-Day Rule is? Listen and learn. Three days is the perfect amount of time to wait before calling a woman after you've seen her. I don't care what category she's in. Whether you've banged her or not, you don't dial her number until the third day. It's not about head games or having the upper hand—it's about keeping her interest. Getting her to think about you. Day one, she's probably reminiscing about the last time she saw you. Day two she's hoping you're going to call and wondering if you had as good a time as she did. On day three—the magic day—she's just about given up hope that her phone is going to ring. She's questioning what went wrong, did she misread your signals, then—*bam*—your call swoops in and makes her day.

I've thought about Dee at random times throughout the day—always with a smile. Her straightforward, wise-ass humor, the way she danced . . . her nipple piercing. But, my phone stays securely in my pocket—because the three-day statute should never be broken.

Saturday night rolls around and it's business as usual. I meet up with Jack and Drew at the opening of the newest hot spot. It's a large club, a renovated warehouse in the heart of the meatpacking district. It's crowded—wall-to-wall bodies with barely any elbow room and a line around the corner. We're sharing a booth with five gorgeous Dutch cruise ship passengers. Amsterdam is wild—it's the modern-day Sodom and Gomorrah. Women from Amsterdam who've been at sea for three weeks could be hard to keep up with—even for us.

I squeeze my way through the throng of people to the bar. I lean forward and try to catch the bartender's eye. A minute later, I'm shoved deliberately from behind. I glance over my shoulder and see a short, Snooki-sized redhead with heavy lids, swaying in her high-heeled brown boots. She points her finger at me and slurs loudly, "I know you. You're the guy I slept with two weeks ago, the one with the motorcycle."

I thought she looked familiar. And her name is trendy, androgynous—Ricki or Remy . . .

Her equally petite but clearly more sober friend puts an arm around her. "Come on, Riley, forget him."

Riley. *So close.*

Riley pouts sloppily. "You never called. Prick."

I'm just gonna put this out there: I'm all for equal opportunity hookups. A woman shouldn't be thought any less of because she wants to get her freak on as frequently as a guy—no name-calling, no slut-shaming. On the other hand, girls need to stop playing the victim card. If I tell you I'm interested in one night only—why am *I* suddenly an asshole when that's all it turns out to be? Listen to what a guy says. Don't assume that there's some hidden meaning behind his actions. Real life is not chick-lit or a romantic comedy; you shouldn't expect it to be.

Still, it leaves a bad taste in my mouth when a girl feels used. "Don't be like that, babe. We had a good time—neither one of us wanted more. I never said I was going to call."

My words fall on deaf ears. Riley's eyes look to my right and she warns, "Watch out for this one, sister—he's a player."

"Thanks for the warning."

And even with the loud, synthesized music at maximum volume, I know that voice. I close my eyes, turn my head, and open them to find Delores Warren standing next to me.

You're not surprised, are you?

Riley fades from my sight and my thoughts as I check out Dee in her club wear. Her blond hair is painted with streaks of purple and blue, a tight, electric blue crop top barely covers her tits, her skirt is nothing more than strips of blue and purple fabric, and fuzzy, calf-high boots adorn her feet. Every inch of her fabulously exposed, body-glitter-covered skin sparkles like diamonds.

She smiles playfully. "Hello, God. It's me, Dee."

I don't try to hide that I'm happy to see her. "Hey. What's up? I left you a message this afternoon."

Today was day three. But Dee seems to be one of those rare

women who is immune to the Rule. She turns to face the bar but replies loudly enough for me to hear. "I know."

"Why didn't you call me back?"

She bops her head in time to the music and shrugs. "I figured you were just being nice."

"I don't do anything *just* to be nice." I hook my thumb in the direction Riley was standing. "Obviously."

I don't kiss ass—unless a girl asks me to—and the only smoke I blow is from my cigarettes.

A few feet away, a dark-skinned, hair-gelled dude in a white T-shirt and skinny jeans yells in Delores's direction. "Yo, Dee—hurry up with the drinks!"

There are two kinds of male Brooklynites—liberal, wealthy transplants who want to immerse themselves in urban living while restoring their historic brownstones to their former splendor, and homegrown, heavily accented, wise-guy wannabes who've watched *Goodfellas* one too many times. This dumbass is definitely the latter. I motion with my chin. "Who's he?"

"That's Mickey."

"Did you come here with him?"

"No. I came with a few girls from work. They're . . . around here somewhere."

Then I ask the more crucial question. "Are you going to leave with him?"

"Probably." The single word hits me like a jab to the chin.

Dee leans over the bar to place her drink order. When she's back on her feet, I move in closer, so I don't have to yell. "You can do better."

She looks into my eyes. Wearing the same expression she had on her face when I left her apartment Wednesday night—yearning mixed with sadness. Resignation.

"Maybe I don't want better."

"You should. Shoot for the moon and you still end up amongst the stars." It's an expression my mother used to say.

Dee lifts one shoulder. "Outer space isn't for everyone. I'm more of a ground-level kind of girl."

A woman's view of herself is like a reflection in a fun house mirror—bent, sometimes warped. The way others see them is always more accurate.

"You're so wrong."

"Mickey's uncomplicated. Easy."

I smile. "If you're looking for easy, I'm your guy—they don't come easier than me."

She chuckles. And I step to Dee's side, blocking her view of the worthless wonder. Out of sight, out of mind, right? Smoothly I ask, "When can I see you again?"

The side of Dee's mouth inches up. "You're seeing me right now."

"I want to see you in a predetermined location . . . preferably in less clothing."

Dee glances down at her outfit. "Less clothing than this? That'd be risking indecent exposure."

I smirk. "Always a sign of a great time."

Her drinks arrive. She picks up the tray and tells me, "I think seeing you again would be a bad idea—for both of us."

"Wrong again."

She smiles softly. "Bye, Matthew." And starts to walk away.

I call, "Hey, Dee." She turns. "Next time, tell him to get his own fucking drinks, okay?"

She holds my gaze for a moment, then nods and disappears into the crowd.

A while later, Drew tells me he and Jack are going to go party with the Dutch world travelers. "Are you coming?" he asks. "Drop some anchor, do a little deep-sea muff diving?"

I scan the dance floor, trying to catch a glimpse of electric blue. "Nah, I'm working on something here." I watch Jack by the door, entertaining the five girls, and ask, "Which one are you going for?"

"The girl in the middle seems like quite the eager beaver." He chuckles at his own joke.

Called it. I snort and Drew asks why. "You don't think it's unusual that out of five Scandinavians, you're shooting for the lone brunette in the bunch?"

Drew gets my point. But he blows it off. "Thanks, Sigmund. If I want to be psychoanalyzed, I'll throw good money away on an actual fucking therapist."

"Whatever you say, man." I slap him on the back.

After Drew and Jack leave, I do a lap around the club. I spot Dee on the dance floor with Tony Soprano Junior and it turns my stomach. His spastic, rough steps are a sharp contrast to Dee's effortless, rolling movements, and I wonder again what the hell she's doing with him.

I find an empty table but get blindsided by an aggressive,

chatty blonde in a short-sleeved cashmere sweater and leather skirt. She sits herself down and seems oblivious to the fact that I'm not paying attention to anything she says.

". . . and I was like, really, Dad? Like, how am I supposed to focus on graduate school with that measly allowance . . ." The droning continues until a dark-haired girl happens by the table. Blondie grabs her hand. "Tracy! Omg, it's been, like, forever. Let's get a pic." She leans her head against Tracy's and snaps a picture with her iPhone. "That's going on my Instagram!"

But, as soon as Tracy's out of earshot, Blondie turns to me with a glower. "I hate that bitch."

You know what I hate? Fakeness. Phony affection. It's stupid and a waste of time. The only falsies I appreciate are on a set of cosmetically altered boobs.

I've had as much of this chick's company as I can stand, and then I see Delores, walking out the door of the club, behind the Italian loser. Determined to salvage the night, I ask Blondie, "Do you want to get out of here?"

She beams. "I thought you'd never ask."

Chapter 7

Blondie doesn't want to ride the Ducati to her place, so she gives me her address and I settle her into a cab before climbing on my bike to meet her there. I'm unusually indifferent about the prospect of getting my dick wet. This girl's like a salad that's included with your meal—you'll munch on it, but only because it's already on the table in front of you. My mind keeps drifting back to Dee, walking out of the club with that undeserving fuckface.

I remember the way she moved Wednesday night and the appreciative, sexy sounds I elicited from her each time I sunk into her, slow and deep. I wonder if he's hearing those same tantalizing noises—and it pisses me the hell off. Not because Dee's screwing another guy, but because the guy is so goddamn unworthy.

At least, that's why I tell myself I'm pissed.

I shake off my conflicted feelings as I find a parking spot, at a meter, around the corner from the blonde's apartment, who I now think of as "Salad-girl." She's waiting for me inside the atrium of her building and opens the door to her first-floor apartment.

"Wow, it's really cold," she tells me in a high-pitched, almost whiny voice. "I can't believe how quick the temperature dropped. I wonder if it's going to snow early this year. I hate the snow. Even at Christmastime, I'll take a sandy beach over . . ."

I kiss her eagerly—just so she'll stop talking.

She squeaks into my mouth before recovering and putting her all into kissing me back. Her tongue flicks at mine quickly—too quickly. There's no rhythm or finesse. Feels like there's a stinger-less bumblebee trapped in my mouth, and its wings are beating the hell out of my tongue. She shoves me back onto the sofa and yanks her sweater over her head, revealing a beige, lacy bra, encasing a set of mega-huge melons.

Like I said before, I'm a breast lover, so I try and focus my attention on this positive attribute, but her idea of dirty talk is a major distraction.

"Oh, yeah," she moans, pushing her tits together. "I'm a bad girl. You gonna be my daddy? Daddy gonna punish his naughty slut?"

There are so many things wrong with that statement, I don't even know where to frigging begin.

First off, the *Daddy* talk is a boner killer. It's as effective as being submerged in a tub of ice water. It makes me think of my father and children and a thousand other things I *don't* want to be imagining during foreplay. The *naughty slut* was a valiant effort—I'm definitely into the name-calling, ass-slapping, dominant role-play thing women seem so fond of these days. But her babyish, breathy voice ruins the effect.

Delores's voice is low, sultry, unmistakably woman. When she begged me to fuck her, or called out *how* she wanted me to fuck her—it wasn't forced or fake. It was unrehearsed and real, because she was so turned on, so caught up in the ecstasy of the moment, that staying silent simply wasn't possible.

I grunt as Salad-girl pounces on my lap. She claws at my shirt but only succeeds in giving me rug burn on my neck. Shirt-burn. Then, with surprising strength, she forces my head between her breasts, holding me so tightly I can't fucking breathe. The Vikings believed dying on the battlefield was a "good death," and normally I'd feel the same way about being tit-smothered . . . but these aren't the tits I want doing me in. I struggle to turn my head, finally succeeding when I grip her biceps and push back. I tilt my head up and reinflate my lungs.

And then, still holding her arms, I look at Salad-girl's face. A cute nose, wet, pink lips, and round blue eyes gaze back at me. She's hot. A solid 8. Any other night I'd be all over this, but tonight . . . I'm not.

Because the eyes I want gazing back at me are light brown with flecks of gold. The lips I want to nibble on are red and full and have the most direct, unexpected responses coming out of them. I'm more turned on picturing Dee in my head than I've been for the last five minutes with this topless alternative grinding on my lap.

"Wait . . . hold up a second. This isn't working for me," I tell her.

"What do you mean?"

Women always say they just want men to be honest with them. Let's see how that plays out. "You're pretty and you seem like a fun girl . . . but, I just realized . . . I'm into somebody else at the moment."

Her neck swivels as she asks, "Excuse me?"

"No offense." She covers her immense chest with her hands.

And now she's glaring at me. "If it makes you feel better, if I hadn't met her first, I'd totally be having sex with you right now."

She scampers off my lap. "You're an asshole!"

I can see why she'd think that.

"Get the hell out of my apartment, you dick!" She picks a coaster up from the end table—the heavy ceramic kind—and whips it at my head. The first one misses. But the second one nails me in the shoulder blade as I dive for the door.

"Ow! Christ, I'm going!"

"Jerk!"

This proves it—whoever said honesty was the best policy, was obviously lying.

I park my motorcycle on the sidewalk and sprint up to the front door of Dee's building. I push her buzzer once, twice, three times for good luck. I wait five seconds, but there's no response.

Next, I do what every other normal human being would.

I push the button down until my motherfucking fingertip turns white.

Buzzzzzzzzzzzzzzzzzzzzzzzzzzzzzzzzzzzzzzzzzzzzzzzzzzzzzzzzzzzzzzzz zzzzzzzzzzzzzzzzzzzzzzzzzzzzzzzzzzzzzzzzzzzzzzzzzzzzzzzzzzzzzzzzz zzzzzzzzzzzzzzzzzzzzzzzzzzzzzzzzzzzzzzzzzzzzzzzzzzzzzzzzzzzzzzzzz zzzzzzzzzz . . .

When that doesn't get an answer, I admit, I start to panic. I walk onto the sidewalk, below Delores's front window, and cup my hands around my mouth. "Delores! Hey Dee—you awake?"

Because this is New York City, a neighbor immediately yells back, "We're all awake now, asshole!"

A few "Shuddups" come from various directions, and I think one woman may have thrown a potted plant at me.

But I'd like to believe it was an accident.

With no other recourse, I throw my head back and go for my best Marlon Brando impression. "Stella!! Steeellllaaaa!!"

Delores's window opens. Fucking finally.

"Matthew?" she calls down, surprised.

My fingers hook my belt loops, going for a nonchalant stance. "Hey," I answer. "S'up?"

"What the hell are you doing?" she asks.

Here is when I realize my grand plan to stop her and Tony from getting busy . . . only reached this point. *Damn*. From here on out, it's all improv.

"I wanted to . . . Can you come down, please?"

Miraculously, she doesn't tell me to go screw myself.

And two minutes later, she's walking out onto the sidewalk . . . with Goomba Johnny trailing behind her. Thankfully, she's still fully dressed in her club clothes. That doesn't really mean much—especially considering the outfit covers little more than a bra and underwear would, but at this point, I'll take whatever bright side I can.

The wise guy wannabe walks in front of Dee and shoves me back. "The fuck's your problem? You some kinda psycho?"

On instinct, my fists rise to a defensive posture. "I didn't come to fight you, but you wanna go? We can go."

Then I notice the tattoo low on his bicep—a tattoo of the Virgin Mary with *AVE MARIA* scrolled below it. And I take a different approach.

"I'm just trying to save my marriage."

Yes, lying is a low blow—but desperate times . . .

His head snaps to Dee. "You're married?"

She's horrified. "No, I'm not married. He's out of his mind!"

I open my wallet to the picture of Mackenzie and force sincerity onto my expression. "My family is my everything. I know you don't know me, but could you just do me a steady and . . . walk away?"

Now Dee is seriously pissed off. She pushes my shoulder and turns to the Jersey Shore reject. "Mickey, that is not my daughter, and he is not my husband!"

He replies, "My name is Mikey."

It's a relief to see I'm not the only one having trouble with names tonight.

Exasperated, Dee asks, "Does it matter?"

For most guys, it doesn't matter—we don't care if you scream the Pope's name while we're giving it to you. But apparently, "Mikey" isn't most guys. Because he throws his hands up in surrender. "This is way too heavy for me. I'm outta here." Then he turns on his heel and walks away.

I watch his retreating form with glee. Then I turn to Dee and hook my thumb over my shoulder. "Some people are so gullible."

That's when she punches me—right in the mouth.

I stumble back and taste blood. Delores may be petite, but she can throw a hell of a right hook. She points and wags her finger as she rails, "I don't know what the fuck this is, but it is *not* okay!"

My hand drops from my injured mouth to my side. And my mind is blank—not a single smooth line or witty comeback in sight. So all I can do is ask, "Why don't you like me?"

"What?"

"We had a great time—the sex was hot, we laughed—but now you don't want anything to do with me."

"This is a new concept for you?"

I snort. "Shit, yeah, it's new. Everybody likes me. I'm a great fucking guy."

Dee massages her forehead with her fingertips the way my mother used to do when she had a headache brewing. Then she sighs and admits, "Okay . . . the thing is . . . it's not you, it's me. I'm the problem."

My eyes crinkle with revulsion. "Jesus Christ, are you serious? I'm practically pouring my heart out here, and you can't even be bothered to make up a decent lie?"

Dee throws out her arms, "I'm telling you the truth. I do like you. You're very cute, you're very funny, and you're fantastic in bed. But I . . . I'm a more content person when I'm not in a relationship. When I get serious with someone . . . I go a little crazy."

"Who's said anything about a relationship? Let's just . . . keep having a good time. See what happens. It's not like we're going to take off for Vegas and get married."

That would just be ridiculous.

Dee shakes her head. "You don't understand. It never ends well. This won't be any different, Matthew. I used to think it was the men I picked, but I've finally accepted the fact that it's me. I make good guys go bad. I'm like . . . a penis pump . . . I turn men into gigantic pricks. *I'm* the girl your mother warned you about—bad news."

And her expression is so serious, I can't not laugh. "No, you're not."

"You don't know me."

"What I know so far is pretty awesome."

She starts to deny what I've said, but I push on. "You're over-thinking this. We can be fuck buddies if it makes you feel better. New friends with fabulous benefits. I'll be the scratch for your itch . . . the booty to your two a.m. call. Just . . . don't screw any other guys—you won't need to."

She begins to shake her head. Until I remind her. "And the world could end tomorrow, remember? The aliens could invade . . . global warming . . . we've got to live for the now, 'cause you never know when the now will be gone."

I hold out my hand. "Take a chance, Dee. I won't let you down."

Her honey-colored eyes look wistfully at my hand. "God, you're good."

I smirk. And it just comes out. "That's what she said."

Dee cracks up.

Then she takes my hand in hers. They're a perfect fit.

Like two middle schoolers experiencing their first crushes, we stand like that for a few moments, smiling at each other. Wordlessly, we turn and walk toward her apartment.

Much too seriously, Dee says, "Hey, Matthew?"

I raise my eyebrows.

"When you've had enough? Just remember I tried to warn you, okay?"

I don't know what kind of fucked-up, douche bags Dee has been going out with, but that kind of talk ticks me off. I'm determined to prove her wrong and lighten the mood. So I lean toward her and whisper, "You're too beautiful to ever get enough of."

Delores rolls her eyes. And I get the distinct impression she thinks I'm bullshitting her. Guess I'll just have to keep calling her beautiful until she believes it.

Chapter 8

Waking up in a place that's not yours is always slightly disorienting. My eyes open to sunlight streaming through sheer purple curtains and to a clothes-cluttered bedroom. Last night, Dee and I talked some more after going inside her apartment. Turns out, she didn't have sex with the homeboy. She said he spent the majority of their time at her apartment on the phone with a friend. *Idiot.* She asked me if it would've bothered me if she had—my answer was yes. But . . . I would've gotten over it.

I slip on a pair of boxers, then I follow the smell of bacon and the sound of music to the kitchen. Dee stands at the stove with her back to me, singing along to "Beneath Your Beautiful" that pours out from the stereo, which is mounted below her cabinet.

Her voice is adorably bad—off-key and screechy—like a mating cat's. Her reddish-blond hair is pinned up with chopsticks—still color-streaked from last night—and the only piece of clothing she's wearing is my button-down, blue shirt. As the song ends, I applaud.

She spins around, spatula in hand. "Morning."

"Nice shirt."

She shrugs. "Since I was making you breakfast, I decided to go full fledged cliché and wear it."

I step up close and plant a sweet kiss on her lips. She smiles, shyly. "Are you hungry?"

"Starved."

Dee hands me two glasses of orange juice and grabs a platter of bacon and scrambled eggs from the counter. We sit at her small, two-chaired dining table and dig in.

"This is good," I comment.

"Organic turkey bacon. It's like crack. One taste, you'll never do pork again."

As we eat, I take the opportunity to check out her place. Before, I was much too preoccupied with making her moan. It's neater than I expected, and eclectic. A red recliner whose fabric has seen better days is stationed next to a round, mosaic-topped table, adjacent to a comfy looking beige couch with a soft, brown blanket thrown across the back. Floral pillows of all shapes are scattered around, and a tall lamp with a beaded fringe shade stands in the corner. Just a few picture frames decorate the walls—one is of Delores, standing next to a thin woman with similar hair color, who I assume is her mother. Another is of Dee, at about thirteen, with one arm around the shoulders of a braces-adorned Kate Brooks, and the other arm around a brown-haired boy, who must be Dee's cousin. All three are wearing roller skates.

I swallow a forkful of mouthwatering eggs and ask, "What are you doing today?"

"I have to hit up the farmers' market in Brooklyn . . . but otherwise, nothing."

"Do you want to hang out?"

"Okay."

"We'll swing by my place so I can shower, and I have to make one quick stop, but after, I thought we could go to Central Park?"

The beauty of living in the city is there's always something to do. Even if your ass is sitting on a park bench and you're feeding the pigeons, it feels like you're doing something.

"Sounds good. I'll get dressed."

Thirty minutes later, Dee's freshly showered and walking out of her building with her hair in a bun, wearing a silver, strapless shirt, black leather pants, and tiger patterned high heels. Luckily, my illegally parked motorcycle didn't get ticketed or towed. Dee gazes at the bike appreciatively. She runs her hand over the seat and it reminds me of how she ran her hand over my stomach, inching lower and lower. I pick up her hand and kiss her palm. "Don't stroke it like that unless you mean it."

She reaches up on her toes and whispers in my ear, "I always mean it."

I pull a cap helmet out of the pack on the back of my bike and place it on Dee's head, buckling it under her chin. She's the perfect mixture of sensual and adorable, sexy and cute—I could eat her out right here on the street.

She climbs on my motorcycle and winks. "Take me for a ride, Matthew."

I rev the engine. "Hold on tight."

Not every girl is cut out for riding on a motorcycle. One or two have clutched me so tight they left nail marks and cut off feeling to my extremities. Another time, a chick didn't grip strong enough—

was too busy "wooting" and waving her hands in the air—and she almost gave me a heart attack when she went sailing off the back. Thankfully, she wasn't harmed. Dee squeezes me just right—one arm around my waist, her other hand on my thigh, the splendid feel of her tits pressed against my back and her chin on my shoulder blade.

I'll gladly give her one long ride after another. Both kinds.

After we arrive at my building, we park in the private deck and head to the lobby. Delores admires the impressive architecture while I retrieve my mail from the box. When we walk into my apartment, I tell Dee to make herself at home and hop in the shower. After I'm dry, I slip on a pair of jeans and a flannel shirt. Leaving it unbuttoned for the moment, I walk back to the living room in search of Delores. She's staring out the picture window.

"I think I'm going to call you 'Upper West Side' from now on," she tells me with a grin.

"But 'God' is much more accurate."

She moves to the bookcase. "These are great pictures." She's looking at one I took of Mackenzie last year, blowing a kiss at the camera. The lighting brought out the brilliance of her baby blues.

"That's Mackenzie," I explain. "The niece I told you about Wednesday night . . . who's technically not." I point to another picture beside it. "And that's my parents." It's a black and white— my mother looks blissfully clueless, my father grumpily oblivious; their everyday expressions.

I pull out my camera bag, making sure I have extra film, checking the lenses.

"Do you have a darkroom?" she asks.

"I do, actually."

A look appears in her eyes that I'm beginning to grow familiar with—one that says she's turned on. "Will you show it to me?"

I put the camera down and raise my arm. "Right this way."

Officially, it's a walk-in closet, but windowless and large enough for a shelf of chemicals and a table with a row of developing trays. The lighting is low of course, with a sepia-tinted hue. I close the door behind us, as Delores looks around. And that feeling of playing seven minutes in heaven when I was thirteen washes over me. But heaven, back then, was never this beautiful.

Dee's eyes rake over me from head to toe. "Do you have any idea how sexy this is, Matthew?"

"A little bit," I admit.

She presses up against me and my back hits the closed door. Dee kisses my chin, then scrapes it with her teeth. "Will you take my picture sometime?" She bends her knees and slides down my torso, her warm hands leaving a trail of heat as they skim my chest and stomach.

I swallow hard. "I will definitely be taking your picture."

She peppers my stomach with soft kisses. "We'll be like a modern day Jack and Rose from *Titanic*."

Breathing heavy now, I say, "Jack was a pussy. If I were him, I would've tied Rose up, gagged her, and tossed her ass in a life boat. Then I would've gotten in after her." I'd like to point out that if Rose had just done what the hell Jack told her to, they *both* would've survived.

Dee wets her lips with her tongue and slides my jeans down over my hips, freeing my already aching dick. She wraps her small hand around the base, pumping slowly. "Until you take those photographs of me, and develop them here, I want you to think about this the next time you're in this room."

Still stroking the base, she covers the tip with her lips, sucking gently and flicking it with her tongue. I lean more weight against the door—my knees going weak. She removes her mouth, peels the foreskin back, and takes me fully in.

And I can't help but moan. "Fuuuck."

Her mouth is hot and wet and so tight, bright dots appear in the darkness of my closed lids. Slowly she increases the suction of her mouth, the speed of her rubbing palm—my hand buries in her hair and tightens.

Dee hums around me, and I beg, "Faster . . ." She grants my request and her head bobs quicker, dragging me closer with every pass of her mouth. I pant. "Dee . . . yes . . . gonna come . . ." She sucks me even tighter, and then I'm coming, groaning raggedly, gripping her hair in my fist—trying not to pull. As soon as she releases me, I sink all the way to the floor, breathing like I completed the New York marathon.

I reach for Delores—pull her up against my chest. I kiss her nose, both cheeks, and finally her mouth, thoroughly. "I'll remember that for a long, long time."

"Mission accomplished."

"You're kidding me, right?"

I take my helmet off and lock it onto my motorcycle. "No, I'm serious."

Dee hasn't gotten off the bike. "I'll wait out here, if it's all the same to you."

"Come on—it's halfway over already—I just have to drop off my envelope."

"Have you never heard the saying, 'As nervous as a whore in Church'?"

"Knock it off with the self-deprecating comments. If that's the standard, I should be sweating bullets. Let's go."

"Do I have to drink blood?"

"Only if you're baptized."

If you haven't figured it out yet, we're at St. Mary's church. It's Sunday—and on Sunday, I go to church, even if it's only for the tail-end of the mass. I have a deeply held belief that something terrible will happen if I don't.

Twelve years of Catholic school will do that to you.

I drag Dee into the vestibule. She steps carefully, like she's walking into a haunted house.

A suited, gray-haired gentleman comes through the double doors carrying a brimming collection basket. *Perfect timing.* I slip my envelope in and bow my head as the priest's voice echoes through the speakers from the main chamber, working up to the final blessing. Dee watches, copying my stance as she stands beside me. Before the priest is finished, a commotion of clattering feet coming up the stairs from the basement draws my attention. Through the side door, Sister Beatrice Dugan steps into the antechamber with a dozen Sunday school students in two lines behind her.

Sister B was my first sexual experience. Well . . . my first self-sexual experience. She was all of our firsts—the closest Drew and I have ever come to a three-way.

Wait, that last part is gross, forget I said that.

Anyway, puberty is a confusing time for a boy. Having a fuck-hot teacher who happens to be a nun made it more confusing. I got carried away when I first discovered the joys of masturbation. Unfortunately, I didn't just "choke the chicken"—I literally strangled the sucker. That's how, at thirteen years old, I ended up diagnosed with CPS—Chafed Penis Syndrome. I don't need to elaborate on that do I?

My mother may have bought into the doctor's explanation that my CPS was caused by keeping a wet bathing suit on too long, but my father sure as hell didn't. In one of our more tender conversations, he told me spanking the monkey was nothing to be ashamed of, that it was like electricity—God wouldn't have given it to us if he didn't want us to use it. But, like all things, moderation was key. I calmed down after that chat, and was able to engage in regular self-pleasure, without inflicting injury.

Sister B quiets the giggling kids with a look. Then with an Irish lilt that time hasn't diminished, she says, "Matthew—how are you, m'boy?"

"Right as rain, Sister B."

"Right as rain and yet still late for Mass? Tsk-tsk."

I shrug. "Better late than never."

She smiles. "I suppose you're right, though offering a few Our Fathers as you pray for punctuality may be in order. I saw your parents at the early mass; they're looking grand as always."

I nod. Then I turn to Dee and say, "Delores, this is Sister Beatrice, my grade school teacher. Sister B, this is Delores Warren."

Sister B greets her. "Pleased to meet you."

Dee waves. "Hi."

Sister Beatrice's brow wrinkles. "You look uncomfortable, m'dear. Why is that?"

Dee fidgets. "I just . . . I'm not Catholic. Not even a little."

Sister B pats her shoulder, and in a hushed voice tells her, "That's quite all right. Neither was Jesus."

When we get to Central Park, I take out my camera and get a few great shots of Dee by the fountain. I take some more nature-themed pictures of the leaves as they're blowing down from the trees. Then Delores and I lay next to each other on a blanket, on a grassy patch, heated by the warm sun of the fall afternoon. And we trade questions—the random, inappropriate kind that are always fun and a great way to get to know a person.

"Have you ever been arrested?" Dee asks me as she plays with the buttons on my flannel shirt.

"Not yet. You?"

She smiles. "Arrested, but never convicted." Then she tells me about the time she, her cousin, and Kate got caught breaking into their local roller-skating rink after hours and had to be brought home by the town sheriff. Her mother wasn't thrilled.

"Have you ever had sex in a public place?" I ask, partially because I'm curious . . . and partially for future reference.

"Mmm . . . public place, yes—but I don't think anyone actually saw us."

I run my fingers through her hair, the sunlight accentuating the red highlights, making it more fiery than golden.

"Have you ever had sex on your motorcycle?" she asks. And I hope that's for future reference too.

"Yes. It's not as easy as you'd think. But, it's something everybody should try at least once." Then I ask, "What's your favorite color? And how do you take your coffee?"

"I don't have a favorite color—it changes, depending on my mood. And I don't drink coffee. I try and stay away from caffeine, it's bad for your skin."

Dee is a foodie. She mentioned going to the farmers' market in Brooklyn later, to stock up on fennel and lemongrass and some other shit I've only heard of in gourmet restaurants where presentation is more important than taste. That's not my idea of a great meal. But she swears her homemade granola doesn't taste anything like rabbit food.

"Is everyone in your family devout Catholics?"

I chuckle. "Devout is kind of a strong word, but we all go to church." I think about it a little more, then say, "Well, all of us except Drew. Besides weddings and baptisms, he hasn't willingly stepped inside a church since we were kids."

She turns on her stomach, resting her chin on my chest. "What made him the black sheep? Did he find a six-six-six tattoo on his scalp or something?"

I smile, because I'm sure several of our ordained teachers held that very same opinion about him.

"No. Drew and God had a falling out when we were about ten years old. That was the year Steven's mother, Janey, was diagnosed with breast cancer. The parents sat us all down, told us she was sick, that she'd be getting treatment from the doctors, and that we had to pray as hard as we could that the treatment would work.

"Drew didn't take the news well. He couldn't understand why, with all the dickheads in the world, God had to afflict someone as nice as Janey with a terminal illness. Anyway, she did chemo and eventually went into remission. But when we were in high school, the cancer came back hard and she was gone within a few months. She was the first person I knew who died. By the time I was born, my grandparents were long gone. My aunts and uncles are still around, but Janey went at age thirty-nine, which, even as a kid, seemed young to me."

Delores's mouth turns down in sympathy.

"But the real kicker came at her funeral. Steven's father, George, was just wrecked. And, unfortunately, useless. That left all the heavy lifting to Steven. He made the big decisions, he played host to the guests at the three-day wake. He was sixteen years old—Alexandra and he had started dating a few months before Janey passed."

I watch a flock of three sparrows, flying with precise synchronization as I continue the trek down memory lane.

"So, on the day of the funeral and burial, there's an early viewing—just for immediate family. Steven wanted to be there first, to have some private time with his mom. Drew and I went with him for moral support. And the priest at St. Mary's at the time was Father Gerald—he was a real old-school, arrogant, prick of a priest, you know? He comes in where the three of us are sitting, and he tells Steven his mother died because she wasn't pure. That if she had been holier, God would have saved her. Then he said her death was also a sign of our lack of faith. That if we had believed more, God would have answered our prayers."

Dee's mouth falls open. "That's terrible. What did Steven say?"

"Nothing. He was too shocked, too grief-stricken to say anything. Drew, on the other hand, has always been quick with a comeback. So he gets up, gets right in Father Gerald's ugly face and says, 'Fuck you, Father, and the donkey you rode in on. Isn't there an altar boy somewhere you should be trying to ply with sacrificial wine, so you can get laid?'"

The corners of Dee's mouth turn up. "The more I hear about this Drew guy, the more I'm starting to like him."

I nod. "Father Gerald turns, like, frigging purple and is just about ready to smack Drew a good one when John, Anne, George, and my parents come in. So Gerald holds off, only to try and get Drew booted out of school the next day. He said if he didn't apologize, he'd have him expelled. Although John didn't like what the priest had said, he leaned on Drew to apologize for being disrespectful. But he wouldn't give—refused to say sorry to such 'an evil fuck.'

"And then, Anne started to cry. She sobbed about how if

Drew got expelled it would ruin his life, and where did she go wrong. That's when Drew caved—'cause he just couldn't handle making his mother cry.

"He wrote a letter of apology to Father Gerald and jumped through every hoop the old bastard gave him for penance. That's why Drew can quote the Bible—word for word—because Gerald made him copy it, down to the last punctuation mark, every day after school. Anyway, by the time his punishment was lifted, Drew was convinced Catholicism was just a racket and that God doesn't give a shit about any of us."

Dee tilts her head and regards me thoughtfully. Then she asks, "But you don't believe that?"

"No, I don't. I asked Sister Beatrice if what Father Gerald had said was true. That if we had had more faith, would God have answered our prayers."

"What did she say?" Dee asks.

In my best Irish accent, I reply, "She said, 'Matthew, m'boy, the Lord answers every prayer . . . but sometimes, the answer is no.'"

Dee thinks that over for a moment. Then she says, "Well . . . that kind of sucks."

I grin. "That's what I said too."

Then I wonder aloud, "What about you? Did you grow up religious?"

"Yeah, you could say that. My mother's always been a spiritual grazer. A taste of Mormonism here, a scrap of Protestant there, but nothing ever stuck. She was interested in Kabala way before Madonna made it all the rage. These days she's into Buddhism—worked out well for Tina Turner."

It's late afternoon by the time we walk back to my bike. I put the folded blanket and camera in the hard-top compartment. And the scent of fresh chili dogs from the sidewalk cart reaches my nose, making my stomach growl. I take out my wallet and ask Dee, "You want one?"

She looks at the hot dog like it's a loaded gun. "Ah . . . no. I prefer to live past the age of fifty, thanks."

I order mine with extra chili, then respond, "The sidewalk hot dog *is* New York." The same could be said for a slice of pizza.

"The sidewalk hot dog is a heart attack in a bun. Do you know how many nitrates are in that?"

"That's what makes it taste so good. You know, for someone who claims to be all 'carpe diem,' you've got a lot of hang-ups."

She caves. "Okay, fine . . ." She tells the vendor, "One please."

"You want chili?" I ask.

"Sure. Go big or go home, right?"

I smile. "I like the way you think."

We stand next to my bike eating our dogs. When Dee is done with hers, a dab of sauce lingers on her chin. Instead of telling her, I take care of it with my mouth.

"Mmm . . ." I smack my lips. "Tastes even better on you."

She laughs. It's a great sound.

Our last stop of the day is the farmers' market in Brooklyn. She was limited by what could fit in the Ducati's pack, but Dee said having me around for the trip was worth the second trek she'd have to make later in the week. I help her carry the groceries into her apartment, and I'm about to ask her out to dinner when she wraps her arms around my neck and kisses me full on the mouth.

Dinner can fucking wait.

I drop the bags on the floor and go right for her ass. Gripping and kneading, her black pants a thin but annoying barrier. Her hands bury in my hair while I lift her and wrap her legs around my waist, giving my rigid cock the contact it craves. I suck on her bottom lip as her hands massage my shoulders, relaxing warmth spreading from her fingertips. I scrape my teeth along her jaw and swing us around, pressing Dee's back against the refrigerator. She moans as our hips rub and grind.

We're both panting hard as I nibble on her neck. Then she moans, "Matthew . . . Matthew, I need . . ."

My lips move against her hot skin. "God, me too . . ."

"I'm . . ."

The next thing I know, Dee pulls out of my grasp and shoves me on my ass in her haste to run down the hall. I lay on the floor, breathing heavy, trying to process what the hell just happened—when the unmistakable sound of upchucking emanates from the bathroom.

Bet you weren't expecting that, huh? Makes two of us.

My stomach rolls as I walk down the hall—the sounds of Dee's sickness making me really fucking queasy. I brace a hand on the doorframe. "Are you all right?"

She sits in front of the toilet, a tissue covering her lips, her eyes closed.

"Do I sound all right, genius?"

"No."

She moans . . . in the not-awesome kind of way. "You and your stupid chili dogs. I think they were bad."

Like any accused man, I launch a defense. "They weren't bad.

If they were bad, I'd . . ." And I can't even finish the sentence. Because heat closes in on my face, and my stomach twists around on itself, and I'm diving for the plastic wastepaper basket in the corner.

Which just makes Dee vomit more.

And I think of Lardass and the Barf-o-rama story from *Stand by Me*. And I'd probably laugh at the entire situation, if I didn't feel so frigging awful.

Eventually, we crawl into the bed and lay next to each other— me stretched out, Dee in the fetal position.

"This is all your fault," Dee whimpers.

"You're right. You're so right."

"I hate you. No—I don't mean that, I like you so much. I think I'm dying, Matthew."

"You're not dying. But I might be dying."

Even though we're naturally stronger than women, it's common knowledge that men are ten times more affected by illness. Just ask your husband or your boyfriend.

Dee opens the drawer of her nightstand, jostling the bed as she pulls something out.

"What are you doing?" I groan. "Stop moving." It's the first time in my life that I've ever said that to a girl.

"I'm writing a note to Katie to have you fucking arrested for manslaughter if I die . . . and the hot dog man as an accomplice."

"You're a cold woman, Delores."

"Better you learn that now," Dee says, even as she moves closer to me. I rub soothing circles on her back until she rolls over and takes my hand in hers. And we stay like that until we both fall asleep.

Chapter 9

It's amazing how close you can feel to a person after you've suffered through the torture of food poisoning together for twenty-four hours. That kind of intimacy can take months—even years—to achieve. I now know Dee's cum face—and her puke face.

We both call in sick Monday morning, both of us still feeling wrung out. We take separate showers and I borrow a pair of her cousin's sweatpants. Normally I'd have issues with going commando in another guy's drawers, but these were clean and folded in the back of Dee's closet, so the time lapse from the last time Warren wore them makes them okay. Plus, the idea of putting on my clothes from last night feels nasty.

Delores sits next to me on the couch, her Stompeez rabbit–clad feet on the coffee table, wrapped in a fluffy, purple robe that would look light-years from sexy on another girl. But because I know there's nothing but smooth, bare flesh underneath it—it's hot.

I flick on the television and we try to agree on a movie to watch. The problem is, Delores has a vagina, which means her taste in movies ranges from awful to nonexistent.

Don't scowl at me—I'm only stating what every man in the world knows. The reason shitty movies like *The English Patient* and *The King's Speech* win Academy Awards? Women have chickboners for Ralph Fiennes and Colin Firth. Sure, *Braveheart* won a bunch of well-deserved awards, but it wasn't just because it's the perfect movie. Mel Gibson, anyone? Enough said.

Dee defends a horrible chick flick suggestion. "I like best friend movies—they're very empowering. *Thelma & Louise, Beaches, Steel Magnolias*—that one's my favorite. I always imagine Kate and me like Ouiser and Clairee when we're old."

"What's a Steel Magnolia? More importantly, what the fuck is an *Ouiser*?"

She looks simultaneously surprised and appalled. "You've never seen *Steel Magnolias*? Are you even human? It was one of Julia Roberts's first movies."

I throw up one hand as I object. "No—no frigging way am I watching Julia Roberts! Drew went through a whole year of Julia Roberts as a kid and he still hasn't recovered. To this day, *Pretty Woman* quotes come flying out of his mouth uncontrollably. Not happening."

"Then what are we going to watch?"

I scroll through the on-demand movies until I spot a winner. "*Conan the Barbarian*. The greatest love story ever told."

Her nose wrinkles. "Normally I'd be into Schwarzenegger-flavored eye candy, but I'm not in the mood. Let's watch *Steel Magnolias*."

I shake my head. "No. It'll be two hours of my life I'll never get back."

Delores tucks her feet under her and rises to her knees. A sly, persuasive smile slides onto her face, which I've come to recognize as a sign she's in the mood to get busy. She leans over me; I angle my head back to keep eye contact.

"Are you feeling better, Matthew? 'Cause I'm feeling a lot better."

I do a quick mental rundown of my faculties. "Yeah, I'm good."

Her smile gets wider—more suggestive. "Then let's make a bet. Whoever can make the other person come first gets to pick the movie? What do you say?"

It's clear to me why Delores is such a successful chemist—she has such an amazingly innovative mind.

I scrape my teeth over my bottom lip thoughtfully. "I say this is a bet I'm going to really enjoy winning."

She tilts back and slowly opens her robe. "Not as much as I'm going to enjoy making you lose."

It was close. If this were NASCAR, it would've been a photo fin-ish—just seconds apart. But . . . Dee was the winner. She got to pick the movie. Although, I wasn't exactly crying about my defeat. If you gotta lose a bet, that's the way to do it.

Anyway, *Steel Magnolias* is well under way. And it just rein-forces my opinion about women and films, because nothing is fucking happening in this movie. It starts off with a wedding and now it looks like Julia Roberts is going to die. Other than that? Just a bunch of girls talking and getting their hair done and talk-ing *some more*.

Dee sits beside me in rapt attention while the lady from *Smokey and the Bandit*—she's Julia Roberts's mother—starts talking to her friends at the cemetery. Dee's nose is already red and her eyes are watery. I turn back to the film and listen as the woman starts to scream and cry and ask how her grandson will ever know how much his mother loved him.

And out of nowhere I start to think about Mackenzie and—God forbid—if something ever happened to Alexandra, how Mackenzie would feel. Who would tell her, how much she would miss out on. Steven's a great guy, an awesome father, but a mother—especially a fierce mother like Alexandra—that kind of love is different. More.

Irreplaceable.

And even though Dee's apartment doesn't seem dusty, some particles must have gotten in my eyes. I rub them, to get the irritation out.

And I sniff. *Goddamn allergies.*

"Are you crying?" Dee asks me with surprise and laughter in her voice.

Disgustedly, I turn to her. "No, I'm not crying."

Then I look back at the television screen. Where Julia Roberts's poor, distraught mother is screaming that she's fine, when she's obviously not. And about all the things she's able to do that her kid never could.

Jesus Christ, this is depressing.

"It's just so fucking sad!" I blurt out as I gesture to the television. "How can you watch this shit and not want to blow your head off with a twelve-gauge shotgun?"

Dee covers her mouth and laughs into her hands. "The fact that it can make me cry is one of the reasons I love it so much."

Okay, that? That is like saying I love the table in my parents'

front hall because I'm gonna stub my toe on it every frigging time
I walk past barefoot.

"Why?"

She shrugs. "Sometimes it feels good to cry. It's cathartic.
You've never cried over a movie?"

I'm offended that she even feels the need to ask.

I shake my head, but then stop as I remember. "*Rocky Three*.
I cried during *Rocky Three,* but that doesn't count. Anyone who
doesn't get choked up when Mickey dies has no soul."

She shrugs. "Never seen it."

"You're missing out. Have you seen *Predator*?" She shakes her
head. "The original *Escape from New York*?" Another negative.
"*The Warriors*?"

"Nope."

Then a thought occurs to me. "Wait, your cousin grew up
with you and your mom, right?"

"From the time I was about six years old, yeah."

"So you had a boy in the house—how is it you've never seen
any of these classics?" I ask, though I'm pretty sure I already know
the answer.

Dee shrugs. "Billy was happy to watch what I wanted."

Sure he was. It's then that I decide to take that poor male role
model–deprived bastard under my wing.

By Monday night, I'm well enough to return to my own apartment. You'd think after almost two full days away, I'd miss it—be
glad to be home. But it feels . . . quiet. Boring, even.

I develop the pictures I took with Dee at the park. And while I wait in the darkroom, I think about the last time I was here. With her. Her wet mouth, the stroke of her soft tongue, the way her cheeks hollowed out when she sucked me dry.

As my memory runs wild, I just barely contain the pussy-whipped urge to call Delores and implore her to come over. I succeed, but only because we already made plans for her to hang out here Wednesday night.

As far as I'm concerned, Wednesday can't come soon enough.

On Wednesday afternoon, I meet Alexandra downtown for lunch.

The weather is mild, so we sit at a sidewalk table outside. I take a bite of my burger while Alexandra crunches a salad with grilled shrimp. Then I tell her, "So . . . I've met someone."

Growing up with Drew, I always regarded Lexi as my older sister, but the fact that we didn't share the same genes, or actually have to live together, made our relationship much less conten-tious than the one she has with her brother. She looks out for me, but she doesn't "mother" me the way she does with Drew. She gets annoyed by my screwups, but she doesn't feel responsible for them. For me, it's the best of both worlds—all the benefits of a big sister without the pain in the ass headaches.

"From what I hear, you and my brother 'meet' lots of women."

I grin. "This one I like."

She nods. "Once again, you and Drew 'like' a whole bunch of poor, unsuspecting ladies. Why is this one worth mentioning?"

"I *like* her, like her."

Alexandra's blue eyes widen. "Wow. A *Wonder Years* reference. This must be serious. Do tell."

My eyes abashedly drop to my burger. "Her name is Delores."

"That's kind of random."

"She's . . . different."

Lexi tries to pull more details out of me. "Like . . . she has three breasts kind of different?"

I laugh. "No. But, for the record, it wouldn't be a strike against her if she did. She's . . . cool. I have a good time talking with her, you know? She says she's not into relationships, but I think I'm hoping I can change her mind. I haven't felt like this since . . ."

Alexandra puts up her palm. "Don't. Do not even say the foul beast's name. I'm trying to eat here."

"Anyway, I'm not sure if it's going anywhere, but I . . ."

I don't get the opportunity to finish my sentence. Because a wave of icy, red liquid splashes in my face.

Tastes like cherry.

"Lying motherfucker!"

I swipe my face, clearing the fluid off my eyelashes. When my vision clears, I see Delores standing on the sidewalk—with a now-empty Slurpee cup clenched in her hand.

Which she proceeds to throw at my fucking head.

"All that talk about not hooking up with other people! Exclusive fuck buddies, you said! I would've liked you if you had just been straight with me! I *knew* it—I knew you were just another false-faced bastard who doesn't like to share his sex toys but has no problem playing with a different one!"

By this time, Alexandra and I are both on our feet. And I have no idea what's going on.

I try, "Delores . . ."

But she cuts me off. "Four days! You tell me four days ago

that you're not interested in screwing anyone else, and here I find you with . . . with . . ."

Lexi holds out her hand for a shake. "Alexandra Reinhart."

Dee's incendiary glare turns to Lexi. But her tirade stops as she wonders. "Reinhart. How do I know that name?"

She lets me answer. Finally. "She's Mackenzie's mother."

If you look closely, you can almost see our previous conversation replaying in Delores's eyes. "Mackenzie . . . the pseudo niece?" Her head turns more fully to me. "That means she's . . ."

"The girl I grew up with—yes. Drew's sister."

Alexandra takes over for me. "Drew's sister, Steven's wife, daughter of John and Anne. I have many designations. One, in particular, is about to be put to good use."

It's times like this I suspect Alexandra knows about her nickname. And it scares me.

A lot.

Alexandra's eyes stay on Dee, but she says to me, "I see what you meant about different." Then to Delores, "You must be Delores. Matthew was just telling me about you. I'd say it's a pleasure to meet you, but I've reached my bullshit quota for the week."

Alexandra circles her slowly—like a shark checking out a wounded seal. "You know, Delores, my mother used to tell me that even though a man wasn't supposed to ever strike a woman, I should never take advantage of that. That I should never act without expecting an equal and deserving reaction."

Dee folds her arms across her chest and stands stubbornly tall under the weight of Lexi's disapproving gaze.

"Matthew's explained our relationship to you. He's like a second brother to me. And of the two of them? He's the nicer one. You should keep that in mind before you think about tossing Icees at his head again."

Dee gives just a little. She looks down at the sidewalk and mutters defensively, "It was a Slurpee."

Alexandra snaps her fingers at me. "Give me your shirt and jacket."

After taking off my tie, I hand the items to her and stand on the sidewalk in a plain white undershirt and gray slacks. Dee reaches for the stained clothes in Lexi's hands. "I'll pay to have them dry-cleaned."

Alexandra rolls her eyes. "The dry cleaners won't be able to get this out. Luckily, I have a homemade paste that should save the day." She says to me, "You can pick it up Saturday."

She puts her hands on my shoulders and kisses my cheek while wiping some remaining red slush off my ear with a napkin. "I have to get going. Good luck—you're going to need it."

Before Alexandra leaves, Dee offers, "I hope the next time we meet, it'll be under better circumstances."

And Alexandra responds, "I seriously doubt we'll be meeting again. Matthew's sweet, not stupid." Then she grabs her purse and walks down the street.

Dee and I watch her go.

Almost to herself Dee says, "Is she always that much of a bitch?"

I smile. "It's what she does." Then I run a hand through my sticky, stiff hair. "What the fuck, Dee?"

The arm folding is back, and she babbles, "I'm not apologizing. It was a natural mistake. I told you I'm not good at this. Apparently, I even screw up fuck buddies. I was walking around on my lunch break, and I couldn't believe it when I saw you. What else was I supposed to think? If you want to blow me off, that's your decision to make, but I'm not sorry."

I grasp her shoulders, dip my head, and shut her the hell up with a deep kiss. Then I tell her, "I'm not blowing you off. And you don't have to apologize."

I know, I know—*are you out of your fucking mind, Matthew?* No, I'm not nuts—I just don't mind a chick with passion, spark. And a little possessiveness is no big deal. Plus, as Barney Stinson has already explained, Delores is hot enough to be as bat-shit crazy as she wants to be, and I still won't kick her out of bed.

Of course, that doesn't mean I'm going to let her get by without payback. Which is why I pull her tight against me and rub my head against her face and hair. Spreading the love—and as much of the Slurpee as I can.

"Ah!" she yells and laughs and smacks me on the back.

Eventually, I lean away and say, "There. Now we're even." I kiss her lips quickly. "I'm going to head home for a shower." Then I get an awesome idea. "You want to join me?"

She's smiling as she rubs the stickiness off her cheek. "I have to get back to work."

I nod. "But I'll see you tonight?"

"Sure."

It's only as she's walking away that I notice the white lab coat she's wearing over her black leather dress, purple tights, and high leather boots. I call out, "Hey, Dee?"

She turns.

"Bring the lab coat home with you tonight. And a pair of safety goggles if you've got them." You may think it's too early in our relationship for role play. But I'll tell you a secret: *It's never too early for role play.*

Chapter 10

For the next few nights, Delores and I hang out. We go dancing at clubs and stay in; we start movies but miss the endings; we have long hours of sweaty sex—the kind you feel dirty about afterward and can't wait to do all over again.

We also talk—surprisingly. In bed or across the dinner table. *On top* of the dinner table.

Dee's chatty. A sharer, an explainer. She also has . . . theories . . . on just about every topic imaginable. Though all of her theories are entertaining, some are pretty out there. Take this, for example:

"John Hughes was a raging sexist pig."

"How do you figure?"

"Look at *The Breakfast Club*. The guys get five main stereotypes—the jock, the criminal, the brain, the ass-hole teacher, the cool laid-back janitor. What do girls get? Two. The beauty queen and the whack job—sub-liminally telling generations of teenage girls they can be beautiful or they can be crazy, but not both. Because at the end, when the crazy girl gets beautiful, she's no longer crazy. It's fucked up. I'm going to start a petition about it."

Or this:

"Microwaves are evil—I'll never own one."
"O-kay."
"The sharp rise in childhood illnesses, allergies, and developmental disabilities can all be traced back to the moment microwaves became common fixtures in the home. It's malevolent consumer abuse. But you have to keep it to yourself. Corporations have ears and eyes everywhere, and there's no lengths they won't go to, to cover it up."
"My lips are sealed."

Then, there's this little gem:

"You actually think the Egyptians built the pyramids?"
"Sure—it's well documented."
"Oh, you poor, gullible man. How were they able to move stones as big as a house? How were they able to make underground, structurally sound tunnels and rooms without any engineering equipment? Or, for that matter, how were they able to shape and cut the blocks at precise and identical angles?"
"Well . . . if the Egyptians didn't build them, who did?"
"Aliens."
"Aliens?"

"Of course. There's tons of proof that aliens have been visiting Earth for centuries—you don't even know."

Nope, and I don't want to. That last one is too freaky—and plausible—for me.

I wake up Saturday morning to the sounds of running water from the shower. And the screechy echo of Delores's singing from inside it. "I Knew You Were Trouble" by Taylor Swift is probably the most annoying song ever written—but hearing Dee's awful rendition just makes me chuckle.

Never one to waste good wood—particularly the morning kind—I grab a condom out of the nightstand drawer, slip out of bed, and step into the bathroom.

". . . trouble . . . ah . . . ah . . ." Her eyes are closed and her head is tilted back to rinse her long hair under the spray. ". . . ah . . ."

I get into the shower and waste no time, going immediately for Dee's succulent nipple that's already pointy and proud. She's not startled. She doesn't yell. Her pitchy "ah" changes to a muted moan, and her hands slide across my shoulder blades, pulling me closer.

I like that she knows it's me, without opening her eyes.

I realize the likelihood of anyone else worshipping her beautiful tits at this place and time *except* me is slim to none. But what I mean is . . . she knows my touch. My sounds, my movements. We've become used to—*attuned to*—each other in the greatest of ways. I know she likes her hair pulled just before she's about to come. And she knows it drives me crazy to watch her finger her nipple ring or when she traces my abs with her tongue.

Once she's rubbing—squirming—against me, I release her breast and devour her lips, sliding my mouth against hers and my tongue inside her warm heat. Without breaking the kiss, I roll on the condom with deft fingers. Then I wrap an arm around her waist and lift her against me with little effort.

Her legs take their natural place around my hips. Cock in hand, I drag the head across her pussy and even with the warmth of the water raining down around us, I feel how hot and eager she is.

I push inside her fully, pressing her back up against the tiled wall. She tears her mouth from mine and moans. Her head tilts back as I start to move—strong, deliberate strokes that fill her completely. I pant against her cheek. She bites my shoulder and I groan.

Her legs squeeze me tighter, and I move faster. Wanting to go deeper. Harder. More.

Always more.

She grunts. "I love your cock. It's perfect." She grinds against me, lifting herself up and down on me, in time with the movements of my hips. "Fuck me, Matthew . . . fuck me with your perfect cock."

Her words get me hotter. Make me harder.

I feel the flutter of her muscles starting to contract around me—tightening—making each thrust of my hips all the more intense and eye-crossingly pleasurable. I speed up even more, wanting us to come together.

Her back is flat against the wall, not an inch of space between our chests as I press into her deeper and deeper. Then she's clenching me, holding me inside as she comes with a high whimper. And I'm right there with her—crying her name as every nerve in my body explodes in a rapturous frenzy.

Dee kisses me again. Slower this time, almost tenderly. I don't let her go right away, but I bury my face in the crook of her neck, content to stay right here with her. All day if I could.

She nuzzles my ear with her lips and whispers, "Good morning."

"I'll say."

I turn, so we're both directly under the spray, and eventually I loosen my embrace and set her down. Wearing ludicrously satisfied smiles, we wash each other slowly then step out into the steamy bathroom.

As I towel off, I glance at my watch. "Shit, I'm gonna be late."

Dee rubs her hair with the cotton cloth. "Late for what?"

I smirk. "I've got a date."

For all of Delores's insistence that she doesn't want to be serious, it's obvious my statement bugs the hell out of her. Her elegant shoulders stiffen, her chin rises, her eyes darken and narrow. She tries her best to keep her voice nonchalant.

Tries—and fails.

"Oh, a date? That's nice. Good for you."

I grasp her hips and pull her up against me so she's got nowhere to look but at my grinning face. "You want to join us?"

She tries to pull away. "It's a little soon for a threesome, don't you think?"

My ears perk right up. "You've done a threesome?"

On second thought, I don't want to know.

"Never mind. Don't answer that. Although I like where your thoughts are headed. I'm not asking for a threesome. I'm asking you to come to the zoo . . ."

"Sounds kinky."

I squeeze her hips. ". . . with Mackenzie and me."

Dee processes my words. Then she smiles—a relieved, grateful smile. She thinks a moment more. "Won't Miss The-Dry-

Cleaners-Will-Never-Get-That-Out have a problem with me tagging along?"

Many families are way too involved in each other's business. You know the kind I mean. Sisters who refuse to speak to each other because one married a guy the other didn't like. Brothers who come to blows because of a bitchy girlfriend, and friends who fall out of touch because someone refused to listen to advice that was never asked for in the first frigging place.

Even if Alexandra full-out hated Dee's guts, out of respect for me, she'd never show it. For months, Drew tried to tell me Rosaline wasn't the girl I thought she was, and even though I didn't believe him, even though he turned out to be right, he didn't rub my face in it.

The best kinds of families try to stop a train wreck—but if they can't, they still show up to give first aid to the walking wounded.

"You'll be with me. She'll be fine with it."

Alexandra and Steven's east side condo is a gorgeous place—I think it was featured in *Architectural Digest* or something. Despite the grandeur of it, Lexi still manages to make it feel like a home, not a museum. She opens the door for Dee and me, and we walk into the shiny, marble-floored entryway.

On her best behavior, Dee says, "Hello, Alexandra. It's so nice to see you again."

"Delores—what a surprise. You'll be joining Matthew and Mackenzie at the zoo today?"

"I will."

Lexi smiles, but there's a teasing shine in her eyes. "That's nice. Only, I do try to discourage Mackenzie from throwing her food, so please remember to set a positive example."

I put my arm around Dee. "We'll try to control ourselves . . . but I make no promises."

At that moment, Mackenzie comes riding into the foyer. She drives her red, bell-ringing tricycle around the circular mahogany table in the center of the room, shaking the ornate arrangement of orchids and lilies in their vase. Reminds me of Danny Torrance from *The Shining* but without the hair-raising eeriness.

Mackenzie parks the trike and climbs her denim-overall-wearing self off. "Hi, Uncle Matthew!"

I get a hug.

"Hey, princess." I tilt my head in Delores's direction. "This is my friend Dee. She's going to come to the zoo with us today, all right?"

Mackenzie's never been a shy kid—she's confident and candid, no matter where she is or who she's with. Traits that run strong in her family.

"Hi, Miss Dee." The "Miss" is all Alexandra. She's drilled titles of respect into Mackenzie's head since she learned to talk.

Delores waves. Then Mackenzie zeroes in on the black fur vest she's wearing. She reaches out and pets it—like a rabbit. Then she asks, "Is that your Halloween costume?"

Dee's wearing tight white pants, a white top, and black sneakers that someone Bejeweled within an inch of their lives. With the vest, I can see why Mackenzie might think it's a costume—a Dalmatian, or a zebra.

"Mackenzie, that's rude," Lexi admonishes.

But Dee waves her hand. "No, it's fine." She crouches down to eye level with Mackenzie. "I like to dress like every day is Halloween."

Mackenzie's face brightens. "That's cool. Can I do that, Momma?"

Alexandra shakes her head. "No. You only get to be Frankenberry once a year."

With that, I get handed a neutral-colored man-purse with all the essentials that have to be in reach whenever any child Mackenzie's age leaves the house. And we head to the zoo.

When I was a kid, I thought zoos were pretty fucked up. You take a bear, or a lion—the king of the jungle—and lock him in a 300 by 300 foot cage, add some greenery, and expect him to be happy? Wild animals are meant to be . . . wild. As I got older, I realized that a lot of the animals were rescued because they were sick or injured and wouldn't survive on the outside anyway. Although there's something to be said for nature taking its course, now I look at zoos as a wildlife retirement home where lions and tigers and bears get to live out the last of their days being cared for and catered to.

It may not be as exciting as living in the wild . . . but it sure beats being dead.

Dee, Mackenzie, and I spend the afternoon visiting all the exhibits in the Central Park Zoo—the lions, the reptile house. Unlike every other woman I know, Dee actually likes snakes. When she was a kid, she wanted a boa constrictor for her birthday, but her mother said no. Her cousin bought her a rubber one in consolation.

We eat lunch—pizza—and I don't even look at the hot dog cart. My days of chili dogs are over.

Dee buys Mackenzie a polar bear balloon and they have a long discussion about how many balloons she would need to be able to fly, like in the movie *Up*. Dee—because she knows about gases like helium—was actually able to figure out how many on her calculator. Mackenzie was totally impressed.

I just hope she doesn't get any ideas.

At the moment, we're eating popcorn and watching the penguins. And Mackenzie asks no one in particular, "Did you know the girl penguins got the boy penguins by the balls?"

Dee chokes on a kernel.

Mackenzie doesn't notice. "Uncle Drew say the girl gets ta pick any boy penguin she wants—they has ta dance for them. Then, the boy penguin has ta carry the egg on his feet for a long time."

"Those girl penguins are some pretty smart cookies," Delores comments. And Mackenzie nods vigorously.

Next we move on to the monkeys. I'm not sure of their breed, but they're small, white little puff balls that can only seem to sit still if they're trying to mount each other. Delores snorts and Mackenzie says, "They wrestle a lot."

I chuckle. And talk low in Dee's ear. "These horny little guys are giving me ideas. We should go before I embarrass myself."

Mackenzie—because she obviously has dog hearing—asks, "Uncle Matthew, whas 'horny' mean?"

I'm quick with the save. "Excited."

She nods . . . and files it away in her adorable, unpredictable mind.

The three of us climb out of the cab back at Alexandra and Steven's. I hold Mackenzie on my shoulder—she's half asleep. Dee carries Mackenzie's balloon and her bag and about a dozen small gift shop items I couldn't not buy her. Alexandra lets us in, and Mackenzie perks up, trying to rub the weariness from her eyes. I set her on her feet, and she hugs us both, thanking us without being told.

Alexandra tells her, "There's a package on your bed—it came while you were out. I think it's the Elizabeth American Girl doll Grandma bought for your birthday, the one that was back-ordered."

Mackenzie's mouth forms a precious O, and she practically vibrates with excitement. "I been waiting for dat! I'm sooo horny!"

Then she scampers out of the foyer to her room.

Alexandra turns stormy eyes on Dee and me. "Care to explain that?"

I rub the back of my neck . . . and then completely throw Steven under the bus. "You should really talk to your husband. He needs to watch his language around Mackenzie."

I'll make it up to him, I swear.

Dee joins in. "Yeah. Kids are like sponges. They just suck up everything around them."

From the look on Lexi's face, she's not buying it.

"We should go," Delores tells me.

"Yes, we should." I yawn. "The amphibians really wore me out. Bye, Lexi."

"Bye, Alexandra," Dee says.

Then we run.

Chapter 11

That night, I blow off clubbing with the guys. Dee and I order Chinese takeout and spend the evening fantastically fucking in every room of my apartment.

I'll never look at my pool table the same way again.

We pass out in my bed, and I sleep the sleep of the exhausted damned . . . until the rustling of clothing and footsteps wakes me up in the middle of the night. I crack my eyes open to find Dee *not* next to me in the bed but bustling around the room, searching for her clothes and pulling them on hurriedly when she finds them.

"Dee? Are you all right?"

Her voice is wide awake and tense. "Yeah, I'm fine. Go back to sleep, Matthew."

Bleary-eyed, I glance at the clock: 3 a.m. "What are you doin'?"

"I'm going home."

I force myself to sit up, shaking the fog from my head. "Why?"

"Because that's where I live, remember?"

I don't know what bug crawled up her ass while I was sleeping, but I'm really too tired to argue with her. I throw the blankets off. "Okay. Jus' give me a minute and I'll drive you."

Her eyes scan the floor, spotting her purse in the corner. "Don't bother. I'll take a cab."

Sensing my time is short, I pull on a pair of sweatpants and grab a T-shirt that landed on the nightstand after it was ripped off of me earlier. "Then I'll take the cab ride with you."

Delores stops and pins me with a sharp frown. "It may come as a shock, but I am capable of getting myself home, thank you very much."

"It's three o'clock in the goddamn morning, Delores."

She shrugs. "It's not like you live in a bad neighborhood."

"It's Manhattan—*any* neighborhood could be a bad neighborhood."

She doesn't respond. And she doesn't wait for me. I clutch my sneakers in my hand and barely remember to take my keys as I jog to keep up with her. Wide awake now, I slip into my shoes on the elevator.

"So, are you pissed off at me about something specific, or is this a more general 'all men suck' kind of thing?"

She folds her arms. "I'm not pissed off."

Translation? You're an asshole, but you have to figure out why on your own, 'cause I'm not telling.

We walk out of the lobby. I wave the doorman off and hail a cab myself. The ride to Dee's place is strained and silent. I sneak sideways glances at her—because the quickest way to get your throat ripped out is staring a skittish dog in the eye.

She sits stiffly—not exactly angry looking, but anxious—like a cornered animal waiting for the chance to bolt. When we pull up to her building, Dee is out of the cab before the driver comes to a complete stop. I ask him to wait for me, then I hop out after her.

As she slides her key into the locked outer door, I put my hand over hers. "Could you, please, give me a hint about what's going on in your head right now? 'Cause I'm . . . kinda lost here, Dee."

She stares hard at our hands, then she faces me with a sigh. "This is just . . . you're moving way too fast for me."

I lean my shoulder against her building. "If you wanted me to go slow, all you had to do was say so. Hard, easy, fast, slow—I always aim to please."

"Don't be cute, Matthew."

Can't help it.

She wiggles her hands, fanning herself—like she's on the edge of a panic attack. "I woke up in your bed and . . . it's just too much. I feel like I'm suffocating. I need . . . space."

Space.

Right.

This is an exclusively female concept. For a man, distance doesn't make the heart grow fonder, it just provides ample opportunity to find someone else he can stick his dick into. When a guy is really into a woman, he feels the same way about her as he does about Sunday football games—more is always preferable.

Still, I see what Delores is trying to say.

This time last week, I offered her casual, but the days that followed have been anything but. They've been intense. Consistently frequent. And it's obviously freaking her the fuck out.

When hanging out with the same person every day becomes routine, it's difficult to remember what your life looked like before . . . or what it might look like after.

Although I'm cool with the time Dee and I have been spend-ing together, I don't want to seem needy. Desperation is a reek that's impossible to wash off once it's been sniffed.

"You need space—sure—I get it."

She opens the door and steps inside. And she turns back to me and smiles insincerely. "I'll . . . call you."

I nod.

Then she slams the door in my face.

She doesn't call.

Not the next day. Or Monday. Or even on the most-holy third day. I haven't been checking my phone every five minutes or anything . . . but I'll admit, the sucker's been fully charged.

Delores blew me off. Just . . . fucking wow.

Yes, I've ditched girls in the past—nice girls who didn't hold my interest. Yes, this is the first time I've been on the receiving end of a blow-off.

And no—it doesn't feel good.

I should forget about her. There are plenty of alternates wait-ing to step up to bat. I should move onward and upward. Down-ward is always fun too.

I should . . . but I don't want to. It's not just that she's beauti-ful, wild, and her tits are the stuff wet dreams are made of. More than all of that—Dee's interesting. Fascinating. Different than any other girl I've dated before. The way her mind works, how she teases, challenges me—I could spend day after day just talking to Delores and never get bored.

She makes me think, she makes me laugh . . . she makes me hard.

And just like a baseball scout can look at a Little Leaguer and see an MVP in the making, I know Dee and I could be great together. Legendary. I feel the potential every time I'm close to her. That's what keeps my thoughts—and my fantasies—coming back to her. Because with a little time and some extra effort, we'll both be reaping some sweet rewards.

By Tuesday night, I take the bull by the horns—or in this case, the bitch by the ears.

I skip the gym and stake out Delores's apartment building, hell-bent on catching her on her way home from work.

She's walking down the block now, briskly striding in shiny, open-toed heels, a flowy white blouse that billows with every swing of her arms, and a green, snakeskin skirt. I trot down to her. Her chin rises determinedly when she sees me, not missing a step.

"Hey, stranger."

"Hi, Matthew."

I walk beside her. "How have you been?"

"Busy."

"Too busy to pick up the phone, huh?"

"Someone call an exorcist—you've been possessed by my mother."

I grasp her elbow, bringing her to a stop. At first she's annoyed, but when her eyes meet mine, I feel it. Electricity. Excitement. Her eyes dance over my face, drinking in every detail. And my own relief at seeing her again—after days of settling for paltry memories—is mirrored in her gaze.

"I'm not him, Dee."

"Who?"

"Whatever jerk-off made you so ready to run—scared of relationships. Of letting yourself actually fucking feel something . . . want someone . . . the way I know you want me."

She crosses her arms and cocks her hip. "You must not fly very often—the airline's baggage weight limit is forty pounds. Your enormous head must weigh at least a hundred."

Depends on which head she's referring to.

I smile. "Very funny."

She turns away, watching the passing cars. And when she speaks her voice is somber. A mixture of sadness and fear. "It wasn't a 'who,' Matthew . . . it was a them. I've been here before. There's no point in sitting through the drama when you already know the ending."

I cup her jaw, brushing the warm, petal softness of her cheek with my thumb. "But I'm not like them."

"That's what they all say, and I let myself believe them. But eventually, the truth comes out, and the guy I cared about—the guy I thought I knew—turns out to be a loser, or a gambler, or married, or just a plain old son of a bitch."

My chest tightens at her wounded expression. At her hurt. And a part of me wants to hunt down every one of the idiots she referred to and smash their faces in for their stupidity.

I lean in close, ghosting my lips along her neck. Because I want to overwhelm her so she'll forget about her doubts and her fears and all the assholes she's ever known. And I'll be the only one she feels—the only one she'll remember.

"Come out with me tonight, Delores. One more time. Even if it's the last."

She wants to say yes. It's there in her eyes, in the way her body turns toward me and her hand naturally gravitates to my arm. But what comes out of her mouth is, "I don't know . . ."

I press my lips to her ear and whisper, "Give me one more night and after that, if you want, I won't bother you again."

She tilts her head back and runs her fingers along my jaw. "You're a tough guy to say no to."

"It's a gift."

She sighs. "All right—one more night. But the clubs are going to be empty."

I smile and hold her hand as we start walking toward her apartment again. "We're not going to a club." My eyes skim her smooth, bare legs. "And, you should probably put pants on."

Curiosity sweeps across her face. "Where are we going?"

I wink. "It's a surprise."

If any of you out there were already wishing I'd marry your daughter? You're gonna go nuts for this next part.

I pull my bike into a parking spot in the almost empty lot. I nudge the kickstand with my foot and climb off. Delores rips the helmet off her head for a better look at the glowing sign.

ROLLER-SKATING CENTER

We're in Newark—the decent part. Because, like drive-in movie theaters, roller rinks are quickly becoming extinct. There aren't any left in Manhattan and only a few still in Jersey. I did some Google searching—figured, given the pictures in her apartment, this would be the kind of date that would make Dee all giggly and gushy.

And after hot and horny, that's the next best thing.

As usual, I wasn't wrong. Dee's smile is blinding as she gets off my motorcycle. She claps her hands and hops up and down. "Oh my God, this is gonna be awesome! I haven't been skating in . . . I can't even remember how long!"

It may sound pansy, but watching Delores smile is quickly becoming one of my favorite things to do. Finding ways to make her smile could easily become a new hobby.

"Do you skate?" she asks as we walk into the building.

Growing up, roller-skating wasn't a frequent pastime for my friends and me. But, I'm pretty sure I can hold my own.

"Once, when I was like, nine."

She grips my arm. "It's like riding a bike; you never forget." Her eyebrows wiggle. "And I do a kick-ass shuffle."

I chuckle. "I'm sure you do."

Inside, the place smells like a mixture of rubber, floor polish, and slightly moldy rugs. After renting our skates and lacing up, we hit the rink.

Where I proceed to fall on my ass. Hard.

But, in a cool way, of course.

Dee stands next to me, laughing, and offers her hand. I take it—then pull her down with me. On top of me. I cover her giggling mouth with mine, and I bite her lip in punishment. But just when things are starting to get good, a pimply faced boy in a white-and-black referee uniform skids to a stop inches from us.

"Um . . . you can't . . . This is a family place . . . You can't do that here."

I smile. "Sorry." Delores covers her chuckle with her hand.

I drag myself up the wall and start again. By our second lap, I'm steadier on my feet and we cruise next to each other. There's only a handful of other skaters on the floor—most of them look under the age of ten. "I think we're the oldest people here," I tell Dee.

"No. Look at them." She points to a Hispanic couple that doesn't look a day under eighty, holding hands, skating in perfect sync. "Aren't they sweet? That's how I want to be when I'm old."

They look . . . happy. Tired, a little worn around the edges, but totally comfortable with each other. It must be gratifying to be with someone who knows you as well as you know yourself—and at the end of the day, still wants to go roller-skating with you.

"Being them when I'm old would be nice. Being Hugh Hefner would be better."

Dee throws her head back and laughs. Then she agrees with me.

Later, Delores is taking a break, sitting down on a bench, while I get some sodas from the snack bar. As I hobble back, a kid with a slick smile and a backwards baseball cap skates up to Dee. Physically, he looks about twelve—but his attitude seems much older.

And he sounds like Joey Tribbiani. "Hey, babe, how *you* doin'?"

Dee smirks. "I'm doin' awesome, thanks."

"How about you and me—next couples skate?"

Before she can answer, I'm there handing her the soda—and answering for her. "I got next couples skate, kid. Called it."

His little punk eyes look me over. Then he tells Dee, "You get sick of the Angus beef over here and wanna try some veal, I'll be over there." He hooks his thumb toward the arcade games that line the wall, then he skates away.

"What the hell was that?"

Delores chuckles. "*That* is exactly how I picture you as a kid."

I shrug. "It's close. I was less obnoxious, much more charming."

"Or maybe you just thought you were," she says, then she takes a sip of soda.

And the DJ's voice comes out over the loudspeaker. "The next skate is couples only . . . and we've got a dedication."

I watch her reaction. Waiting.

"'All I Want Is You' by U2 is going out to Dee from Matthew."

Her eyes widen, and her teeth clasp her bottom lip—with excitement and awe—because she never saw it coming.

I stand up and hold out my hand.

Dee shakes her head a little, then she smiles up at me. "You just made every dream of my thirteen-year-old self come true."

She stands and kisses me sweetly. Then she holds my hand and we move out onto the floor. And—thank Christ—I don't fall. The lights dim so only multicolored spinning spots illuminate the rink. Bono's voice howls out of the speakers as Dee and I smile at each other and skate. And it's ridiculous and immature—silly and stupid.

And more fucking perfect than I ever thought possible.

Riding back into the city, we're stopped at a red light. I know Delores enjoyed herself tonight, and I'm almost certain she has no problem spending the rest of it at my place.

But . . . I want to hear her say the words.

Women liked to be chased, want to be shown that they're desired, needed—valued. And guys like me revel in the chasing—but only if catching is a possibility. I want Delores to admit—to acknowledge—that she's caught. That she's in this with me. That she wants it just as bad as I do.

I turn in my seat so I can see her face. "Do you want to call it . . . or are you gonna stay with me?"

My words are heavy with double meaning. And when her brows furrow with deliberation, I know she understands what I'm asking.

"Tell me this is you," she demands softly. "Tell me this is . . . real."

"This is as real as it gets, Dee."

She mutters to herself. "What the hell . . ." Then she holds on to me tighter. "I want to stay with you."

I grin—with relief and delight. Then I rev the engine and take us home.

Chapter 12

On Friday night, there's an art show at one of my favorite galleries downtown—the Agora. For the upper crust of New York, art appreciation is like a girl going out for the cheerleading squad in high school. Often, it's got very little to do with a love of the "sport," and a whole lot to do with the status symbol.

But I actually enjoy art—beautiful paintings, interesting sculptures. Although I could do without performance and certain modern pieces—pissing in a jar and calling it art is not my idea of fucking talent.

I swing by Dee's at seven, but I leave my bike at home. Delores told me she's wearing a dress, so she'll definitely prefer taking a cab to the gallery.

And what a dress it is. When she opens her apartment door, all I can do is stare. My mouth hangs open—drooling is definitely possible.

It's sleeveless and short—accentuating her long, toned limbs. Bright blue and green geometric-dotted fabric covers her ample breasts and the lower half of the dress. But the stomach and chest area are cut away, covered by a thin, sheer black material. I've never seen a dress like it—the definition of sexy.

Finally closing my mouth, I hold up the large bouquet of red roses I bought for her.

'Cause, yeah, I'm smooth like that.

Dee's extremely grateful. Holding the roses in one hand, she trails the other down the lapel of my charcoal gray suit, over my stomach, and cups my junk in her hand.

It's unexpected, but always a pleasant surprise.

"They're beautiful. Thank you," she whispers while stroking my dick, before pressing her strawberry-flavored lips to mine.

After she pulls back, I murmur, "The priceless art doesn't seem so interesting anymore. Maybe we should just stay in?"

"Oh no, this is a dress that needs to be seen. And . . . you look way too hot in that suit to stay home."

Can't really argue with that.

Unlike the exhibitions at major museums like the Met, private gallery shows are smaller, more intimate affairs. Although it's open to the public, typically only serious buyers attend, and the wine and hors d'oeuvres served by the white-gloved attendants are chosen specifically to cater to the expensive tastes of those patrons.

Both of us enjoy a glass of white wine as we peruse the photographs and paintings on the walls. The floors of the gallery are natural wood—the walls, stark white, with dramatic overhead lighting accenting each piece. Guests are scattered around the maze-like rooms, voicing their opinions of the works in hushed, pretentious tones. Delores and I are alone in one partitioned area, whose walls are dotted with vibrantly colored and variously sized canvases depicting a wide range of subjects.

"Which one's your favorite?" I ask.

"Why? Are you going to buy one?"

The prices aren't displayed, but I know from experience that any of these pieces will easily go for tens of thousands of dollars.

"Thinking about it."

But that's not why I asked.

Art preference is very personal, almost subconscious. It's the same as learning if a guy prefers boxers, briefs, or going commando—art teaches a boatload about the kind of person you are.

Dee strolls the perimeter of the room, stopping in front of a painting of a white farmhouse on top of a hill, with a fiery red-and-orange sky on the horizon.

"Katie would like this one."

"How come?"

She tilts her head. "It's very neat—cozy and safe. But the sky . . . there's kind of a wild side to it too."

I point to a piece on the opposite wall. "Drew would go for that one."

She glances at it. "Because it's a picture of a naked woman?"

I chuckle. "Yes. And . . . because it doesn't try to be something it's not. It's not a picture of a flower that's really a vagina—like it or hate it, it is what it is. Drew's a big fan of the direct approach."

"Which one do you like best?" she asks.

Immediately I point to a Jackson Pollock that's not for sale. It's busy with splashes and swirls of every color against a black background. Dee approaches it, looking closer, as I tell her, "Looking at it never gets old—I see something new every time." I glance back at Dee. "Which brings me back to my original question: Which one is your favorite?"

She opens her small green purse and takes her phone out. She scrolls through the pictures on it before handing it to me.

"That's my favorite."

I look at the screen. "That's the periodic table."

She shrugs. "To me, it's a masterpiece. Harmonious. Perfectly organized. Dependable."

"Aren't some of the elements unstable?"

She smiles. "Sure, but the table tells you which ones they are. No surprises. No disappointments."

And this right here is the perfect example of who Delores is. Safety-goggle-wearing chemist by day, glitter-covered club girl by night. She wants excitement, spontaneity, but a part of her—the part that's been dicked around by one too many pricks in the past—craves reliability. Honesty. Truth.

I want to give her both. I want to be her roller coaster and her merry-go-round, her adventurer and her protector. Her impressionist and her periodic table.

❧

As the show winds down, most of the guests congregate in the main reception room of the gallery. While Dee goes to the ladies' room, I stare at a huge sculpture in the corner, trying to figure out what it's supposed to be—either an endless cavern or a swamp monster.

I don't notice the person who comes up beside me until she speaks.

"I'm thinking of acquiring this piece for my music room. It has a very inspirational energy, don't you agree?"

It's Rosaline. She's well put together in a strapless beige dress, with her dark hair piled on top of her head—not a strand out of place.

And she's smiling at me . . . like the spider to the fly.

"I'd say more confusing than inspirational. It doesn't seem to know what it is."

"Perhaps that's because it's willing to be anything you want it to be."

The tone of her voice, the playfulness in her eyes—I'm pretty sure she's coming on to me.

"Do you still dabble in photography, Matthew?"

"I do."

She giggles softly. "Do you remember that time we went out to Breezy Point and drank too much of that awful Chablis? Your camera got a lot of use that day."

I remember the day she's talking about. We were young and worry-free and drunk on cheap wine and each other. But I don't look back fondly on any moment with Rosaline. If you have a can of white paint and add a drop of black, the whole batch will be tainted. Gray.

The memories that should mean the most—the starry-eyed, first-love kind—they just make me sick. Because every touch, every word and kiss . . . none of it was real.

Before I can respond, Delores is back at my side, holding my arm comfortably. "There are paintings hanging in the ladies' room! How do you think those artists feel? Their work is in a respected, renowned gallery . . . but only in the shitter."

For just a second, Rosaline's expression turns sour. Then—like the actress she is—she covers it with courtesy. "Well . . . hello. I'm Rosaline Du Bois Carrington Wolfe. And you are?"

"I'm Dee."

"Dee what?"

With a toss of her hair, like some blond bombshell from the forties, she says, "Just Dee."

"Do you and Matthew . . . work together?"

Dee just laughs. "Do I look like a banker?"

"No . . . I wouldn't say you do." Her eyes cut to Dee's dress, and her voice takes on that bitchy, passive-aggressive tone that I can't stand on a woman. "Your dress is much too . . . bold . . . for a banker. Not every woman would be so . . . brave . . . to wear something so *unusual*."

Delores smiles sweetly—but there's a bite to it. "So nice of you to say. And *your* dress, it's so very . . . beige."

Rosaline caresses the fabric modestly. "Well, you know what they say—less is more."

Dee looks her right in the eyes. "And sometimes less is . . . just less."

She lets the jab hang for a moment. Then she turns to me. "I love this song. Do you want to dance?"

Instrumental music has been floating around the room all night. The song Dee loves is a jazzy, wordless version of "Unforgettable" by Nat King Cole.

Rosaline chuckles. "My dear, that's just background music. No one actually dances at these things."

Delores shrugs. "Life is short—I never pass up the chance to dance to a good song. Matthew, what do you say?"

I take Dee's hand and kiss it softly, so proud of her right now. "I say, I'd dance with you anywhere."

TAMED   123

Then I lead her to the middle of the room. As we pass Rosaline, Dee whispers, "Lovely to meet you, *dahling. Ta-ta.*"

I take her in my arms and begin a smooth, easy fox-trot. Dee follows my lead effortlessly. "Wow, look at you, Fred Astaire. I didn't know you could dance like this."

"I'm very talented."

She grins. "Believe me, I know." Her eyes slide in Rosaline's direction. "Sooo . . . is every woman you introduce me to going to be a bitch?"

I think it's over. "No—she was the last of them."

"Is she an ex-girlfriend or something?"

No man wants to tell the story of how he was played—made a chump. It's embarrassing, uncomfortable—we generally choose to block it out and replace it with stories of our winning touchdowns and all-night fuck fests.

"Or something. Why do you ask?"

"It feels like she's trying to slit my throat with her eyes."

Skillfully, I turn us, so my body obscures her view.

But Dee still says, "She's very beautiful—like a Victoria's Secret model."

"Baby, she doesn't hold a candle to you."

She stops dancing. Fully. Immediately. And her face—her gorgeous face is a mixture of hurt and doubt . . . and a trace of resentment.

"Don't do that."

"Don't do what?"

"Don't feed me a line like I'm a girl you just met in a bar. Tell me you hate her, or tell me you want to fuck her brains out, and either way, I'll deal. Whatever you say, just . . . mean it. Be here with me . . . be real."

She's right. Right on the money. Reflexes are a body's reaction without input from the brain. They happen independently—without thought or consideration. Insecurity is not something I'm used to hearing from Dee. And I sure as shit don't want to keep talking about Rosaline, so I said the first thing that came to my lips. Without thinking.

Without meaning it.

And she deserves better than that.

"I . . . I'm sorry." I pull her back to me, and we're dancing again, slower than before.

Dee rests her cheek against mine, and I kiss the shell of her ear before whispering, "What I meant to say was, she's beautiful—but only on the outside. You, on the other hand . . . you're like a diamond. Clear . . . and flawless . . . through and through."

She tilts her head up to look at me. And she's smiling again. And I feel like a master of the universe.

"I like that much better."

I brush my hand up her arm, over her shoulder, under her hair to the back of her neck. Then I kiss her softly. Tenderly. I worship her lips, venerate her tongue. It's wet and wonderful—the kind of kiss that makes you forget you're in a public place—or if you do remember, that makes you not give a flying fuck.

When the music and the kiss end, Delores licks her lips. "Let's get out of here."

"Great idea."

When we get back to my apartment, Delores takes off her heels, dropping each one with a thud as she walks straight to the stereo system.

"Do you want some wine?" I ask.

Her eyes rake over me appreciatively. "I'm not thirsty for wine."

As she plays with the buttons, I press up behind her, skimming my lips across her neck and my fingers up her sides. The speakers come alive with "Demons" by Imagine Dragons. Dee presses the REPEAT button and swivels her ass against me.

"I likc this song," she says.

"I like this dress."

She turns to face me. And her breath tickles my ear as she whispers, "You're going to like what's underneath it a lot more."

She drags my jacket off my arms and drops it on the floor. I take her mouth, and she makes quick work of my shirt. Her hands glide over my chest as she backs me up, wordlessly guiding me to the couch. I sit back, expecting her to follow me down.

But she doesn't. Instead she stands up.

And the heat in her eyes—the hunger—makes my heart pound. She retrieves my camera from the coffee table, then she kneels between my spread knees, presenting it to me, like an offering.

"Take my picture, Matthew."

I breathe heavy—almost a grunt. And my cock aches with anticipation. Of watching her, touching her, and yes, photographing her.

On some level, every guy wants to be a porn star. I mean, really, can you conceive of a more awesome way to make a living? Disneyland may be the happiest place on earth, but Silicone Valley is the place men's wishes come true. Homemade sex tapes and photographs allow men—and women—to taste that fantasy. To reminisce and relive the most erotic experiences of their lives.

If that's too wild for your tastes, you may want to skip this next part.

Dee smiles when I take the camera from her hands. I double-check the film and the battery while she stands up and sways her hips in time with the music. Her eyes close, her head rocks side to side, her shiny, strawberry-blond locks fan out around her as she spins.

And she looks so . . . free. So beautifully unrestrained.

It takes my breath away.

I capture the moment with eager hands. *Click, click, click* goes the shutter.

She reaches behind her, pressing her tits forward, releasing the zipper on her dress. Unhurriedly, she peels it off her body. Revealing a sheer, black, strapless bra trimmed in bright blue with a matching thong. Her breasts are firm and high and completely visible through the shadowy fabric—including my favorite play-thing, Dee's sparkling diamond nipple piercing.

Her dress lays forgotten on the floor as she gyrates and turns. I lick my suddenly dry lips, refocus the lens of the camera, and shoot.

Click, click.

Delores's hands slide down her thighs then skim up her stom-ach, cupping her breasts the way I want to. My fingers twitch and I grip the camera tighter.

Click, click.

My voice is rough as I say, "Come here, Dee."

And miraculously, she actually does. The moment she steps close enough, I pull her down on top of me, one hand fisting in her hair, the other kneading her smooth, tight ass.

She moans against my lips. Then her hands fumble with my belt, pushing my pants and boxers down in one fell swoop. Taking her—and the camera—with me, I slide from the couch to my knees, then down onto the floor. The fabric of Dee's lingerie feels whisper soft against my straining cock—but not as soft as her skin.

I lay her down flat, then I rear back. Keeping eye contact, I slide her almost nonexistent panties off first. When I tug at the peek-a-boo bustier, it rips up both sides, but I don't let that stop me.

"I'll buy you a new one," I promise gruffly.

Dee gives the slightest nod.

When she's beautifully bare, ready and writhing, I pick the camera back up.

Click, click, click, click.

I set the camera down, close by, and cover Dee's body with my own—giving all my attention to her amazing breasts. I squeeze with one hand while I worship the other with my mouth. I lick around her nipple, then I encase it with my lips—scraping with my teeth, flicking with my tongue, suckling hard until Dee cries out in that stunning symphony of elation and pain.

Then I start all over again with its exquisite twin.

"Do you like my tits, Matthew?" Dee moans.

I rub the pink peak with my firm tongue, then answer, "I love them. They're perfect. I could do this all fucking night."

"You like licking them?" She whimpers.

"Yes."

"Pinching them?" She sighs.

"Yes."

"Sucking on them?"

"Shit, yes."

"Do you want to fuck them, Matthew?"

White-hot need goes straight to my cock—making me moan. Because giving her breasts a thorough fucking is a fantasy I've courted since the second I laid eyes on them.

"Yes," I practically beg. "God, yes, I fucking want that."

She smiles, tantalizingly. A perfect seductress—the face and body of an angel with a devil's desire. All willing and wanting.

"Me too."

Delores glides down beneath me, trailing kisses as she goes, pausing when her face is directly under my raging erection. As I hover over her, she takes me into the superb wetness of her mouth, all the way—until I feel the tightness of her throat. She eases back, leaving a heavy coating of moisture behind when she removes her mouth.

I rise up onto my knees. Dee lies between them, her breasts overflowing in her own hands, perfectly aligned with my cock above them. Gently, I sit back, bracing most of my weight on my calves. She presses her breasts together, encasing my rigid dick between their perfect, slick softness.

I savor the sensation. My eyes squeeze shut.

"Fuck me."

There's a smile in her voice as she tells me, "That's my line."

I want to move—I want to pound against her in a frenzied rush until I find that paradise that I know is just waiting to be reached.

But I hold back—and force myself to go easy. To let her take the lead. I open my eyes and meet Dee's fiery gaze. She pushes her tits up and down—jerking me off with them—again and again.

The feeling—*Jesus Christ*—it's more incredible than I ever conceived.

Dee's hands still, just maintaining the snug fit, while I drive my hips forward and back—slowly—drawing out the indulgence. Then I hunch over and speed up—my breaths come faster, my heart tries to break out of my chest.

Dee pants beneath me. "Use the camera, Matthew. I want to see the pictures. After."

I hiss and I groan. Then I do what she demands. I grab the camera from the floor. And take the pictures.

Click, click.

But it's not the view of my cock sliding between her luscious tits that I capture—that image is already seared into my brain until the end of time.

Click, click.

It's her lips—open in pleasure. *Click.*

Her wet, seeking tongue. *Click.*

Her amber eyes blazing with intensity . . . and trust. *Click, click, click.*

Those are the images I immortalize. The ones I need to hold on to.

Because outside of this moment—beyond our searing attraction and erotic endeavors—Delores doesn't trust me. Not fully. Not yet.

She wants to. She hopes I'm worthy. But doubt still lingers, protecting her heart—preventing her from putting her faith in me completely.

And it's okay. I don't know what scars she carries. I don't know the experiences that taught her to be so guarded. I'll wait until she's ready to show me. I'll work at convincing her, that I'm one of the chosen few she can give her trust to.

Because Delores is worth waiting and working for.

But here—now—Dee's body already believes what her mind is still wary of. That I'll never hurt her. That I want her—desire her—more than any other woman before her.

That I'll cherish every part of her—her body, her mind . . . her heart—for as long as she'll let me.

The song's drumbeat pounds. And the singer's words resonate.

This is my kingdom come.
This is my kingdom come.

My cock slides smoothly between her breasts in a sensational, steady rhythm. Then Dee lifts her head. She leans forward and wraps her lips around me, pulling as much of me into her mouth as she can reach—sucking hard.

And it feels so fantastic, I swear I could frigging cry.

Pure undiluted ecstasy rips through me. I moan her name as I come hard and deep—from the marrow of my fucking bones.

After Dee swallows every drop, she releases me from her mouth. Then she smiles mischievously. "That's what I was thirsty for."

I keel over to the side, my legs no longer able to hold me up. And I try like hell to catch my breath.

After a minute of silence, Dee asks, "Did I kill you?"

I chuckle. "Pretty damn close. That was certainly better than I ever imagined heaven being."

I drag her to me, holding her against my chest. Our skin is slick and all kinds of sticky wonderful. "That was amazing."

"Yeah, I know." She giggles.

"But it's about to get even better."

She looks up into my eyes. "Is it really?"

I smile and nod. "It really is. Because . . ." I lift her up and slide under one of her legs so she's straddling my chest. And her sweet pussy is mere inches from my mouth.

Then I hand her the camera. ". . . now it's your turn."

Chapter 13

Dee stays at my place that weekend.

On Saturday, I bring her to the gym with me, looking very come-worthy in my rolled-up boxing trunks, a sports bra, and gloves. She made a few jabs at the speed bag and was convinced hers was broken, but I showed her it's just a lot harder than it looks.

Delores was proud of herself by the time we left—almost as proud as I was of her. She hadn't mastered the bag, but she was a hell of a lot better than most beginners.

Then Sunday morning rolls around.

I'm awakened by whispered arguing—that raspy, not at all quiet sound that's as annoying as frigging fingernails on a chalkboard.

"No—Mom, he's sleeping. God, would you just stop! I hate when you do this! Fine—I'll wake him up. Fine!"

Hands poke and push at my shoulder.

I tell myself it's just a dream.

"Matthew. Matthew—wake up, my mother wants to talk to you."

My eyes open. And I see Delores isn't fucking with me—she holds out her cell phone.

Parents love me—always have. But, my first interaction with them is not usually over the telephone while I'm in bed with their daughter at six o'clock in the goddamn morning.

It's a little off-putting.

I whisper roughly, "I don't want to talk to your mother."

"Yeah, well, join the club. But she'll keep calling—just get it over with so we can go back to sleep."

"No," I hiss. "I'm naked. I don't want to talk to your mother butt-ass naked."

She rolls her eyes. "It's a fucking telephone, not Skype—get over it." She pushes the phone at me.

"No."

"Yes."

Then she actually presses the phone to my face so I've got no choice but to take it. My voice comes out forced—unwillingly respectful—like a class of grade school kids giving their teacher a group greeting.

"Hi, Ms. Warren."

Her voice is clipped—strong. And I wonder if she has any military training in her background. "Good morning, Mr. Fisher. I am told that you are having relations with my daughter—please confirm or deny."

I look at Delores incredulously.

She just mouths, "I'm sorry."

I clear my throat. "Well . . . um . . . not at the moment."

She harrumphs. "I realize that Delores Sunshine is an adult and can make her own decisions. But given the state of the world today, I would appreciate it if you would indulge me by answering a few questions to ease the mind of a concerned single mother?"

I cover the mouthpiece with my hand. And smirk. "Your middle name is Sunshine?"

Dee hides her face in the pillow.

My attention goes back to Ms. Warren. "Fire away."

She clears her throat. "Have you ever been arrested or convicted of a crime?"

"No."

"Have you ever been treated for a mental disorder?"

"No." But I'm starting to suspect Ms. Warren has.

"Are you gainfully employed?"

"Yes."

"Do you live in a structure that does not have wheels attached to it?"

"Yes."

"Have you fathered any children that you are aware of?"

It feels like I'm being interviewed by the scariest life-insurance company ever.

"No—no children—aware of or otherwise."

"Do you practice safe sex with my daughter?"

And that concludes the trivia portion of our game show . . . thanks for playing.

I sit up a little straighter in bed. "Here's the deal, Ms. Warren—I think your daughter's awesome. I treat her with respect, I care about her, I make sure she has a wonderful time whenever we're together." Delores watches me with warm, adoring eyes. "But frankly, the answers to these questions are none of your goddamn business. That's between Dee and me—only."

Ms. Warren grunts. Then she says, "Well, it was nice speaking with you, Matthew. Hand the phone to my daughter, please."

"Yes, ma'am." I pass it over to Dee.

"Okay, Mom. Yes. I love you too. Good-bye." She ends the call with a sigh.

Then she lays her head on my chest, wraps her arms and legs around me—and squeezes tightly. I kiss the top of her head and run my hand up and down her spine.

"Please don't hold her insanity against me," she pleads.

I chuckle. "You haven't met my parents yet. Like Ferris Bueller said, every family has weirdness in it."

"Well . . . the good news is, she likes you. You're welcome to stay in the bunker."

"I . . . I don't know what that means."

Dee closes her eyes and explains. "A few ex-boyfriends back, Amelia dated a guy that was a survivalist. He built an underground shelter in our backyard. He didn't last, but the bunker has. She keeps it fully stocked, and the people closest to her are invited to hide out there, when, according to her—inevitably—the government tries to enslave the populace and take her guns away."

The hum of Dee's voice is just about to lull me back to sleep . . . when her words finally register.

I pick my head up. "Wait. Your mother has *guns*?"

Monday night, I walk into my apartment and throw my keys down on the front hall table. And right away, something feels . . . off.

The air feels different. It's like a sixth sense when you live alone—you can just tell when someone has been in your place.

Or if they're still there.

Nothing in the living room is disturbed. The same goes for the kitchen and dining room, which I scan as I walk down the hall toward the closed bedroom door. I open it and walk in.

And there, laid out in the middle of my bed, in a pale pink lace teddy with matching garters and stockings is . . . Rosaline.

For a lot of guys, this is a fantasy come to life. Right up there next to a hot, horny chick showing up at your door in a trench coat with nothing on underneath.

But for me? Fantastic fantasy—wrong girl.

Her dark hair falls over my pillow in shiny waves. Her blue eyes gaze at me while her red lips stretch into an inviting smile. "Hello, Matthew."

"How the *fuck* did you get in here?" She doesn't acknowledge the shocked disdain in my tone. Or maybe she doesn't hear it.

Her ruby smile stays perfectly in place. "I told your doorman I was an old friend. After a little persuasion, he let me in. You really should complain to the manager. After what you paid for this place, the security is appalling. Although, I suspect at the moment, you're quite pleased about that."

She trails her hand down her stomach, teasing the thin fabric of her panties. Although my eyes are tempted to follow her hand, I keep them trained on her face. "And you'd be wrong about that."

She rises from the bed and stands in front of me, eyes downcast, hands folded—the perfect picture of sexy vulnerability. "I was *wrong* to leave things with you the way I did. Seeing you again has made me realize how much I've missed you. I was hoping, now that I'm back in the city, you'd give me a second chance."

I'm not going to lie. Hearing her say that is a rush. My ego does a fist pump. Isn't that what every jilted lover craves? To hear the former object of their affection say that they were wrong? Beg and plead to be taken back?

"You're leaving Julian?" I ask, stupefied.

She giggles. "Leaving him? Of course not, silly. If I leave, I get nothing—the prenup was very specific about that. But that doesn't mean I can't enjoy my own . . . distractions. You and I can enjoy them together. Frequently."

A few weeks ago I may have taken her up on the offer. Screwing Rosaline was always a spectacular event. And I'm a *guy*. Regular sex without attachment is the pot of gold at the end of the frigging rainbow. Something all of us dream about finding but don't really believe exists.

But here—now—not even my dick is interested. Which is really saying something considering she's almost naked.

Rosaline steps forward and moves to put her arms around my neck. But I grasp her forearms and hold her at arm's length. "Get dressed."

She looks genuinely surprised. Confused.

But before I can elaborate, there's a knock on my door. And Delores's squawking, singing voice drifts down the hallway. "How ya call ya loverboy? Come 'ere, loverboy . . ."

Motherfucker.

This is bad. Like building a house on an ancient Indian burial ground whose bodies are reawakened and really pissed off kind of frigging bad.

I walk away from Rosaline and make my way to the door, going over my options. I could stash Rosaline in a closet or under the bed, but if Dee finds her, I'll look guilty. I could try to rush Delores away from the scene of the crime, but if she ever finds out why, I'll look really fucking guilty.

The only viable choice is to lay it on the line—tell Delores the truth—appeal to her trusting nature and God-given faith in the honesty of her fellow man.

Yeah—you're right—I'm totally screwed.

I open the door. Delores holds a *Dirty Dancing* DVD up for me to see as she dances in place. "This is the perfect movie for us! I'm sure you haven't seen it yet—since your testosterone-drenched eyeballs have been too busy watching action movies and war porn. But lucky for you, I own the director's cut with extended scenes. We can reenact the 'lift' scene. I also do a hot cha-cha."

I slide out into the hall before she's done talking and close the door behind me. That's when she notices the look on my face and stops dancing. "What's wrong?"

I put my hands on her shoulders and say, "I need you *not* to freak out."

Of course saying that is just going to make her start to freak out sooner. *Stupid*.

"Why would I freak out?"

I try to do better. "You have to trust me, Delores. I swear it's not what it looks like."

That's not any better, is it? *Shit*.

Her apprehensive tawny eyes shift from my face, to the door behind me, and back again. She doesn't assure or agree, but demands, "Open the door, Matthew."

Might as well just get it over with.

I open the door and Delores marches in ahead of me. Whatever she was bracing herself for, she doesn't find it. She looks around the living room. "What are you . . ."

It's then that Rosaline comes striding down the hall—still covered in garters and lace.

Because if I didn't have bad luck? I'd have no luck at all.

"I think you're being rather childish about . . ." Rosaline stops short when she sees Dee—but doesn't seem even a little bothered. "Well, this is awkward."

I grind my teeth. "I told you to get dressed."

"I thought you were being coy. I didn't think you were serious."

I turn my back on her and face Delores. "Dee . . ."

Half a dozen emotions swirl in her eyes—shock, surprise, hurt, betrayal, anger, humiliation. Faith and trust are nowhere to be found.

But she doesn't run.

And for just one moment, I think I might have gotten through to her. That she'll remember my promises—think of my actions—over the last several days and she'll come to the inevitable conclusion that I'm not a cheating dickwad.

I'll give you a second to guess what she does next. Just to keep things interesting.

. . .

. . .

. . .

. . .

. . .

. . .

. . .

. . .

. . .

She slaps me. Hard. Straight across the face.

Slap.

Then she runs out the door like a bat out of hell.

"Goddamn it!"

I want to go after her—I will—but first I have some exterminating to do.

With an oblivious smile, Rosaline says, "Now, where were we?"

"I was just about to toss your ass out the door. Still am. I don't want to resume anything with you, Rosaline. We're done. Don't try to speak to me at parties. If you see me on the street? Turn around and walk the other fucking way. If you ever pull something like this again, or try to interfere in my life? I'll make damn sure your husband and every society acquaintance you have learns that you're a conniving, cold-hearted, two-faced bitch. Understand?"

Her confidence evaporates and her expression turns wounded. But it only lasts a second. Then her eyes ice over. Angry, but controlled. Like a rat hell-bent on survival, even if it means chewing off her own leg. "Very well."

I give her a final glare as I walk out the door. "Don't be here when I get back."

◦◦◦

By the time I catch the next elevator and make it down to the lobby, Dee is nowhere in sight. I jog out to the sidewalk and search through the sea of busy New Yorkers until I spot her blond head retreating down the block.

And that's when it starts to rain. It's pelting and icy, like a giant sky-wide showerhead turned on cold full blast.

Thanks a lot, God. Way to cut me a fucking break.

I weave between pedestrians—trying my best not to get an eye gouged out by the flurry of umbrellas along the way. When I catch up to Dee, I grab her arm, spin her around, and yell, "Would you stop running! I told you not to freak out!"

She motions back toward my building and shouts, "How am I supposed to not freak out when you've got a naked girl in your apartment?"

"Because I'm not up there with her! I'm down here—probably contracting pneumonia—chasing the fuck after you!"

"Why?"

And it's then that I realize I've asked Dee to trust me—to believe that I'm different from the assholes of her past—without really giving her a reason to. Any guy can show a girl a good time—thoughtful presents, fun dates—but that doesn't mean he's honest. He could just be putting up a convincing front. Shielding an ulterior motive or a player persona.

To prove you're not hiding anything, sometimes you have to empty your pockets, open your bag, submit to a pat down. Even if it's uncomfortable or embarrassing. Trust has to be earned . . . sometimes by stripping yourself bare.

"We dated for two years in college. I wanted to marry her— and I thought she wanted the same thing. But she didn't. She was cheating on me the whole time with an older, richer guy, and I was too fucking blind to see it. She dumped me when he got her pregnant. She broke my fucking heart . . . and . . . and now, I'm so glad she did. Because if not . . . I never would have met you."

Delores looks surprised. Then sympathetic—but lingering doubt is there too.

"She's so beautiful."

I gaze at Dee's wet, matted hair, her mascara-smeared face, her blue tinged-from-the-cold lips. Then I shake my head.

"Not to me."

She takes in my words, and after a moment gives me a small smile. I hold out my hand. "Can we please go back inside now?"

She takes it. "Okay."

We walk quickly back to my building. As we get close, I see Rosaline step out of the lobby door—wearing dark sunglasses despite the weather, an impeccably belted trench coat, with her hair pulled back into a low, neat knot. Her driver holds an umbrella over her head as she walks to the open door of the limo. I don't bother to watch her drive away—I'm just relieved that she does.

⚬⚬⚬

Back in my apartment, Dee wraps her arms around herself, but that doesn't stop her teeth from chattering. We strip out of our wet, cold clothes, and I fill the double-wide Jacuzzi with water, just short of scalding. Although few things are better than a splashing, slippery screw in a bathtub, that's not what this is about. I'm not going to get all corny and say I just want to "hold" her—I want much more than that.

Just . . . not right now.

I relax against the back of the tub, my arms on the edges, with Dee's head resting on my chest, her body laid out beside me, turned toward mine. I close my eyes, enjoying the feel of the hot water as it loosens my muscles and warms our skin. The mirror-fogged room is quiet, peaceful—both of us content just to be.

Until Dee whispers, "What's the worst thing you've ever done?"

I open my eyes, tilt my head so I can see her face. "You ask the weirdest questions."

I see her smile. She explains, "Good deeds are easy to talk about. But bad things tell you more."

I inhale a gulp of steam and do a mental rundown of all my transgressions. Then I confess. "I . . . cheated . . . on every girlfriend I ever had, in high school and college . . . before Rosaline. And the few times I got caught, I made them feel like it was their fault."

There's no judgment in Delores's expression. No horror or revulsion. Just curiosity. "Why did you do that?"

Why do guys cheat? It's an age-old question with varied answers. The simplest is—because they're guys. But that doesn't tell the whole story.

Some guys get bored. Tapping the same ass—even if it looks like Kate Upton's—can get old. For others, it's a game. The thrill of getting away with something they shouldn't, the excitement of possibly getting caught. A final few are just cowards. They don't have the balls to admit to a girl who loves them that they don't feel the same way. They think they're shielding her from hurt by letting her believe their commitment means more than it actually does.

"Because I was young and stupid. Selfish. Because I wanted them enough to bang them, but not enough to stop banging other women. Because I didn't know how fucking awful and humiliating it felt to be lied to like that.

"Karma's a righteous bitch, though. After Rosaline . . . then I knew. And I swore I'd never make someone else feel like that again."

In a messed-up way, Rosaline did me a favor—taught me a much-needed lesson. Made me a better man. For the women who came after her.

For Delores.

I touch my finger to Dee's chin and bring her eyes to mine. "I would *never* do that to you. You know that, right?"

Please, God . . . please let her believe.

She searches my eyes, trying to read me—then she gives me a crooked smile. "Yes, I know that." She lays her head back down against me. "But, I'll still need a reminder once in awhile."

"What about you?" I wonder. "What skeletons are in your closet?"

She doesn't answer right away. When she does speak, her voice is hushed. "I had an abortion when I was sixteen years old. He was my first—good-looking, cocky, came from the better end of town. He said he loved me and . . . I believed him."

She watches her hand move under the water, creating a ripple effect. "And, I know I'm supposed to have this . . . regret . . . about it. Guilt. But I don't. It was the right decision at the time."

"Still," she continues, "every now and then, I'll think to myself—I could have a kid right now. He or she would be about nine years old. And I'm not . . . sad . . . exactly, but I wonder what my life would be like, if things had been different."

She looks up into my eyes. "Do you think I'm awful?"

"Not even a little." I pull her closer against me and kiss the top of her head.

Her tone is less weighted when she comments a moment later, "I mean, wouldn't that be crazy? Me—raising a little boy or girl?"

"Do you want kids?" I ask. "Ever?"

She shrugs. "I don't know—I'm not sure I'd be any good at it. My mom wasn't exactly the finest example. I don't think she was ready to be a mother. I was an accident; Billy was a charity case. She loved us and tried really hard, but nothing was ever . . .

stable . . . when I was growing up, you know what I mean? She was always changing jobs, trying to reinvent herself, looking for love in all the wrong places. She's more of a friend than a parent. I'm afraid her inconsistency could be hereditary."

Even though this conversation has gotten way more serious than I ever would have predicted, I can't stop myself from picturing Dee as a mom. Cruising the city streets in her heels and halter tops, with an infant strapped to her chest in one of those baby-backpack contraptions.

And in my imaginings, the infant is the perfect blend of us: Dee's strawberry blond locks, my hazel eyes.

"I think you'd be a great mom."

Warm appreciation melts in her eyes and radiates from her smile. "Really?"

"Really."

Delores reminds me a lot of Alexandra, actually. Fierce—fervent in her affection. A giver of tight hugs and plentiful kisses. That's the makings of the best kind of mom.

There's no more talk after that. We stay in the tub until the water turns cold, enjoying the comfortable silence—together.

Some women won't appreciate hearing this, but I'm going to say it anyway: You don't need love to have great sex. The most fantastic sexual experiences of my life didn't involve emotions at all. They involved women I was pretty indifferent to, actually. I didn't know them well enough to like them or dislike them. For some, I didn't even know their names.

But I knew they were hot—I wanted them, was attracted to them, on a purely physical level.

Lust is easy. Clear. Exhilarating.

Love is messy. Confusing. Sometimes scary.

Lust is powerful. Primal. Driving.

Love is dubious. Transitory. It can fuck with your head.

I realize this opinion isn't absolutely exclusive to men—but statistically speaking, guys are much more likely to get satisfaction from a random, emotionless sexual experience than women are.

Google it, if you don't believe me.

Most women crave feelings with intercourse—they might not even be able to get off without it.

But Delores Warren isn't most women. She screwed my brains out the first time we went out. Without knowing me well enough to feel anything, except lust. And it was awesome. For both of us. In fact, she seemed to have preferred it that way.

Like I said . . . lust is easy.

But the night after Rosaline invaded my apartment, something changes. Shifts.

Transforms.

I don't just want Dee to come hard, I want to please her. I want her to feel happy, cherished—in or outside the bedroom. And I want to be the reason she feels that way.

She sighs in her sleep, and the sound awakens me. She's on her stomach, the blanket only covering to her waist, exposing the flawless expanse of her back. I watch her face and wonder what she's dreaming. Her features are relaxed, smooth—making her appear vulnerable and young.

Innocent.

And an ardent protectiveness fills my chest, clenching at my heart. My hand touches her first, softly trailing up her spine. Followed by my lips. My tongue. I taste the sweet saltiness of her skin, from her backbone to her neck.

"Matthew." She sighs. And I know she's awake too.

She rolls over onto her back, her alert eyes finding mine in the darkness. I push the blanket away, and her thighs open for me. Welcoming me.

I move onto her, chests pressing, thighs aligning, her hips cradling. And when I kiss her lips, it's so much more than just a kiss. Different than the others we've shared.

I want her to know what I feel. I want to show her—with every caress, every stroke—what she's come to mean to me. And more than anything . . . I want to know I mean the same to her. I want to feel it from her.

I slide into her fully. Her gloriously tight wetness stretches, yields, then clutches at me as I pull back for another thrust. My mouth hovers above hers, our breaths blend, our pants mingle.

It's fucking splendid.

She touches my face, and I kiss her chin, her cheek, her hair, her ear, showering her with my newfound feeling. Our movements are tender . . . not gentle or calm per se, but . . . meaningful.

Profound.

Her hips rise up to meet mine, fusing us deeper. I swallow the sob that falls from her lips as she comes before me. I plunge into her, unrelenting, through her orgasm, until I follow with an earth-shattering one of my own.

Her legs wrap around me, keeping me magnificently imprisoned in her embracing heat. We kiss as we come down, nibbling and biting at each other's lips. I turn my face into her neck, resting my head against her clavicle, breathing in her scent. Her hands skim my arms and settle on my shoulder blades.

A few minutes later, I reluctantly pull out. Dee's arms tighten around me, so I don't move off of her. We fall asleep in that same position—with my body serving as her heavy blanket, and hers my supple pillow.

Chapter 14

Over the days and nights that follow, Delores and I literally spend every night together. She finally opens up and tells me all about her ex-boyfriends. There weren't as many as you're probably thinking, but the ones she had were some real winners.

There was the first prick, of course—the kid who knocked her up, then kicked her to the curb.

Douche bag number two turned out to be older than he'd first said. Like . . . ten years older. And married. With a kid.

The asshole after that—this would be during Delores's college years—stole her bank account information, cleaned the frigging thing out, and took off for Vegas. The dickhead left her a note explaining he had a rampant gambling addiction that he'd been able to keep hidden from Dee for the months they were together.

And finally—there's the last gash. The motherfucker who hit her.

Delores said it only happened once, but once is way too many times for me. She wouldn't give me his name, but I swear on everything that is holy if I ever learn it? I'll track the fucker down, go to his place, and break every bone in the hand that touched her.

Then I'll break the other one, just to be sure he won't forget.

Oh—and then there's the story of her parents. Delores said her mother and father hooked up hot and heavy, swearing it was instant but lasting love. Until her mom got pregnant. Then her father turned into a ghost and disappeared . . . never to be heard from again.

Now that I know the details about Dee's losing streak, everything makes so much more sense. Why she was so nervous in the beginning, even though she liked me—*because* she liked me.

It's a wonder she even trusts me now. After her history, I wouldn't have been shocked if she threw in the towel and went full-out lesbian.

But—as cool as that would be—I'm really glad she didn't.

The night before Thanksgiving is officially the biggest bar night on the calendar. Every year after the Day-Before-Thanksgiving Office Party, Drew, Jack, and I hit the clubs and party until the sun comes up. It's a great time. As traditional as turkey, stuffing, and cranberry sauce.

Although, can I just say, I never got the cranberry sauce thing. Even homemade, it's fucking nasty.

Anyway, this year I invite Dee along for the ride—the office party and the after-festivities. I haven't hung out with the guys in more than two weeks. It happens that way sometimes. When a kid gets a new shiny toy for Christmas, the last thing he wants to do is let his friends play with it. He hordes it, hibernates with it, keeps it to himself, maybe even sleeps with it under his pillow. Then, after a week or two—he'll let someone else have a turn.

Not that Jack or Drew are going to have a frigging "turn" with Dee the way they'd probably like—but it's time to bring her around. Let her get to know the boys so they can see she's a cool kind of girlfriend. The kind that plays darts and shoots pool and doesn't put a damper on the good times.

I call Dee's cell from outside her apartment building so I don't have to search for a parking spot for my bike. Then I smoke a cigarette while I wait for her to come down. When she exits the building, I smile appreciatively at her outfit. Black satin pants hug her legs so tightly, they look like they're painted on. Hot-pink stilettos match her halter top, and she carries a short black jacket in her hand. Her hair is pinned up and curled, drawing attention to the diamond necklace that falls just above her cleavage.

"Nice necklace," I tell her as I hand her a helmet.

She shrugs. "Junk jewelry from QVC."

I make a mental note to get her a real one. And the image of Delores dripping in diamonds—and nothing else—brings a leer to my face and a boner to my pants.

She puts on the helmet but doesn't climb on the Ducati right away. She stands on the sidewalk, hands on her hips, looking thoughtfully at it.

"What would you say if I said I wanted to drive your motor-cycle to the party?"

"I'd say you're shit out of luck. I don't ride bitch."

She knocks me upside the head—but my helmet softens the blow.

"Then let me take it for a ride myself. Just around the block."

"I . . . don't think so."

She pouts.

I sigh. "Have you ever driven a motorcycle before?"

"No, but I've always wanted to."

"Well, I've always wanted to fly, but that doesn't mean I'm gonna strap on a squirrel suit and skydive from the goddamn Empire State Building."

She steps closer and rubs her placating hands up my chest. "Come on, please? I'll be really careful and grateful. Really grateful. Like . . . deviantly, let you handcuff me to the bed kind of grateful."

Forget the national broadcast system—this is the test.

Am I going to stick to my man-guns, keep my pride, and protect my cherished vehicle from almost certain carnage? Or, am I going to be ruled by my dick and swayed by the promise of kinky, have-Dee-at-my-mercy-all-night-long sex?

No contest.

"Riding bitch it is."

I slide back in the seat so she has room to climb on in front of me. Then I show her the clutch, the gas, and—most importantly—the brake.

You know that saying about your life flashing in front of your eyes before you die?

By the time we make it to the office building, I can say— without a shred of doubt—it's totally fucking real.

I saw my whole life laid out before me. Three times.

Once for the bus Dee veered in front of. Once for the garbage cans she took out like bowling pins, and once for the cab that almost knocked us sideways.

Although, that last one wasn't totally Delores's fault. New York cabbies are fucking crazy—they'll take you out without blinking an eye and won't even check the rearview mirror to make sure you're dead.

Leaving my bike safely in the parking deck, Dee and I walk hand in hand into the large, festively decorated conference room. Classic, upbeat music emanates from the DJ's speakers stationed in one corner, mouthwatering aromas waft from the buffet table along one wall, and the sounds of chatter and laughter fill the room.

John Evans is good at many things—but throwing a great party is at the top of that list.

I make the rounds with Dee, introducing her to my coworkers, my executive assistant. We get some drinks from the bar and hang out with Jack O'Shay, who gives us the toned-down version of his latest weekend exploits. I spot my parents across the room—as we head in their direction, Jack catches my eye, points to Dee, and gives me a thumbs-up.

My mother's petite—more than a foot shorter than my father who, even now in his later years, stands at six foot two. She's getting on in years, her poofy light brown hair is a bit grayer since the last time I saw her. But her eyes—the same hazel color as my own—still sparkle with the lively sweetness they've always had.

She was a true debutante, raised to be elegant, poised . . . and silent.

Legend has it, she met my father when he crashed her coming-out party, and there was an instant infatuation. He was rowdy in those days—a partier—but he was captivated by her calm serenity. She was helplessly attracted to his passion. And despite my grandfather's threat to disown her, they eloped four weeks to the day after they met.

My mother doesn't have a mean bone in her body. She's soft, virtuous. Her voice is naturally quiet—almost lyrical, like Jackie Kennedy in those historical White House interviews. My father has always been brutally protective of her, and there is nothing— *nothing*—I remember her ever asking for that he didn't immediately provide.

My father greets me with a handshake. "Son."

"Hey, Dad."

Dee stands beside me as I get a hug from my mom. "Darling."

Introducing a girl to your parents can be stressful, particularly if your mother is one of those overly critical, judgmental, no-one-is-good-enough-for-my-boy types. My college roommate's mother was like that. She cut his girlfriend to pieces for wearing white frigging shorts after Labor Day. Needless to say, she wasn't his girlfriend for long after that.

But my parents are easy. My dad, in particular, knows I'm not a saint. He thinks that if I can find a woman willing to put up with me, that's good enough for him. My mom just wants me to be happy. Her definition of happy is married with 2.5 children and a family pet. Any chick who can make that happen will be welcomed into the family with open arms.

If she's able to persuade me to sell my motorcycle—she'll be extra adored.

"Mom, Dad, this is Delores Warren."

Delores smiles brightly. "It's so nice to meet you, Mr. and Mrs. Fisher."

My father nods. "Likewise."

My mother comments, "Those are adorable shoes, Delores."

"Thank you. They're my latest favorite pair—and a lot more comfortable than they look. I can even dance in them and they don't pinch a bit."

"Are you a dancer, dear?" my mother asks.

"Not professionally."

"When I was your age, I loved to dance. I would make Frank take me every chance we had."

Since Dee's glass is almost empty, I take the opportunity to get us both refills from the bar. I see Kate Brooks walk in and recognize the guy standing next to her as Delores's cousin, from the pictures in her apartment.

I hand Dee her fresh drink, and when there's a lull in her and my mother's conversation, I tell her, "Your cousin and Kate just walked in."

My mom excuses us with, "It was nice meeting you, dear. I hope to see you again soon."

"Same here," Dee says warmly.

As we walk through the crowd she tells me, "We should take your mom out dancing sometime. I can tell there's a twerker inside her just waiting to bust out."

"Bust out or bust her hip?" I chuckle.

We reach Kate and Billy, and Delores introduces me to her cousin. He gives me a firm handshake. "Good to meet you, man."

I nod. And Delores teases her cousin. "Kate finally got you into a suit, huh? It looks good—never thought you'd clean up so nice."

He pulls at his collar uncomfortably. "Don't get used to it. The only way this thing's coming back out of the closet is if I've got a funeral to go to."

Kate rolls her eyes. Then John Evans joins us. Introductions are made and we talk shop for a few minutes. I see Drew across the room, making his way over to us. Having known him since birth, I'm kind of an expert on reading his facial expressions—even the ones he tries to cover. At the moment, he's pissed. Royally.

Not entirely sure what it's about. He and Kate lost Saul Anderson—the client they were both aiming for—a few weeks back. Although his old man was disgruntled, Drew was inordinately pleased with himself for telling the bastard off, so I know it's not that. He was also able to smooth things over with his father, so that can't be what has him riled either. For a second I consider that maybe seeing Kate—the first woman I know of who has shot him down—here with her fiancé could be what's got him all hot under the collar.

But I discount that as soon as I think of it. Drew's possessive of his car, his clients—not women. He doesn't do jealousy any more than he does relationships. So I just can't imagine him getting upset that a chick he wants to nail is nailing somebody else. Even a woman as attractive as Kate Brooks.

"Drew!" his father greets him. "I was just telling Mr. Warren about that deal Kate closed last week. How lucky we are to have her."

"It's all an act," Delores goads. "Beneath her corporate suit and that good-girl persona beats the heart of a true rebel. I could tell you stories about Katie that would put hair on your eyeballs."

Kate shoots Delores a warning glower. "Thank you, Dee. Please *don't*."

Billy chuckles and puts his arm possessively around Kate's waist.

Drew frowns. And although he's joking, his words are cutting.

"That's right. You were quite the little delinquent back in the day, weren't you, Kate? Dad, did you know she used to sing in a band? That's how you supported yourself through business school, right? Guess it beats pole dancing."

Dee looks sharply at Drew—obviously not appreciating his tone.

Kate coughs. Drew hands her a napkin, chivalrously. But then directs his lethal wit at Warren. "And Billy here, that's what he still does. You're a musician, right?"

"That's right," Billy answers.

"So, tell us, Billy, are you like a Bret Michaels kind of rocker? Or more of a Vanilla Ice?"

"Neither."

"Why don't you grab your accordion, or whatever you play, and pop up onstage? There's a lot of money floating around this room. Maybe you could book a wedding. Or a bar mitzvah."

Billy glares—like he's just dying to knock Drew on his ass. "I don't play those types of venues."

And with his next comment, it seems like Drew is dying for him to try. "Wow. In this economy, I didn't think the poor and jobless could be so picky."

"Listen, you piece of—"

Kate tries to diffuse the tension—like a referee in a ring, breaking up two boxers hell-bent on getting a piece of each other. "Billy, honey, could you get me another drink from the bar? I'm almost done with this one." She tugs on Warren's arm.

He huffs. But heads over to the bar anyway.

Then, sounding as livid as Drew looks, Kate says, "Drew, I just remembered I have some documents to give you about the Genesis account. They're in my office. Let's go."

"It's a party, Kate," John states jovially. "You should save the work for Monday."

"It'll just take a minute," she tells him with a smile. Then her smile drops as she grabs Drew's arm and drags him away.

While John chats with an associate next to him, Dee leans in and tells me quietly, "I don't like how your friend was running his mouth at my cousin—and Kate."

I put my arm around her. "He's just competitive. It's business—a dog-eat-dog kind of thing."

And I have no doubt Drew would give up his right ball for the chance to eat Kate Brooks.

Dee's not pacified. "If he comes back and decides to be a dick again, I'm going to tell him he's risking getting his cut off."

In the weeks since meeting her, I've seen many sides to Delores—carefree, seductive, tender, silly. But this is the first time I've witnessed her protective side. I've got a lot of respect for loyalty. The fact that Dee is so violent about expressing hers is goddamn adorable.

I press my lips to the top of her head. "Let's just hope it doesn't come to that."

When Kate and Drew didn't return to the conference room within a couple of minutes, I'm guessing Billy went searching for them. Because ten minutes later, Billy and Kate appear at Dee's side—both looking uncomfortable. Tense. Definitely not happy campers.

Drew doesn't come back to the party at all.

When Jack takes his leave a half hour later, I assume he and Drew made plans to start bar-hopping early. Given her recent threats against Drew, it's probably not the best night to bring Dee out with the guys after all. So when the office party winds down, Kate, Billy, Dee, and I hit the city together. We walk a few blocks and grab a table at a just-starting-to-get-crowded tavern that's hosting an open mic night on its small stage.

Delores and Kate harass Billy to sign up to perform. Billy nudges Kate with an elbow. "Sing with me. Like old times."

Kate shakes her head. "No way. My singing days are over. I've hung up the microphone for good."

Although her tone is joking, Warren looks . . . disappointed. Maybe even a little wounded.

After downing our first round of drinks, his name comes up and he takes the stage—borrowing one of the tavern's guitars. He sings a cover of "Here's to Us." I don't remember the name of the original band, but I know their sound leans toward heavy metal and their lead singer is a smoking hot redhead with killer pipes.

And I have to say—I'm pretty frigging impressed with Billy Warren. His guitar playing is really good and his voice is awesome—smooth, with just the right amount of gravel.

Dee raises her glass, claps, and calls, all while bobbing her head in time to the tune. Kate, however, watches Billy with proud—but serious—eyes. I guess some of the lyrics are kind of sad, in a way. Poignant.

They talk about toasting love, good times, mistakes, and moving on.

Warren hits the last note of the song perfectly, and the whole place erupts in applause. Kate smiles and stands when he comes back to the table, telling Billy he did a great job. I shake his hand and say the same. While Dee goes for the more exuberant approach. "Awesome job, Jackass!" Then she hugs him until he turns red.

Kate excuses herself to the bathroom. And I turn to Delores. "So . . . I guess your cousin got all the musical genes in the family, huh?"

Billy adds, "I see you've sampled Dee-Dee's singing skills."

"Screw you both—I'm an excellent singer."

Her cousin chuckles. "Sure you are, Rain Man. Cats come from miles around just to hear you—hoping to get lucky."

I laugh and tap my beer bottle to Warren's. Then he ducks as Dee whips a pretzel at his head.

Kate sits back down next to Billy, and I can't help but notice the space between their chairs. Billy leans forward and says, "So . . . I've got some news. That music producer who came to my gig a few months back called. He wants me to come out to California . . . says he can get me into a studio."

Dee smiles joyously. "Oh my God! That's fantastic!"

But judging by the look on her face, fantastic isn't what Kate thinks it is at all.

"When . . . when did this happen?" she asks.

Billy shrugs. "A few days ago." He sips his beer.

"Why am I just hearing about it now?"

Tension sweeps across the air like a swarm of locusts.

Billy stares hard. "When was I supposed to tell you, Kate? You're never around."

Her frown deepens. "We live together."

"And even when you're at the apartment, you're not there."

She looks away and pushes a hand through her hair. Delores watches them—worriedly—like a child of divorce stuck between two bickering parents.

"I can't . . ." Kate starts. "I can't go to California now."

Billy keeps his eyes on his beer bottle. "Yeah . . . I know. That's why I'm going by myself."

Kate looks completely blindsided—hurt, and a little angry.

"But . . . we had a plan. You supported me when I was in school and now I . . . it's my turn to do that for you."

Billy pushes his chair back from the table. Defensive frustration makes his hands clench and his expression tight. "Well, plans change, Katie. I mean really, will you even fucking notice when I'm gone? 'Cause it sure doesn't feel like you will."

She's about to ask what he means. It's right there on the tip of her tongue. But she stops short and says, "I don't want to fight."

This just pisses Warren off more. "Of course you don't want to fight. You don't want to do anything with me these days! You're too busy to go anywhere—"

"I'm working!"

He ignores her. "You don't want to argue, or talk; you don't want to have sex . . ."

Kate's cheeks flush pink, but I can't tell if it's because she's embarrassed or mad.

"All you want to do is look over your fucking files and decide what suit you should wear to the office."

"That's not fair!"

"I know business is a man's world, but I didn't know you had to dress the part."

Delores jumps in. "Don't be a dick, Billy."

"Stay out of it, Dee-Dee."

With fire in her eyes, Kate gets in her finance's face. "Screw you."

He laughs in a bitter way. "Interesting choice of words. I'm not sure who you've been screwing lately, but it hasn't been me."

Kate stands up and rips her purse off the back of the chair. "I'm going home. Good night, Matthew. Dee, I'll call you."

As Kate walks out the door, Warren stands up to follow her, but Dee grabs his arm.

"Billy! Don't . . . don't say things you can't take back . . . things you and I both know you don't mean."

All he does is nod. Then he's out the door too.

Dee takes a long drink of her martini. "Well, that just happened."

"Think they'll be okay?" I ask.

"No. I'm sure they'll make up, stay together—do the long-distance thing. But they haven't been okay in a long time. Their relationship is like a morgue . . . lifeless. And Billy's right. I can't remember the last time they argued before tonight."

"Isn't that a good thing?" I wonder, finishing off my beer.

"Not for them. They don't not argue because they're happy—they don't fight because, I think, deep down where neither of them wants to admit, there's nothing worth fighting for."

The most successful marriages and relationships are between best friends—who want to fuck each other. Trusted confidants who can't keep their hands off each other. When you've been with the same person for years, it's supposed to get comfortable. Broken in. Like a well-worn favorite pair of sweatpants.

But there has to be heat—desperate attraction. A craving need. Sometimes, like Steven and Alexandra, it comes in waves. They indulge it, when the demands of life let them. But if the passion is gone and you can't be bothered to even try and rekindle the flame—all you have is friendship. Companionship.

At eighty years old, that may very well be enough. But at frigging twenty-five? You're just settling for the status quo.

"You ready to head out?" Delores asks.

"Yep. Looks like it's just you and me tonight."

She pumps her fist. "Weekend warriors . . . on a Wednesday. Let's do it."

Delores and I spend the next few hours bar-hopping. We play darts and pool. She takes me for fifty bucks on our last game because I didn't realize I was dealing with a practiced hustler.

I should have known.

Ultimately we end up at a club—pressing and grinding together on the crowded dance floor. But the whole time, Dee's more subdued than usual. She seems weighed down. Disquieted. Not the unpredictable and jovial girl I've come to know the last few weeks.

I call it a night—much earlier than past years—and we go back to her place. Once there, we crash on the couch and talk about nothing . . . and everything. Eventually, the subject of pets comes up, and I tell her all about King, the massive black Great Dane I grew up with. I genuinely loved that big hairy bastard, so I'm kind of horrified when Delores tells me, "I never had a dog."

"Really? Never? Not even like . . . a Chihuahua?"

She shakes her head. "I had a hamster—they're pretty self-sufficient. My mother never wanted the responsibility of a dog. Plus, there was the drool phobia."

I grin, 'cause I can already tell this is gonna be a good one.

"The what?"

"Drool phobia. I have a long-standing aversion to any man or animal with over-productive saliva glands."

"You're kidding me."

"I can handle wet kisses—you already know that. They're hot when I'm caught up in the moment. But too much saliva is nasty. And spitting, drooling—those are deal breakers. Makes me nauseous."

Delores isn't bothered by dirt or sweat or sloppiness. She's not afraid of rodents—even the cat-size rats that scour the city and are pretty fucking frightening if you ask me. She's in love with my motorcycle and actually likes snakes. So, I can't help but find this quirk—this chink in her otherwise "doesn't give a shit" armor—cute. Funny.

And I want to fuck with her about it.

The nine-year-old boy inside me—the one who was amused by dangling a long-legged spider in Alexandra's face, despite the consequences that always followed—takes over my body. It's the only explanation for what I do next.

"So . . . it would bother you if I did this?" I scrape my nasal passage loudly then hawk the thick ball of phlegm up to the back of my throat.

Delores leans back, closes her eyes disgustedly, and holds up her hands. "Do *not* do that."

I swallow my spit and taunt, "And I guess you really wouldn't want me to do a John Bender in front of you."

•   John Bender—*The Breakfast Club*. If you don't know what I'm talking about, watch and learn.

She actually looks a little panicked. "Don't you fucking dare!"

I smile wide. Then I tilt my head back, open my mouth and launch an impressive loogie wad up into the air. It gets some distance, hangs for a moment, then falls back into my waiting mouth. Before I can say "tasty," Dee is up on her feet screaming.

"Ah! That's sooo gross!" She dances around like there's ants crawling under her dress and points at me as she shrieks, "You are no longer Clit-Boy or God! You're Loogie-Man and you disgust me! I'm never kissing you again!"

"Is that a challenge?"

She laughs nervously and backs away. "No . . . no, you and your foul tongue stay away!"

In a flash, I'm off the sofa with my arms around her waist. Dee struggles to get away and we both fall to the floor in a screeching, rolling, laughing heap. I'm able to get on top; I straddle her stomach and pin her wrists above her head. There's no chance for her to buck me off, but that doesn't stop her from trying.

And maybe it's the friction from her writhing body underneath me. Maybe it's because I'm having so much fun. Or maybe it's the fantastic sexual escapades we had in this particular position—but whatever the reason, I'm instantly and totally turned on.

Still, I ignore the boner. He's not going anywhere anytime soon, and I've got some torturing to do. Like a tentacle in a sci-fi horror film, my outstretched tongue slowly lowers toward Dee's face. Her head thrashes and her screams turn ear piercing.

Then she tries to bite me.

So I go in for the kill. I lick her cheek and her forehead—making sure to leave a heavy slime trail, like a slug that's been mutated from a radiation leak. I get her closed eyes next, and I'm about to move to her neck when there's a loud knock at the door.

I wonder if a neighbor heard Dee screaming and called the cops. I roll off of her. She gets up, making snorting but revolted sounds as she wipes at her face vigorously. Then she threatens, "You're ass is grass, Fisher, and I'm the lawn mower. Do not close your eyes tonight."

I just laugh.

Dee opens the door without looking out the peephole. And standing there, head down, guitar case in hand, is Billy Warren. He looks up at Dee and asks, "Can I stay here tonight?"

Dee opens the door wider to let Billy walk in.

"Yeah—sure. What . . . are you okay?"

He drops his guitar in the corner. His eyes are moist, like he's fighting to hold back tears, but losing. "Kate and I . . . we . . . I broke up with Kate."

Chapter 15

After giving Delores the barest of details, Billy insists she go check on Kate—sounds like she's pretty much a train wreck. Dee grabs her coat and makes eye contact with me from the door. Then she tilts her head in her cousin's direction, silently telling me to hang out with him while she's gone.

I nod firmly. She gives me a thankful smile then walks out.

Leaving Billy-boy and me on our own.

I feel like I should play host, but this is his cousin's apartment—he's obviously comfortable in it—'cause he knows where the hard liquor is. As soon as the door is closed, he walks to the kitchen and comes back with a bottle of vodka, two shot glasses, and two beers.

He sits on the couch, sets the on-my-way-to-shit-faced paraphernalia on the table, and pours two shots. He slides one in my direction and immediately downs his own. By the time I swallow my shot, Billy's already finished with number two.

He blows out a deep breath and stares at the table. Without

looking up he informs me, "You're good for my cousin. You make her . . . happy. Dee's got crap taste in guys—always has. Assholes are her usual type—but you, you seem decent."

I crack open my beer. "I like to think I am. She makes me happy too."

He nods. Then he looks up at me. "She's worth it—the hell she'll most likely put you through. Delores can be a major pain in the ass, but it's only because she's been hurt—trusted the wrong people . . . and now's she's scared of being wrong again. But . . . she loves . . . deep. She gives everything she's got. If she lets you in—she'll never let you down."

"I know she's worth it." I chuckle. "And I'm working on getting her to let me in."

Billy takes a drag on his beer. "Good."

He offers me another shot—I shake my head and he drinks it himself.

Then he says, "I know you don't know me, man, but I'm hoping you'll be straight with me. Is something going on between Kate and that Evans guy?"

The words hang for a moment, and I ask cautiously, "Did Kate tell you something was going on between them?"

He drinks his beer and shakes his head. "Nah—just a feeling. She's always mentioning him—either because he's pissed her off or he's helping her out or he's done something fucking brilliant."

In situations like these, I don't like to lie. I was raised on the idea that how you treat others is how the world will turn around and treat you. At the same time, Drew is my best friend. So while Billy seems like a good guy, if I need to have someone's back here, it's not going to be his.

"Kate really doesn't seem like the type to cheat, Billy."

"She's not. At least, she never was before."

I nod. "And Drew . . . well, he doesn't screw around with girls from the office. It's kind of a rule he lives by. He's never broken it before. Not once."

He leans back on the couch, mollified—relieved—by my statement.

Then, roughly, he says, "This sucks."

I agree. "Breakups always do."

He snorts. "This is my first one. Kate and me . . . we've been together forever—since we were fifteen. She's been my first everything. I thought she'd be my last everything too. My only."

I just nod and let him talk.

"But the last few years . . . it feels like we've just been holding each other back, you know? I don't think I'll ever stop loving her . . . but it's not the same. It's not enough. We don't . . . fit . . . anymore."

Sympathetically, I tell him, "That happens—a lot. People change."

He nods too. "Yeah." He takes another swig of beer. "Still fucking blows chunks though."

"It gets better."

We sit silently for a few minutes—our heart-to-heart time over.

So I pick up the remote and pull up the on-demand movies. "You want to watch *Predator*?"

Billy pours himself another shot. "Sure. Never seen it."

I grin. "It'll change your life."

A few hours before sunrise, Delores comes walking back into her apartment. I'm half asleep on the well-used recliner while Billy's passed out cold on the couch.

The vodka bottle sits empty on the coffee table—its purpose fulfilled.

Dee kicks off her shoes with a sigh. Then she sees me. And she's surprised. "You're still here?"

"Am I not supposed to be?"

"No, no, it's fine."

She covers her cousin with the throw blanket, brushing his hair back tenderly, like a mother with a feverish toddler. Then, she walks past me into her bedroom. I get up and follow her.

"How's Kate?"

Delores takes off the outfit she's still wearing from the party—letting the clothes fall off her to the floor. Leaving them there. Revealing tiny leopard print panties and a matching strapless bra.

"Kate's a mess. She's hurt . . . Billy said some messed-up stuff during their argument. Harsh shit. And she feels guilty. Billy worked his ass off to support Katie while she was in school. She hates herself, now that she won't be able to return the favor."

Dee keeps her back to me when she removes her bra, only turning around after she slips a red Phillies T-shirt over her head.

"Thank you for staying with him, Matthew."

"Of course."

She sighs, but her shoulders are stiff. "I'm really tired."

I start to unbutton my shirt, to join Dee in bed. I'm not looking to get laid—although with the amount her cousin drank tonight, I don't think even a full-fledged fuck fest would wake him up. But I'm not expecting what Dee says next.

"You can go now."

My fingers freeze on the buttons. "What?"

"I said, thank you, I'm tired—you can go." And her eyes are flat, her face taught—like a mannequin in a department store.

I step toward her, trying to make it past her attitude.

"Dee, I know you're upset . . ."

"Or maybe I just don't want you here, Matthew!" she lashes out. "Maybe I just want to be alone."

And, yes—in case you're wondering—this is my pissed-off face. Jaw clenched, lips tight, eyes alive with adrenaline. I'm angry at her words—her outlook—her stubborn fucking inability to look at me and our relationship without the black cloud of her past hanging over it.

"You don't want to be alone—you're just fucking scared. You see Kate and your cousin and you don't want to feel what they're feeling . . ."

She claps her hands slowly. Sarcastically.

"Brilliant deduction, Watson. Forget Chippendales—if banking doesn't work out, it sounds like you want to be a therapist."

I push a hand through my hair, trying to rein in the frustration that makes me want to put my hand through her bedroom wall.

"This pushing me away shit is getting really fucking old, Delores."

"Well there's the door." She points at it. "Why don't you go find yourself something brand spanking new."

My voice is low—but fuming. "Good idea. I'll do that."

Then I turn around and walk out of the goddamn room.

I make it all the way to the living room—my hand on the apartment door—before I stop. Because this is exactly what she's expecting. For me to give up. On her.

On us.

Dee would rather hit first and then throw in the towel than risk getting sucker punched later on.

I know this. As well as I know the last thing she really wants is for me to leave.

To leave her alone.

My hand drops from the door and I walk purposefully back into her bedroom. She sits ramrod straight on the edge of her bed, facing away from me.

"I'm not leaving. You want to yell? You can yell at me. Feel like hitting something? I can take a punch. Or, we don't have to talk at all. But . . . I'm not going anywhere."

I sit on the bed and take off my shoes—the rest of my clothes quickly follow. Dee slides under the covers, then switches off the lamp, but the room doesn't plunge into total darkness. There's just enough light from the window to make out her silhouette—on her back, staring up at the ceiling. Boxers on, I climb under the covers next to her. And as soon as my head is on the pillow, she moves closer, turning on her side and resting her forehead against my bicep.

"I'm glad you didn't go."

I wrap my arm around her, pulling our bodies together—her cheek now on my chest, her hand on my stomach, our legs entwined. Delores whispers, "What am I supposed to do tomorrow? It's Thanksgiving. Kate, Billy, and I were going to spend the day together—go out for steak."

My brow wrinkles. "Steak?"

I feel her shrug. "Everybody eats turkey. I hate doing what everyone else does."

And I can't help but smile.

"I can't choose between them," she continues. "This is going to be hard enough—I don't want either of them to feel lonely." Dee lifts her head and looks into my eyes. "If Steven and Alexandra broke up, who would you pick to spend the day with?"

I stroke her back lightly and answer in the most unhelpful way possible.

"I don't know."

She lies back down on my chest. And I add, "You don't have to choose. You could blow them both off equally and come to Drew's parents' place with me for dinner."

She snorts. "No, I can't do that."

I didn't actually think she'd go for it.

I suggest an alternative. "Your cousin is going to be sleeping it off for many hours to come. And when he does wake up, I can guarantee he's not gonna want to eat steak. Leave Billy a note, meet up with Kate for brunch, spend the afternoon with her, then take him out for a late dinner."

"But they'll both still be alone, for part of the day at least."

"They're adults, Dee. They'll deal. And who knows, maybe tomorrow they'll patch things up."

"I don't think so," she says softly. "It's probably for the best if they don't."

"That's pretty much what your cousin said too."

She kisses my chest lightly—one sweet peck. "It's just . . . sad. The end of an era."

I squeeze her. Dee tilts her head back to look at me. "Matthew, these last few weeks with you and me . . . I . . ." She pauses and licks her lips. "I . . . I'm really glad you stayed tonight."

"Me too."

After a few minutes, her breathing turns steady and deep. I think she's fallen asleep, until, in a small voice she says, "Just . . . don't hurt me . . . okay."

I run my hand through her hair and hold her tight. "Not ever, Delores. Promise."

They're the last words we speak before we both fall asleep.

Early the next morning, Dee wakes up just long enough to kiss me good-bye. I walk past Billy—dead to the world—on the couch and go home for a long shower. Then I drive up to Drew's parents' country place for the day's festivities.

All the usual suspects are in attendance—John and Anne, Steven and Alexandra, George, and my mother and father. I make my way through the handshakes and hugs to the back sunroom, which affords a panoramic view of the pristine backyard. And a view of Drew—with Mackenzie—riding opposite ends of the very same seesaw we played on, as kids, a lifetime ago.

Although they seem to be engaged in a serious conversation, I walk out the back door anyway to join them. Drew lets Mackenzie know I'm here and she hops off, turns, runs, and throws herself into my arms like she hasn't seen me in months. But I eat it up and give her a long hug, letting her legs wrap around my back.

Then I set her down and we shake hands. "Hey, man," he greets me.

"What's up?" I ask. "You go home early last night? You never came back to the bar."

He shrugs. "My head wasn't in it. I hit the gym and went to bed."

Huh. That kind of behavior is weird for Drew, and I wonder

if it has anything to do with his pissy attitude toward Kate and Billy at the party.

"You hung out with that Delores chick?" he asks.

I nod. And test the waters. "Her, Kate, and Billy."

He shakes his head. "That guy licks ass."

Mackenzie walks over to us and holds up the Bad Word Jar—Alexandra's invention—to keep us in check around her kid. It's simultaneously a bane of my existence and completely fucking hysterical.

"He's not so bad."

Drew says, "Idiots annoy me." And he loses another dollar.

I think he does it on purpose—actually curses more than he would if the jar didn't exist. Like a twisted sort of reverse psychology, just to buck the system and show his sister that he won't be controlled.

And maybe you're wondering why I haven't told him about Billy and Kate's breakup? The answer is simple: Guys don't fucking gossip. We don't talk about shit like that—other people's relationship issues. We barely talk about our own relationship issues. It's just that simple.

Plus, Drew would be on Kate like white on rice, if he knew she got dumped. Because everyone knows dumped chicks are low-hanging fruit. Easy pickings. I think it would give him an unfair advantage in their little battle of the sexes. One he doesn't need.

Lastly, people break up all the time . . . only to get back together the very next day. Despite what Dee said, Billy seemed pretty devastated over Kate. I have a feeling he's going to try for one more at bat before that particular game gets called.

There's no point in getting Drew's hopes up in the meantime.

"So what's the deal with you and Delores?" he asks.

I smile. And keep it simple. "We're hanging out. She's cool."

"I'm assuming you've nailed her?"

I frown. Because even though I know he doesn't mean to be disrespectful, Dee's not just some random chick. Hearing him talk about her like she is *feels* disrespectful. So I set him straight. "It's not like that, Drew."

Now he's confused. "Then what's it like, Matthew? You haven't hung out in over two weeks. I can understand you being too pussy-whipped to come out if you're getting some. But if not, what's the deal?"

I wait for Mackenzie to approach us with the Bad Word Jar . . . but she doesn't. Guess she didn't hear that one.

Then I try to get Drew to understand, but since he's never been in love with anyone except himself, I really don't know if he can. "She's just . . . different. It's hard to explain. We talk, you know? And I'm always kind of thinking about her. It's like the minute I drop her off, I can't wait to see her again. She just . . . amazes me. I wish you knew what I meant."

He warns me. "You're in dangerous territory, man. You see what Steven goes through. This path leads to the Dark Side. We always said we wouldn't go there. You sure about this?"

I just keep smiling. And in my best Darth Vader voice I tell him, "You don't know the power of the Dark Side."

This Thanksgiving dinner is definitely one for the record books. Or the scrapbooks. If I'd had my camera handy, I totally would have documented the entire hilarious, horrifying debacle. It was stupid of me to think the all-hearing Mackenzie didn't pick up on Drew calling me "pussy-whipped." She heard, all right. The reason she didn't charge him was because she didn't know it was a "bad word."

After she repeated it at the Thanksgiving Day dinner table? Then she knew. And all hell broke loose.

I can't help but chuckle again. Her asking Steven, "'Wha's *pussy-whipped*, Daddy?'" will forever live in my brain as the funniest fucking thing I've ever heard. I was so shocked, I spit out the black olive in my mouth and almost blinded Steven when it hit him right in the eye. Drew's father practically choked to death on his turkey and my mother knocked over her glass of wine— leaving a permanent reminder on Anne Evans's lace table cloth.

Good times.

Alexandra was rightly and truly pissed. Of course, if her ire was directed at me, I probably wouldn't find it so awesomely amusing. But it's aimed squarely at Drew, so I laugh over Mackenzie's parody and its aftershocks the entire ride home.

I only wish Delores had been with me to see it. Speaking of Dee, before I get back to the city, I stop for gas and call her to see how her day went.

"Better than expected," she says. "But, can I stay at your place tonight? My cousin is channeling his feelings into his music. And while I love listening to him sing, if I have to hear one more fucking song about his heart breaking, I'm going to make our food poisoning episode look like a hiccup."

And my life just got a whole lot more perfect. I know when things first started with Dee and I, she said she wasn't into relationships. And I know she's had her moments of insecurity— but look at us now. She's coming to me, asking to stay at my place. That's a huge tell. It means she wants the same things I do.

That we're on the same page. That she's invested—interested in a future—with me.

I chuckle against the cell phone. "Sure, I'll be at my apartment in thirty minutes. Come on over, baby."

It's always darkest before the dawn. It's a common saying. What's less common, but equally true is, *Pride comes before the fall.*

Remember a while back I told you that women needed to stop playing the victim card? Stop reading into a guy's actions, thinking they mean something more than they do, and just accept what a man is telling them, straight up? I was so into Dee, so eager to take what we had and run with it all the way into the end zone, I ignored my own advice.

Ever heard of the myth of Icarus?

You probably weren't expecting a Greek mythology lesson, but indulge me anyway—this is important. Icarus was the son of a master craftsman. His father made him a pair of wings out of feathers and wax and warned him, before he took off, to stay on the flight path. Not to fly too high. Icarus agreed.

But once he was airborne, he was so caught up in how amazing it felt—the beauty and warmth of the sun—he forgot all about the warning. He ignored the signs that were right in front of him because he was positive he knew where he was going, thought he had everything under control.

You can guess what happened next. Yep, Icarus got burned. His wings fell apart and he came crashing back to earth.

Unfortunately . . . I can relate to that.

Chapter 16

The Bible says there's a time for all things under heaven. A time for peace and a time for war, a time to reap and a time to sow . . . a time to love . . . and a time to *tell* a girl you love her.

It doesn't actually say that. But it should. Because many poor bastards make the mistake of telling a woman at the wrong fucking time.

Like after sex. *Wrong*. That's just asking for trouble.

Or during an argument. *Really wrong*. There's a reason the Doors' song "Love Her Madly" is still popular today. Because the lyric, "Don't you love her as she's walking out the door" is timeless. Men don't like to lose. Not a bet, their favorite T-shirt, or a girlfriend. In the attempt to keep from losing the latter, we could say something stupid—things we really don't mean.

But for me, tonight is the perfect time to take my and Dee's relationship to the next level. I had a key to my apartment made for her, and when I put it in her hands, I'm going to tell her I'm falling in love with her.

You're not surprised, are you? Jesus, you had to have seen this coming.

I've been thinking about it a lot lately. It happened gradually, but that's the best way. In four weeks, Dee's gone from a girl I wanted to nail, to a girl I wanted to hang out with, to a girl I really liked . . . to someone I don't want to live without.

I think about her all the time, I crave her—miss her—when we're apart, no matter how long we were just together. She's funny and beautiful and interesting . . . and sure she's a pain in the ass too, but—like I told you in the beginning—I love her because of her quirks, not in spite of them.

The last week and a half has been amazing. Billy's still crashing at her apartment, so except when she's there checking on him, she's been here with me. But I still want more. There were plenty of times that I could have dropped the bomb on her during the last few days, but I wanted it to be memorable. Special. Something she'll proudly tell Kate about, or someday—our kids. Girls love that shit.

I haven't talked to her yet today. I was out of the office all day, visiting with one client after another. But she's coming over tonight and I have the whole thing planned. You want to hear about it?

We'll start with an excursion to the Jersey shore. My parents used to take me there all the time when I was a kid. It's December, but most of the rides and boardwalk games are open year-round. There's an indescribable magic to the place—an aura of simpler days—a nostalgic beauty. I'll hold Delores's hand, spend thirty bucks to win her a two-dollar stuffed animal on one of those games where you have to knock the weighted cans over with a baseball. We'll ride the bumper cars, maybe a roller coaster, and we'll share a delicious but incredibly bad for you funnel cake.

Then we'll kick off our shoes and walk down the beach, near enough to the water so we can watch the waves in the moonlight without getting wet. It'll be cold, so she'll lay back against me and I'll wrap my arms around her to keep her warm. And then, with the thunder of the crashing waves in the background, I'll tell her.

That she's changed my life. That I want to share the rest of it with her. That nothing looks or feels the way it did four weeks ago—because of her—it's unbelievably better. I don't think she'll freak out, although it's possible. If she does, I'll tell her she doesn't have to say anything back. I'm a pretty patient guy. I can wait.

Then we'll make out. And it'll be awesome. Sex on the beach isn't all it's cracked up to be. Sand is not a friend to genitalia. But . . . if Dee is interested, I'm sure as hell not going to turn her down.

When I hear my unlocked apartment door open, I check my hair in the bathroom mirror. *All good.* Then I walk out to the living room. Smiling—until I see Delores's face.

She's furious. The teeth-grinding, pacing, nostrils flaring kind of fury. And words shoot out of her mouth—like a hail of bullets. That I walk right into.

"Your friend is an asshole! And I want you to tell me where I can find him."

"Which friend?"

"Drew-I'm-gonna-cut-his-pecker-off-and-feed-it-to-him-Evans.

I chuckle, even though I shouldn't. "Easy there, Lorena Bobbitt. Calm down."

Calm down. What the hell am I thinking? Those two words are like pouring water on a grease fire—just makes it hotter. It's the second most direct way to piss a woman off even more than she already is. The first, of course, is to ask if she's on the rag.

"Calm down? You want me to calm down?" Dee yells.

"What the hell is wrong with you?"

"What's wrong with me, you insensitive ass, is I just left Kate's apartment. She's wrecked—completely devastated. Because your buddy, Drew, played her like a violin and then treated her like a whore that he couldn't even be bothered to pay afterward."

I knew Drew had a thing for Kate, but still, I can't keep the surprise out of my voice. "Drew and Kate hooked up?"

Dee crosses her arms. "They sure did. He's been all comforting and kind to her since the breakup with Billy. Made her believe he actually gave a shit. She spent the weekend at his apartment. And then this morning, after they got to work, he pretty much told her she sucked in bed—wasn't worth another go around."

I press my fingers to my forehead, trying to digest the information Dee's telling me—that just doesn't make any sense. Drew doesn't take women to his apartment, any woman. Drew doesn't screw the same chick twice . . . at least . . . not if he remembers he's already done her. And spending the weekend with a girl? No frigging way.

"Are you sure Kate said Drew?" I ask.

"He called her a fucking 'project,' Matthew! One that he was 'done with.' And I'm gonna make a project out of his face. Kate is the best person I know. She puts on a tough front, but inside she's soft. Breakable. He doesn't get to treat her like this."

Underneath Dee's anger, there's pain. She's hurting, because her friend is hurting. I move forward to touch her, to comfort and calm her, but she steps back.

I put my hands up in surrender and try to reason with her. "Drew's not that kind of asshole, Dee. He has a lot of respect for women . . . in his own way. He likes to have a good time, no hard feelings. He doesn't get off on making girls feel bad about themselves. He wouldn't go out of his way to hurt someone, especially . . . Jesus, especially not Kate."

"Well he did!"

I shake my head. "Kate must've misunderstood him."

For a moment she just stares. Her gaze rakes over me, up and down, like she's seeing me for the first time. Then her expression changes from righteous fury to cold disbelief.

And her voice drops to a harsh whisper. "Are you defending him?"

"He's my best friend. Of course I'm defending him!"

Her chin lifts sharply, almost like she's absorbing an uppercut. She hisses, "Well then fuck you too!"

"Excuse me?"

"If you think there's nothing wrong with what he did then you're not the person I thought you were. Not even close."

And I shout, "Are you fucking serious right now?"

"Yes! A serious idiot is what I am. To think that I let myself believe . . . I should've never let things get this far. We're done Matthew. Don't come to my apartment; don't call me! You and your asshole friend can just stay the hell away from us!"

Her words hit me like a sledgehammer to the stomach. They're wrenching. Bruising. And fucking maddening. Dee's rant continues, but I'm not listening anymore. All I think about is how stupid I've been.

Blind.

Again.

It's almost funny, in a depressing, ironic kind of way. Dee told

me—more than once—that she couldn't do this. That her relationships never ended on a happy note. But I didn't listen. I heard
what I wanted to hear and believed I could change her mind.
That if I was charming enough, smooth enough, she'd see—like I
did—how great we could be together.

What a fucking moron.

It's really no different than Rosaline. The red flags may not
have been there for the same reasons—but they were there. And
I missed them.

"Goddammit!" I kick the coffee table but it doesn't break. So
I kick it again—until it does. The leg collapses and the glass top
cracks against the floor, bringing Delores's rant to an immediate
stop.

She takes two steps back, looking cautious—almost afraid
that she's pushed me too far. And I hate that I've made her look
like that. But I'm too pissed, too disappointed in her to stop. So
instead, I lash out.

"You say Kate puts on a tough front but she's soft inside? How
about you look in a fucking mirror, Dee? You're terrified—nothing but a scared little girl. You'd rather be alone and tell yourself
it's what you choose than take a chance on something that might
be better. Something that could've been amazing. I have bent over
backwards for you! I've spent weeks walking on fucking eggshells
trying not to scare you away! And where's it gotten me? Nowhere!
You think you're done? *I'm* done! 'Cause it's not worth it."

Her arms cross over her waist, holding herself together. And
she doesn't look angry anymore. She looks . . . sad.

I take a breath and push a hand through my hair. And I laugh
at myself—because I'm an idiot. Pathetic. "I had this whole thing
planned. I was going to take you to the boardwalk and win you a
bear. I was going to tell you that I think you're the most incred-

ible, beautiful, fantastic woman I've ever known. And I was going to tell you that I'm completely in love with you. And now . . . now I can't say any of those things." I shake my head. "Because you're just waiting . . . . looking for a reason . . . because I can't love someone who's so fucking eager to run out the door."

Her voice is quiet now. Softer. "I told you . . . I told you I wasn't good at this."

And mine is raw. "Yeah, well I guess I finally believe you."

I look into Dee's honey-brown eyes. Eyes that always said so much, even if she didn't speak a word. And I turn my back on her. "Just go, Dee. Just leave—it's what you've wanted to do from day one."

I hear her breathing. Waiting. And then I hear her footsteps. They stop near the doorway, and for a wonderful, awful moment I think she's changed her mind.

Until she whispers, "Good-bye, Matthew."

I don't answer, and I don't turn around. Until I hear the door close behind her.

Chapter 17

"Fuck!"

I spend the thirty minutes after Dee walks out cursing and pacing and kicking shit around my apartment—generally pissed off at the entire world.

"Shit!"

I'm angry at myself for letting things get as far as they did—for losing my patience and my temper—and for even falling for Dee in the first place. My self-flagellation is hot and varied and doesn't make a whole lot of sense—even to me.

I'm furious with Delores—for not trusting me, for not even fucking trying. For not thinking what we have is worth the risk. For thinking I'm a goddamn risk at all, when I've done everything possible to show her I'm not.

And I'm beyond irritated with Drew—but I'm not sure what the fuck for yet. Maybe he cut Kate down just like Dee claimed. And if he did, it was an asshole move. One that's unjustly blown back on me. And I'm kind of pissed that he even screwed Kate at all—breaking his precious, stupid fucking rule that was there for a reason. *This* reason. Because—like a goddamn suicide bomber—his actions have had painful consequences for everyone around him.

But most of all, I'm infuriated that Drew won't pick up his fucking phone so I can find out what the hell happened.

"Goddamn it!"

Guys aren't chatty. The telephone is not a necessity for us—unless it's to find out where we're meeting up or what the latest baseball scores are. But this is one time I actually need to talk to him—and he's MIA. I call Erin, Drew's secretary, who's still at the office. She informs me that he went home sick this afternoon—that he probably has the flu.

Fucking perfect.

Screw it. I drop my phone, grab my keys, and head over to Drew's apartment—to get the story straight from the ass's mouth.

But when I get to his place, he doesn't answer.

I bang on the door for the third—or thirtieth—time. "Drew! Open the fucking door! What the hell happened today? Drew!"

Nothing. I stop and listen for any sign of life inside the apartment, but all I hear is silence. Not even the rustle of footsteps or the squeak of couch springs. There's an excellent chance he's not even home. Which means, for now, I'm shit out of luck.

Breathing hard, I leave the building. I get on my bike and ride—fast and sharp. Probably not the best idea at the moment, but I do it anyway. I get through the tunnel, onto the turnpike, where traffic is thankfully scarce.

And I really open her up. The wind blows so cold and harsh, my face goes numb. But it's a good thing. Because feeling nothing is so much better than feeling the loss. Of what Dee and I had—of everything we could've had.

I ride for hours. Trying to let go. Trying to forget today . . . and the entire four weeks that came before it.

❦

I park my bike in the garage and climb off—stiff and frozen from the ride. I didn't think I was hoping that Delores would be here, waiting. That she'd realize she made a terrible mistake and show up at my door to beg and apologize. *Especially the begging part.*

But I realize it's exactly what I was hoping for . . . when I reach my apartment door and she's not there.

And the disappointment is crushing.

The letdown intensifies when I scroll through the missed calls on my phone and see that none of them are from Dee.

But I'm not tempted to call her.

I'm frustrated, and I miss her—but I'm not calling. I'm not chasing her. Not this time. Not ever again, if it comes to that.

Drew hasn't returned my calls either. I'm looking forward to work tomorrow, where I'll see him, get the story . . . and most likely punch him in his stupid face. That'll make me feel better.

Don't worry—I won't actually do any damage. Even though he doesn't box as often as I do, Drew's no wuss. He can take care of himself. And unlike Delores's and my relationship, our friendship will survive. A few punches, between friends, really isn't that big of a deal.

I have no appetite, so I skip dinner. I just take a shower and collapse—naked and wet—into my bed. But when my face burrows into the pillow, I smell her. The scent of her skin, her hair—it's sweet and spicy, apples and cinnamon, distinct.

And it makes my chest ache.

Instead of getting up and sleeping on the couch, like I probably should, I pull the pillow closer and wrap the sheets tighter—surrounding myself in Dee's memory—until I fall asleep.

Kind of pathetic, right?

Yeah, I fucking think so too.

Tuesday morning, I drag my ass into work—grumpy, disheveled, and feeling shitty—even though I slept like a rock. There, I hear all about the show Billy Warren put on for Kate in the lobby, and I wonder if they got back together. As far as grand gestures go, you don't get much grander than a public serenade and a lobby full of flowers. But if Kate is back with Billy, why would she give two shits about what Drew thinks or feels about her?

Throughout the rotten day, I check to see if Drew shows up. He doesn't. And I wonder if he really is sick. Or if whatever happened between him and Kate—and the possibility that she went back to her ex right after—busted him up more than he let on.

I spend my time wondering about that . . . so I don't have time to think about Dee. But, of course, my mind finds a way to squeeze thoughts of her in.

Plentiful, pain-bringing thoughts.

About where she is—what she's feeling. If there's any way she's doing as badly as I am.

Erin gathers Steven, Jack O'Shay, and me together and asks

us to cover for Drew while he's out. Like the man himself, his clients are fucking spoiled, and they tend to freak out if he isn't close by to hold their hands. I take a couple of his files because, even though I think he's a shithead at the moment, I'm not gonna let his career tank over it.

The extra work makes the day go faster, and before I know it, it's quitting time. I go to the gym—even though I'm feeling craptastic—and undergo a brutal workout and sparring session.

Because this is what most guys do when they're hurting. Punish themselves or—like the barking boss in desperate need to get laid—everyone around them.

After the gym, I stop by Drew's apartment again, significantly calmer than last night. He still doesn't answer the door, but this time, I hear the television on inside. Sounds like he's watching *Anchorman: The Legend of Ron Burgundy.*

I pound on the door. "Open up, jerk-off."

The only response I hear is the growl of Sex Panther—a punch line from the movie. I knock again. "Come on, douche bag. You're not the only one with problems, you know."

When he still doesn't answer, I genuinely start to worry. "Drew, you seriously need to give me a sign here. If not, I'm going to assume you're actually dying and call nine-one-one."

A minute goes by. Then another. And just as I'm about to pull out my phone, something bangs against the inside of the door. Like it was purposely thrown against it. A baseball maybe.

Bam.

"Drew? Was that you?"

Bam.

"Do you need me to bust the door down?"

Bam . . . Bam.

I think for a moment. Then, to make sure I'm right, I ask, "So it's once for yes, twice for no?"

Bam.

Guess it'll frigging have to do for now. I sit on the floor and lean my back up against Drew's door. And I start to talk, ask yes and no questions—feeling kind of like an idiot. Like some teenager in a horror movie, communicating with the other side through a Ouiji Board, who's too much of a moron to remember those interactions never end well.

"Erin said you texted her. Do you really have the flu?"

Bam.

"Did you and Kate hook up last weekend?"

Bam.

"Was it as good as you imagined?"

Bam . . . Bam.

You might be confused by his answer. I'm not.

"Was it even better?"

There's a meaningful pause. And then . . . *Bam.*

"Were you a dick to her afterwards?"

Bam . . . Bam.

No. So Dee did have it wrong. But then, Drew elaborates. Sort of.

Bam.

No and yes. Drew was a dick to Kate . . . but he seems to think he had a reason to be. I move on.

"Delores broke up with me. Because of the way you treated Kate. And I was really into her, man. I . . . I fell in love with her." My voice gets stronger. Irritated. "Do you even care? Are you fucking sorry at all?"

There's another meaningful pause. Then . . . *Bam.*

Although his remorse is nice to hear, it doesn't help me at all.

And, the bottom line is, it wasn't really Drew that ended Dee and I. That was all on us. Her refusal to trust me . . . my refusal to keep trying to earn it.

Whatever Drew said to Kate, he's obviously suffering because of it. So, I let him off the hook. "The truth is, it's not all on you. We had . . . issues. Problems I thought I could get us through . . . but . . . she didn't want it as much as I did. You know how that goes."

Bam.

"You plan on staying in there forever?"

Bam . . . Bam.

"Do you need anything? Is there anything I can do?"

Bam . . . Bam.

I nod, even though it's only to myself. "Do you want me to come back tomorrow?"

There's a moment of silence, when I assume he's thinking it over. Then he answers.

Bam.

I go back to my apartment and do nothing but watch TV the rest of the night. My face has one expression the whole time—grim. As I flick through the stations, one of those long-as-hell commercials comes on, advertising the ultimate soft rock eighties collection. And "One More Night" by Phil Collins plays loud and clear. It's the part of the song where he's wondering about calling the girl.

And it's like a freaky science fiction movie—like the television is reading my fucking mind. I stare at my cell phone. Contemplating.

Trying to Jedi Mind Trick it.

Ring, you bastard. Ring.

I pick it up, brushing my fingers over the numbers. And I punch in nine of Dee's ten digits . . .

Until the next lyric out of the TV reminds me that maybe she's not alone.

I toss my phone away, like a scorching Hot Pocket fresh from the microwave. Then I plant my face in the couch cushion and yell into it.

"Fuck me!"

The music on the infomercial changes. And now it's "Against All Odds"—a song about a guy who has so much to say to a girl, but she just won't turn around and let him.

You know, somebody must've really screwed Phil Collins over. Big-time.

I sing a few of the lyrics 'cause it's just you and me here. And for an eighties song, it's pretty good.

And—oh look—"Total Eclipse of the Heart" just came on. Completing the trifecta of spirit-crushing, why-don't-you-just-kill-yourself eighties tunes.

Yay.

Excuse me while I go slit my wrists in the bathroom.

Chapter 18

Wednesday morning brings a staff meeting in the conference room. I sit comatose through it—only half listening. After it's over, everyone files out, except for Kate, who's still at the table, sorting and organizing a stack of papers and folders in front of her.

She's Delores's best friend—and yes, that means there's a code. As impenetrable as the blue wall of silence. But, at this point, I've got nothing to lose.

"Hey."

She smiles softly. "Hi, Matthew."

I don't beat around the bush. "Does she . . . does she ever talk about me?"

Kate looks down at the conference table. "Not a word."

Yeah—motherfucking ouch.

But I don't surrender all hope just yet. "Does she think about me?"

Kate's eyes meet mine and they're sympathetic—a little sad.

I'm not sure if the sadness is for me or for Delores. She whispers, "Every day. All the time. She hasn't gone out she just . . . mopes, and watches movies. She won't admit it, but I know it's because of you."

Well . . . that's something at least. Misery loves company—and Delores's gives me a sick jolt of comfort. Reassurance. That at least I'm not alone.

"Matthew, why don't you just call her? People in relationships have arguments sometimes; it doesn't mean it has to be over."

I'm already shaking my head. "I can't do that. Delores likes to be chased—I get it. But, at some point, she needs to stop running and let me catch her. I've put myself out there for her—to show her how important she is to me. That I'm in this for the long haul—if she wants it. But now it's her turn. She has to show me she wants it too."

Pride isn't always a sin. Sometimes it's a savior that keeps you from making an asshole of yourself. Of not just looking like a fool—but being one too.

"I've been with someone who . . . wanted something else. Some*one* else. I'm not going there again."

Kate nods her head, with a small smile. "Okay. For what it's worth, I hope Dee wises up soon."

"Thanks."

I take a few steps toward the door. But then I stop. Because even though I haven't actually seen Drew, every instinct I have tells me he's hurting. Licking his wounds.

The fatal kind.

And my hunch is, Kate's nursing the same kind of injury—she's just better at hiding it.

"Listen, Kate . . . about what happened between you and Drew . . ."

All signs of friendliness drop from her face. Her eyes go hard, her lips pinch, and she cuts me off in a sharp voice. "Don't, Matthew. Just . . . don't."

I guess Drew's not the only one who's hell-bent on keeping radio silence.

"Okay." I squeeze her shoulder. "Have a good day."

She smiles tightly and I head to my office.

Later that evening I swing by Steven and Alexandra's to keep an eye on Mackenzie while they go out to the movies. Lexi opens the door for me, looks at my expression for longer than necessary, then glances behind me. Seeing only the empty space there, her face softens with pity.

She pulls me into a tight hug and says, "You know, Matthew, there is such a thing as too different."

I swallow hard. "Yeah, I know, Lex."

There's no time for a pity party because a blond blur comes tearing down the hall, wearing a blue princess nightgown, with a floppy teddy bear grasped in one hand. She crashes into my legs and wraps her arms around my knees. "You're here!"

I reach under her arms and pick Mackenzie up. "Hey, princess."

"You wanna play tea party, Uncle Matthew? You can be Buzz Lightyear and I'll be Miz Nezbit."

"Sounds like the most fun I'll have all week."

I'm rewarded with a gorgeous baby-teethed smile. And for the first time in days, the weight sitting on my heart feels a little lighter.

Steven helps Alexandra into her coat, and they each kiss Mackenzie good-bye.

"Bedtime at eight," Alexandra informs me. "Don't let her try and negotiate more time."

"I'm not sure if I can hold up against the big, blue, puppy-dog eyes."

She grins. "Be strong."

They leave and I lock the door behind them. For the next hour and a half, I play tea party with Mackenzie. And Barbie dolls. Then we build a block wall and take it out with her remote-control Humvee. Just before bed, we shoot some hoops with the Fisher-Price adjustable basketball net I bought her for her birthday.

Once she's all tucked in, she asks me to read her a story and pulls a thin Disney book out from under her pillow.

Cinderella.

Mackenzie hugs her bear and regards me with long-blinking, sleepy eyes. When we get to the part about Prince Charming's proclamation, she asks, "Uncle Matthew?"

"Mmm?"

"Why didn't Cinderella go to the prince with her glass slipper? Why didn't she say 'It's me'? How come she waited for him?"

I think about her question and can't help but make the comparisons to Delores and me.

"Maybe . . . maybe Cinderella wasn't sure how the prince felt about her. Maybe she needed him to be the one to come to her—so she would know he loved her."

This is just fucking sad. Talking about my love life with a four-year-old?

Oh, how the mighty have fallen.

Mackenzie nods her understanding and I read on. Until . . .

"Uncle Matthew?"

"Yes?"

"How come da prince didn't know it was Cinderella? If he loved her, he woulda bemembered what she looked like, right?"

I think of Dee's teasing smile, her perfect lips, the warm tenderness in her eyes when she wakes up beside me, how it feels to caress her cheek with my fingertips—like touching a rose petal.

My voice is thick when I answer. "Yes, Mackenzie. If he loved her, he wouldn't have forgotten what she looked like. Not ever."

She yawns, long and wide. Then she turns on her side and nestles into the down pillow.

With a drowsy sigh in her voice, Mackenzie says, "I think Uncle Drew is right. Prince Charming really is a douche bag."

And those are the last words she says before sailing off into dreamland.

⸻⸻

Thursday at work, my father stops by my office and informs me my mother is expecting me for dinner that evening. Disappointing my mother is a capital offense, and the last thing I need at the moment is to have my name at the top of the old man's shit list.

I arrive at five thirty on the button. My parents' place is a four-bedroom multi-floor brownstone, originally built in the 1920s, with original molding, three ornate fireplaces, a sitting room, den, a music room, a butler's pantry, and a spacious formal dining room.

Do they really need this much space? No. But they wouldn't dream of moving. Especially once I was out of the house and, as my mother used to say, they could finally have "nice things" again.

I figure it'll only be a few more years before we'll need to install one of those cool automatic chairs to get them up the staircase.

After the housekeeper, Sarah, who's worked for my parents for years, answers the door, I find my mom in the sitting room, enjoying a glass of sherry by the lit fireplace.

When she sees me, she smiles, stands up, and hugs me close. "Hello, darling. I'm so glad you could come tonight." She peers up at my face. "You look tired. You must be working too hard."

I give her a smile. "No, Mom, I'm really not."

We sit and she tells me about the mums she's growing and the latest goings-on at the country club. When my father exits his study, that's the cue that dinner is served.

The dining room table's not overly large—six chairs—but my father eats at one end, looking over the newspaper that he's just getting around to reading, my mother dines at the other end, and I'm in between.

As she slices into her chicken cordon bleu, my mother asks, "Are you still seeing that young lady from the office party? I liked her very much, Matthew. So spirited. Right, Frank?"

"What?"

"The girl Matthew brought to the office party—we liked her, didn't we? What is her name again? Deanna?"

"Delores," my dad grunts—proving he actually is aware of what's going on around him.

Sometimes I think he just acts clueless—and deaf—so he won't have to participate in conversations that don't interest him. It's a handy trick.

I force the food down my suddenly tight throat. "No, Mom, Dee and I . . . we didn't work out."

Her tongue clicks in disappointment. "Oh, that's a shame."

She sips her wine. "I just want to see you settled, dear. None of us is getting any younger."

Here we go.

My mother is awesome—kind and gentle—but she's still a *mother*. Which means any second now, she's going to start talking about how I need someone to take care of me and about seeing her grandchildren before she dies.

It's a discussion we've had before.

She leans my way, and in a conspiratorial tone whispers, "Was it . . . a sexual problem?"

My bite of chicken gets stuck in my esophagus. I pound my chest and dislodge it—but my voice is scratchy.

"What?"

She straightens back up in her chair. "It's nothing to be ashamed of, Matthew. I used to wipe your bottom—there's no reason we can't have an adult discussion about your sex life."

"Used to wipe your bottom" and "sex life" should never, *ever*, be used in the same sentence. Unless your name's Woody Fucking Allen.

I clear my throat again. Still burns. "No, Mom. We were fine in that area."

"Are you sure? Some ladies don't always feel comfortable expressing their needs . . ."

No way this is happening.

". . . communicate their desires. My book club is discussing a novel this month on this very subject. *Fifty Shades of Grey.* Would you like to borrow my copy, Matthew?"

I take a long drink of water. "No, I'm already familiar with it, thanks."

The fact that my dear, sweet mother is familiar with it, however, will definitely be giving me nightmares.

She pats my hand. "All right. You let me know if you change your mind. That Mr. Grey is certainly creative with a necktie."

Thankfully, the rest of the dinner conversation revolves around less nauseating topics.

After the plates are cleared, I stand up and kiss my mother's cheek. "Good night, Mom. And . . . thanks . . . for your advice."

She smiles. "Good night, darling."

My father wipes his mouth then throws his napkin on the plate. "I'll walk you out. Going to have a cigarette."

My father has smoked my whole life—but he doesn't know I do. Doesn't matter if I'm thirteen or thirty—if he ever finds out, he'll break my frigging fingers.

We walk downstairs and stand in the open doorway where he lights up. The smell of my father's cologne and the freshly lit cigarette smell familiar. And weirdly . . . comforting.

"What's the matter with you?" he barks in his rough, old-man voice. "The last few days, you've been walking around looking like you did the day we had to put King down."

See? He may not comment a lot, but it's only because he's too busy listening and watching—and pretending like he's not.

I kick a pebble off the front step. "I'm fine, Dad."

I feel his eyes on me. Scrutinizing. "No, you're not." He snubs out his cigarette in the sand can. "But you will be."

And then he hugs me.

Strong—like a bear. The same way he'd hug me when I was a kid, just before he left for a business trip.

"You're a good boy, Matthew. You always were. And if she can't see that? Then she doesn't deserve you."

I hug him back, because . . . I just really fucking need to. "Thanks, Dad."

We break apart. I swipe at my nose and he smacks my back.

"See you at the office."

"Good night, son." He closes the door behind me.

I don't go home right away. I walk a dozen blocks trying not to think—or see—Dee's face in my mind with every step. I walk one street down, to Drew's building.

The doorman greets me, and when I get to the penthouse, I sit down in the hallway, leaning my back against Drew's door.

I'm not entirely sure he's listening, but it feels like he is.

And I laugh. "Dude, I hope you're sitting the fuck down—'cause you're not gonna believe the conversation I just had with my mother . . ."

Friday is a rough one. I just . . . miss her. It's acute and relentless. The memories, the image of her face, are in my head every second, taunting me. I can't concentrate; I don't want to eat. My body feels weighted and heavy; my chest is tight, achy, like the tail end of bronchitis. I miss everything about her. Her laughter, her ridiculous theories, and yes—not gonna lie—I miss her exquisite tits. I've gotten used to sleeping next to Dee—or on top of her—skin to skin, with my arms either draped around her or my head nestled on the soft comfort of her breasts.

My goddamn down pillow just doesn't compare.

What I really need is to get laid. You may not like hearing that, but too fucking bad—it's the truth.

When your car irreparably dies, do you sit inside it, remembering all the times it drove you to work or to a friend's or on some great road trip? Of course you don't. That's stupid. The logical thing to do—the only thing to do—is go shopping for a new car. That's the only way you'll ever be able to move forward.

For a man or a woman—getting laid after a breakup is a lot like that. It feels good—even if just for a few moments—and it reminds you that life doesn't stop. That the world isn't ending just because your relationship did. Getting some instills confidence in a brighter tomorrow. In a future not immersed in misery.

But while the idea occurs to me, and I know it's something I should do . . . I don't want to. I have no desire to fuck anyone who's not Delores Warren. And to tell you the truth—there's a small, admittedly pussy-whipped part of me that's afraid to. Scared about even trying.

It's the same part of me that sags with disappointment every time I come home and she's not here. The part that still thinks there's a chance she'll realize how great we are together, that she's completely in love with me, that she'll come running back to me. And if any or all that were to happen, I would never want to have to break the news that during our downtime, I screwed another woman. Right or wrong, the trust I've worked so hard to build with Delores would be destroyed. So, in the end, it's just not a risk I'm willing to take—not for some random piece of ass I don't even want.

⬥

Saturday isn't any better. Jack pleads with me to go out with him—complains that he feels abandoned, that he's missing his wingman.

But I'm just not up for it.

Instead, I grab a six-pack and a pizza and have a pity picnic outside Drew's apartment door. I do most of the talking: He only "bams" his answer when I ask if he's still alive. It sounds like he's moved on to watching *Blades of Glory*. What's up with the Will Ferrell fixation, right? Weird.

Anyway, after I'm done with the pizza and making my way to the bottom of the last beer, I lean my head back against his door—a little buzzed. And I get downright philosophical. I talk about the weekend, when we were kids, and my uncle took Drew, Steven, and me camping at his cabin in the Adirondacks.

Steven's highly allergic to poison oak—he blew up like a tick.

But not even that stopped him from joining us in our search for buried treasure. My uncle had given us a map he and my old man had made when they were kids—to a box of silver dollars they thought would be a brilliant idea to bury.

For the entire first three days up there, all we did was hunt for it. But then . . . as kids tend to do . . . we gave up. We turned our attention to climbing trees, and beating the crap out of each other with sticks, and watching the girls from the local college go skinny-dipping in the lake.

I think about those days and, of course, Delores—always her. And I wonder sadly, "Do you think if we had just held on a little longer, looked a little harder, tried just a little bit more—do you think we could've made it to the treasure, Drew?"

He doesn't answer. And I'm a lot further past buzzed than I thought. So before I knock out here in his hallway, I pack up my stuff and take a cab back to my own bed.

And like every night before, I dream of Dee.

Chapter 19

When a guy's nursing a broken heart, he engages in one of three behaviors: he drinks, he fucks, he fights. Sometimes all three in one night.

It's been six days since I've seen Delores and I haven't fucked anyone. Drinking has been minimal—but I'm definitely ready to fight. I've been going to the gym every day, working out harder than usual, trying to channel the feelings of missing her into something positive.

On Sunday afternoon, when I walk through the gym door, Shawnasee's is the first face I see. You remember him, right? The prick I mentioned awhile back, who's in dire need of a good beat down?

Looks like today's his lucky day.

He grins menacingly. "You wanna go a few rounds, or you gonna pussy out again?"

Something inside me tears—like the Hulk when he shreds his T-shirt—and I answer, "Let's do this."

I can't wait to get in the ring. To hit something—to vent the frustration and guilt and generally bad feelings that have been churning inside me for the last six days. I bounce on my toes, roll my head left to right—cracking my neck. Then I duck under the ropes, tap my gloves together, and walk to the center of the ring.

Shawnasee's already waiting for me, looking both confident and eager. Ronny stands between us and recites the typical directions about clean fights and good sportsmanship. We hit gloves, go back to our corners, and wait.

Then the bell rings.

I come at him, hard and fast, but my head's not in it. If you want the truth, I've got no fucking business fighting right now. Because my focus isn't on my opponent at all. It's on the unfairness of life. The bitterness of wanting something—someone—that doesn't want me the same way. At the moment, I'm all about pain and heartbreak—feelings I'm hoping punches will purge.

Shawnasee and I dance and dodge in a circle around each other . . . and then movement from the front door distracts me. And I forget all about footwork, defensive postures, jabs, right hooks, and body blows.

Because standing there in the doorway is Delores Warren.

In a nanosecond, my mind takes her in from head to toe—her hair's pulled back in a ponytail, revealing a makeup-free, beautiful face. Her plain white T-shirt is tied at the hip over tight blue jeans and black Converse sneakers. I don't have time to greet her or even wonder why she's here.

Because the instant after I see her, Shawnasee's fist makes contact with my chin—like an uppercut from Thor's hammer.

My teeth crunch together and my head jerks back. My eyes close automatically as I fall straight back and crash to the floor.

I don't know how long I'm out, but it must only be a few moments. The next time I open my eyes, Ronny's stubbled face is inches from mine. My vision is blurry—colors and lights stretching and bleeding into one another. Sound roars in my ears, like static from an out-of-commission television set.

Through the din, Ronny's voice breaks through. "Fisher! Can ya hear me, Fisher?"

I blink and answer, but my speech sounds muffled, like I'm talking underwater. "Yeah, I . . . I hear you."

"Can ya see me all right?"

"Sure, Ronny. I see a whole bunch of you."

Ronny turns and talks to someone next to him. I only make out a few words: ". . . concussion . . . hospital." Then he leans back over me. "I need you to get up, Fisher."

My legs don't think that's a good idea.

"I'd rather just stay here, if it's all the same to you."

"You need to stand, Matthew."

Nope. My legs still say "Go screw yourself."

"I don't think I can."

Then I see her. She kneels down next to Ronny—next to me. Her warm hand touches my bicep where my T-shirt ends. And she whispers, "Get up, ya son of a bitch . . . 'cause Mickey loves ya."

Instantly, I'm choked up. Not because of the stirring movie quote—but because of what those words could mean.

For us.

"You watched *Rocky Five*?"

Delores nods. "I watched them all. Mickey dying was the saddest thing I've ever seen in my life, you bastard."

Then her face crumples, and she's crying.

She doesn't try to hide it. Her hand doesn't cover her face or stifle her sobs. Because she doesn't pretend to be someone she's not. Take her or leave her, what you see is what you get.

That's what I love about her. One of the many things I love.

My arm is heavy, but I raise it. One still-gloved hand brushes at her tear-trailed cheek. "Don't cry, Dee."

"I'm sorry. I'm so sorry. I was awful to you."

"No . . . I was an asshole. I promised you I'd be patient, and then I . . . wasn't."

"No, you were right. You were right about everything."

I'm reminded of our audience when Ronny cajoles, "All right, boys, let's hit the lockers for a few. Give these two lovebirds some time to cry all over each other." As the other guys follow out, Ronny shakes his head at Dee and me. "This is exactly why I don't want women in my gym."

Once we're alone, I force myself to sit up. This is not a conversation I want to have on my back. Well . . . unless I was naked and on my back.

Dee helps me take the gloves off my hands, and then I rest my upper body against the corner of the ring.

She asks, "Are you okay?"

"Yeah. It feels like a semi ran over my face, but otherwise I'm good."

With vengeful eyes, she glances toward the locker room door where Shawnasee entered. "I'm going to slash that guy's tires before we leave. Will that make you feel better?"

I chuckle. "Never change, Dee."

She sobers and looks down at her hands. Then she confesses, "The thought of having feelings for you—real 'forever' kinds of feelings—scares the shit out of me."

Her declaration doesn't bother me. She's not telling me anything I didn't already know. But the fact that she's here . . . that means *everything*.

"I know."

"I didn't want to get used to being with you, because I knew once I did, when you left . . . I'd be miserable. But it's too late. I was miserable anyway. These last few days . . . I've never felt so sad. And lonely. Empty."

"It's been the same for me."

She smiles at that, though there are still tears in her eyes. And in her voice. "But when I'm with you . . . when you're here next to me . . . it feels perfect. You make me happier than I ever thought I could be, Matthew."

"Well that's an easy fix. I'll just have to stay with you . . . all the time. It won't be too difficult. Because . . . I'm kind of . . . totally in love with you."

"You're an amazing man, Matthew. You're funny and warm, you're thoughtful and sexy as all hell. You're . . . you're the best thing that's ever happened to me." Her eyes are soft and tender as she looks into mine. She touches my face gently. "I love you, Matthew."

Even though it feels like my jaw is going to splinter off at any moment, I smile. It's impossible not to.

My hand slides to the back of Delores's neck and I bring her forward. My mouth brushes hers—lightly at first—then deeper, with more meaning. I pull her across me, full into my arms. Our tongues touch and taste, slow and unrushed, with the promise of more to come.

Dee sighs and rests her forehead against mine. "I didn't imagine telling you I loved you, like this."

"Me, neither. But . . . it's something we'll remember, right? It works for us."

"It sure fucking does." Then Dee hops to her feet and holds out her hand to me. "Why are we still here?"

I'm able to get up without her help. But once I'm standing, I remember what brought us to this moment in the first place. "Dee, about Drew and Kate . . ."

She puts her finger over my lips. "No. We're not talking about them. Ever. You're not your bastard best friend—I know that. I don't want him coming between us."

She's right. This isn't about Drew or Kate or Rosaline or any of the douche bags from her past. They shouldn't affect us—can't touch us.

This is about me and Dee.

As we make our way out of the ring, I ask, "Did you take a cab here?"

"Yeah—why?"

I grin. "I drove the Ducati."

Dee's pleased. "I've missed feeling the power between my legs."

I throw my arm around her shoulders. "Oh, you'll feel the power—*after* I get you back to my place."

Delores loops her arm around my waist and shakes her head. "So cheesy." Then her voice becomes firmer, more insistent. "But we're both going to have to wait to feel the power, because before we go home, we're taking a cab to the emergency room to get you checked out."

"What? No, I'm fine, really." I whine like a six year old who doesn't want to go to the dentist.

Dee shakes her head. "Don't want to hear it—you're going. Concussions are nothing to fool around with. I just got you back, I'm not taking any chances on losing you now."

I open my mouth to argue—because I really am fine—and I'll be fucking fantastic as soon as I get Dee back in my bed. Or, on my kitchen counter, the dining room table, the living room wall—you get the point.

But before I can disagree, she adds, "Besides, for what I have planned for you? We're going to need medical clearance."

Well, when she puts it that way . . .

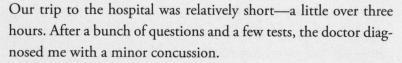

Our trip to the hospital was relatively short—a little over three hours. After a bunch of questions and a few tests, the doctor diagnosed me with a minor concussion.

Frigging Shawnasee.

Payback is a bitch—and you can bet your ass I'll be driving that point home the next time I'm at the gym.

The doctor told me to watch out for nausea, blurry vision, blah, blah, blah. At the same time Dee and I asked if sex was okay.

He said it was.

Which is why the moment my apartment door closes, Dee and I are kissing, tearing at clothes, mauling each other—with six days of desire and want driving us on. My clothes are easier to get off than Dee's, so by the time we step over the threshold of my bedroom, I'm completely naked.

Hard, hot, and thick, I need to be inside her more than I need to take my next fucking breath.

Dee's shirt? Gone.

Her bra? On the pool table in my dining room.

I touch her, hold her against me—drowning in the sensation of our bare chests pressing and the velvet texture of her perfect skin. My fingers work on the button of her jeans. But Dee stops me. Her hands cover mine and she backs up a step. Her chest rises and falls rapidly as she tries to catch her breath. "Matthew . . . there's something I have to tell you. I . . . did something. Last night."

Fuck. Me. Hard.

Last night was Saturday. My first thought is, "Dee screwed another guy last night," and I almost double over from the sheer agony of it. And the rage.

I know, technically, we weren't together. We were broken up. I can't get mad.

Fuck that—I'm going to lose it.

I'll forgive her. I'll get over it . . . *after* I smash something into a thousand pieces and pound on the walls like a gorilla on crack cocaine.

I sit down on the bed. "What'd you do? Whatever it is I'll . . . fuck, just tell me what it is."

And then she does the strangest thing. She smiles. And unbuttons her own pants, sliding them down her legs as she talks. "I thought all week about what you said. How I was scared, how I didn't want to take a chance . . ."

"I was angry when I said that, Delores."

"But you were also right. So I wanted to do something, to show you, to *prove* that I do trust you. That I want this, and you—permanently."

She slips her panties off, and I'm momentarily hypnotized by the sight of her stunningly smooth pussy. Until I notice the white bandage covering a small patch of skin below her pelvic bone.

She peels it off, revealing the bright blue tattoo emblazoned on her skin underneath. A tattoo of my name.

MATTHEW

I'm speechless—can only stare. Then I drop to my knees in front of her and kiss the soft, still-tender flesh beside my name.

"I fucking love it. I love you." I dust my fingers over it, very gently. "Now you're really stuck with me."

Delores tilts my face up and runs her hands through my hair. "Yeah, I really am."

I stand, swing her around, and toss her on the bed. Then I jump in after her.

Chapter 20

Later, when the sun has gone down and the sheets on my bed are fantastically rumpled, after fevered "I love you"s and "I missed you"s and "Don't ever leave me"s are whispered between desperate touches and gratified moans, I force myself to get up.

It's not easy. Dee lays naked in my bed, her lips swollen and well used, her hair alluringly tousled. I stand for a moment—pants in hand—just looking at her.

"God, you're beautiful."

This time, she smiles. And I know it's because she believes me.

She reaches out her hand. "Then don't go. Come back to bed, Matthew."

I groan—'cause getting back in bed is all I really want to do. But I shake my head. "I won't be gone long. I just have to check on Drew real quick—it's a guy-code thing. What kind of friend would I be if I didn't make sure he hasn't hung himself in his walk-in closet?"

"The kind who wants to make the world a better place."

Then she spots my camera on the bedside table. She turns it over in her hands, biting her lip. "I guess I'll just have to occupy myself . . . by taking X-rated selfies on your camera. We can develop them together when you get back."

I take a second to enjoy the images that pop into my head—that hopefully will be showing up on my camera.

Then I hand her two extra rolls of film.

I take my time kissing her good-bye before I compel my legs to move to the door. Just before I walk out, Dee calls, "Matthew?"

I stop and turn to her.

"I love you."

And just like every other time she's said it today, a goofy, ridiculously happy grin appears on my lips. I walk back to the bed and kiss her yet again.

"For the record? I'm never going to get tired of hearing you say that."

She smiles contentedly. "Hurry back."

And I end up running the whole way to my bike—so I can do just that.

Outside Drew's apartment door, it's the same old same old. I pound on it and I call, but the only response I get is one bump of a base-ball thrown against the door when I ask him if he's still breathing.

I sigh and rest my hand on the door.

It's time for some tough love. Well past the time for it, if you want to know the truth.

"Dude, you gotta man up. Whatever happened between you and Kate—however badly you fucked up—it's not gonna get any better if you don't come out and deal with it."

No response.

I try taunting him. "In all the years we've known each other, I never would've guessed you were capable of being such a gigantic pussy. You realize you're completely wrecking my image of you, right?"

Still nothing.

"Come on, Drew. Open the door. Remember how I was after Rosaline? You were there for me . . . let me return the favor."

Third strike, and I'm out.

I tap the door, the way I'd tap Drew's fist if these were better days. "Okay, man, have it your way. I'll be back tomorrow, all right?"

Bam.

The door vibrates from the impact of the ball on the other side, and I know he's heard me.

I shake my head as I walk back to the elevator. Because tomorrow, when I come back, I won't be alone. I really didn't want to have to do this—but it's been a frigging week. He's left me no choice.

It's time to go nuclear.

I exit the lobby of the building, stepping out onto the sidewalk. Then I take my phone out and dial.

She picks up after two rings, greeting me by name.

"Hey, Alexandra. Listen, I need your help . . . it's about Drew."

And the rest, as they say, is history.

So now you have the full story. The parts you didn't get to see before, the answers to some of the questions that might've been bugging you.

When it comes to advice, I'm kind of tapped out at the moment—there's not a whole lot left to give. But I'll leave you with this:

Life is a short, wild ride. Don't try to put the brakes on, don't overanalyze or try to control it. If you're lucky, like I was, you'll find that perfect someone who'll sit next to you and hold your hand through every curve, every up and down.

And that? Just makes it even more fun.

Epilogue

Six months later . . .

Las Vegas, Nevada. The Elvis Chapel. It's technically called
A Little White Wedding Chapel, but because there's an
Elvis impersonator officiating the services, it'll always be the
Elvis Chapel to me. We wait in an adjoining room for our turn,
surrounded by signed photographs of the celebrities who've
exchanged vows here over the years.

It's been six months since our first kiss on the dance floor.
Maybe you think that's too fast. Maybe you think we're crazy. But
for Dee and me?

Crazy is actually pretty normal. Let's look at how we became
engaged, for example:

*"Mr. Fisher, please lay back down!" the nurse yells in a com-
manding voice, but I ignore it.*

What a fucking disaster.

Instead of a private, romantic evening at Dee's favorite restau-

rant, I've somehow ended up in a hospital gown, on a gurney, in the back room of the goddamn ER. The only thing that could make it worse would be if the engagement ring was to get stolen by a sticky-fingered nurse or random homeless person.

I designed the ring myself, and it's perfect. A flawless two-carat diamond surrounded by emeralds, rubies, and sapphires. It's color-ful, unique, just like Dee. Now I just have to give it to her.

I dig my pants out of the standard-issue plastic hospital bag and pull the ring box from the pocket. Then, before the nurses can stop me, I sprint down the short hall to the emergency room waiting area where Delores is. She stands up as soon as she sees me.

I walk to her and drop to one bended knee. "I want you to belong to me. And I want to be yours. I want to be the reason for your smiles. I want to spend the rest of my life listening to all your theories and teaching you the difference between a good movie and a bad one. I want to be eighty years old, holding your hand during couples skate—and I promise to love you every single moment from now until then. Will you marry me, Delores?"

Yeah—so that was my romantic proposal.

Dee didn't want to have a long engagement, and I was thrilled about that. The "why wait?" philosophy is how we started, and it hasn't let us down yet. So, here we are—me, Dee, Drew, and Kate—in Vegas for a quickie wedding and kick-ass celebration.

I look in the mirror and try to straighten my tie, but it doesn't cooperate.

"Are you sure about this?" Drew asks from behind me, dressed in his own custom-tailored tuxedo.

"Never been more sure, buddy."

I give up on the tie. *Screw it.*

"Are you really sure?" Drew asks. "It's not too late to back out."

I smirk. "It's way too late."

His eyes drop to my crooked tie, and he steps in front of me to fix it—like a father helping his teenage son on prom night. Once it's straightened to Drew's satisfaction, he puts his hands on my shoulders, looks me in the eyes, and says, "Are you sure you're really sure?"

Kate's frowning voice calls from across the room. "Drew?"

"Yeah, babe?"

"He's sure. Don't ask him again or I'm not going to be happy. And you won't like it if I'm not happy."

I think they've been watching *Incredible Hulk* reruns recently.

Drew nods. But as soon as Kate's back is turned, he silently mouths, "Are you sure? Really sure?"

I laugh. Because I'm sure.

And because I never—ever—thought I'd see the day when Drew would be cowed by a chick. But it looks like he has.

Haven't we all?

I adjust my cuff links as Dee walks up beside me, warm contentment in her eyes. She's wearing an all-white, all-lace, long-sleeved minidress with baby blue stilettos. Her strawberry-blond hair is pulled up at the sides, and a shoulder-length veil cascades over her hair like a halo, held in place by a small diamond tiara that sits atop her head.

"What are you thinking about?" she asks me.

I wrap an arm around her waist, pulling her close. "I was thinking about the first time I called you. I didn't want to admit it at the time, but I think I was kind of nervous." I kiss her temple, gently. "I'm not nervous now."

She rests her head against my chest. "Me, neither."

Just then, the double doors to the chapel open, and a crystal-encrusted Elvis steps into the room. "Are we ready to get this show on the road, kids?"

Drew and I take our places near the altar as the doors are closed once more. Instrumental guitar music begins, the doors open, and Kate steps into the archway. Out of the corner of my eye, I see Drew smile wide as he follows Kate's every move. When she gets down the aisle, he winks, and Kate answers him with an adoring smile.

Once Kate stands in her assigned spot, the doors reopen again, revealing Dee on Elvis's arm. As he escorts her down the aisle, he sings our wedding song, "Can't Help Falling In Love."

Delores and I stand side by side, hand in hand, as Elvis asks us our vows. "Do you, Matthew Franklin Fisher, take Delores Warren as your lawfully wedded wife?"

"I do."

"Do you promise to never treat her like a 'Hound Dog,' 'Don't Be Cruel,' or leave her 'Lonesome Tonight'?"

"I do."

"Do you promise to be her 'Big Hunk O' Love,' her 'Teddy Bear,' and love her tender and true until death do you part?"

I cup Dee's cheek in my hand. "Always."

Dee smiles and tears up as I slip the platinum band on her finger, next to her engagement ring.

Then Elvis asks Delores, "Do you, Delores Sunshine Warren, take Matthew Fisher as your lawfully wedded husband?"

Her voice is clear and sure as she answers, "I do."

"Do you promise to never step on his 'Blue Suede Shoes,' never cause him to have a 'Suspicious Mind,' or leave him 'All Shook Up'?"

"I do."

"Will you always have him on your mind, always show him the 'Wonder of You,' and always keep that 'Burning Love' for him until death do you part?"

"I will."

With that, Dee slips the ring on my finger. And in a deep drawl, Elvis proclaims, "By the power invested in me by the State of Nevada, I pronounce you husband and wife." He slaps my shoulder. "You may kiss your bride."

I don't have to be told twice. I wrap my arms around her and press my lips to Dee's—pouring every ounce of love, excitement, and gratitude I feel for her into it.

I don't know if it's proper to use tongue in a wedding kiss, but I don't let that stop me.

Before I can sweep Delores up, she jumps right into my arms, and I cradle her as we kiss. Kate claps and Drew whistles. After we take a thousand pictures, we thank Elvis and head out. And the four of us spend the rest of the night laughing and dancing until we can't stand up.

It really is the best of times. And it's just the beginning.

Turn the page for a bonus from *New York Times* bestselling author

Emma Chase!

Kate, Drew, and Billy make an interesting cast of characters at Matt and Dee-Dee's wedding. Can they behave themselves long enough to let Matt and Dee-Dee have their special day?

HOLY
FRIGGING
MATRIMONY

Chapter 1

I sit in a high-backed chair in the corner of the bedroom in a suite at the Plaza Hotel, flipping through the advertisement-packed pages of *Bride* magazine. Female-targeted ads are ridiculous. I don't care how "flawless"-looking the makeup claims to be; if you don't already look like a Victoria's Secret model, no cover-up in the world is gonna make you look like one.

Another thing I don't get—everyone always raves about the Plaza, but the room is wall-to-wall florals—the bedding, the upholstery, the framed pictures. It looks like it was designed by a deranged Mistress Mary, quite contrary–obsessed grandmother. I shift in the chair, trying to get comfortable, but the seat is obviously made to be "looked at," not "sat in." I give up on the magazine and wait.

Waiting for what, you ask?

For Kate, of course.

She's behind the closed bathroom door, probably taking a bath. And she doesn't know I'm here yet. It's going to be a surprise. A lust-filled, haven't-seen-her-in-twenty-four-hours-and-I-can't-wait-to-get-inside-her kind of surprise.

You have no idea what's going on right now, do you? Well, hang on; you'll figure it out shortly.

Because the bathroom door opens, and Kate steps into the bedroom. And like a dog who hasn't seen his master all day, my lonely cock lifts its head at the sight of her.

She holds a champagne glass filled with bubbly, orange liquid. Her hair is twisted up in a high knot while delicate, curling strands brush against her damp neck. She's wearing a short, red, silk robe that leaves little to the imagination—which is exactly why I bought it for her.

I smile when she sees me. Her beguiling brown eyes widen. "Drew?" She glances at the door. "What are you doing here? You're not supposed to be here."

"I know. I snuck in. I'm stealthy like that."

She steps toward me. "If Dee sees you, she's going to freak out."

I scowl at the mention of Kate's psychotic best friend, whose mission in life is to interfere with mine. "Screw Dee. I wanted to see you."

Last night was the first night we've spent apart since Kate moved in with me. Now, you might think that one night shouldn't be that big a deal—but you're wrong. Ask any recovering drug addict which night of detox was the worst? When they were hungriest for a fix? The initial hours of withdrawal are always the hardest.

Kate smiles forgivingly but reminds me, "The guys aren't supposed to see the girls before the reception. It's a tradition."

I stand up and pull Kate flush against me because seeing her, smelling her vanilla- and lavender-scented skin, makes touching her a must. "It's a stupid fucking tradition. And that's not even accurate—the actual rule is the *groom* isn't allowed to see the *bride* before the *ceremony*. Delores just made this shit up to make me miserable."

Are you starting to figure it out now?

Kate giggles. "Because everything is always about you, right?"

"Well . . . yeah."

I lean in to kiss her lips, but she leans back. "You can't stay here."

I counter her dodge with a move toward her neck. I kiss and suck the sensitive skin above her collarbone. *Delicious.*

I mumble against her, "Sure I can."

Kate tilts her head with a sigh, giving me more room to taste, even while she argues, "And when Dee finds out you're here?"

"If Delores comes in this room, she's going to get an eyeful." I chuckle. "Maybe she'll go blind. Or she'll learn something— lucky Matthew."

Kate sees the wisdom of my words. Or else she's just as horny as I am. Her body relaxes against mine, and her arms tighten around my shoulders, giving in.

Victory is mine.

My hand slides beneath her robe, palming her soft, gorgeous tit. And I whisper, "Tell me you missed me last night."

She pushes against my hand, wanting more. "I did."

I trail light, tickling kisses down her chest and bend my knees to reach my target. I rub my face against the velvet flesh of her breast, breathing lightly on her aroused nipple. "Tell me you thought about me, Kate."

"Mmm . . . I always think about you."

I reward her words with the flick of my tongue. I lave her gorgeous nipple then suck it into my mouth. Kate holds on to my head for dear life. And just as my hand makes its move up her thigh . . .

There's a knock, then a voice comes from outside the bedroom door.

A grating voice, like the one those Satan-worshipping teens from the '80s probably heard when they played their heavy metal records backwards.

"Kate? Hey, Katie, did you fall asleep in there?"

Delores thought it would be a *great* idea for her and Kate to share the two-bedroom suite for the night. Their mothers shared an identical one a few doors down.

Kate tenses and I close my eyes, praying Dee'll go the hell away.

But not surprisingly, my prayers go unanswered. The doorknob jiggles. "Kate, open up."

I get in one last drag on Kate's tit, then I release it with a pop. She closes her robe and drags me toward the door, pushing me to the corner so I'll be hidden when it opens. Then she breathes deeply, brushes her hair out of her face, and cracks the door open just enough to see Delores.

Kate tells her, "I'm here. I was just taking a bath—what's up?"

"The photographer's on his way. Get your buns moving—he'll be here in an hour." Delores pauses, then asks, "Are you okay?"

"Yeah, of course. I'm fine."

Suspicion swims in Dee's tone. "You look flushed. Why are you all flushed?"

Kate is good at almost everything she does. Except lying. She sucks at that.

She waves her hand at her face. "I . . . I don't know."

"Were you masturbating?" Dee teases.

Oh, to all the angels and saints—how I wish she fucking was.

Watching Kate get herself off—in front of me—would be epic. It's a major fantasy. But she's hesitant, self-conscious. I'm trying to get her comfortable with the idea. Two birds, one stone and all that.

For guys, it's a phenomenal turn-on. So if you ladies are looking to spice things up a bit? Try a little self-diddling. Trust me—your audience will be begging for an encore.

Kate scoffs, "No, Dee, I wasn't masturbating."

Delores still isn't convinced. "Are you having phone sex with the Goatfucker?"

Phone sex.

Also at the top of my to-do list.

"I told you to stop calling Drew that," Kate scolds.

"I know—you're right. I can't help it. I picture his face and it just comes out of my mouth."

Now Kate sounds impatient. "Okay—yes, all right? I'm having phone sex with Drew."

"Eww! Why did you tell me? I don't want to know that."

Kate sighs. "Then why did you even ask? Look, Dee, you worry about *you* right now, okay? I'll make sure I'm ready when the photographer gets here."

Begrudgingly, Delores says, "All right. Your mom's almost dressed if you need any help." Then she suggests, "Hey—maybe you should leave him hanging? Dipwad's balls could be our something blue."

"*Good-bye,* Delores." Kate closes the door.

After we hear Dee close the door to her own bedroom, Kate locks ours and turns to me. "She's onto us. I'm going to have to make sure she's completely occupied before you sneak out. You might be here awhile."

I grin. "Oh, no . . . however will we ever fill the time?"

Kate turns and walks toward the forgotten chair. The silk robe sways teasingly, revealing the barest glimpse of her sumptuous ass.

"*You'll* be filling the time perusing *Bridal* magazine while *I* get dressed. Not all of us can look presentable in five minutes flat."

I shrug. "Seven, if I need to shave."

"Regardless. There's no time to mess around—even for a quickie."

I stalk toward her. "A—there's always time to mess around. B—it depends on your definition of quickie. My interpretation happens to be how *quickly* I can make you scream my name. Past experience has shown I can make that happen pretty damn fast."

For the first time, I notice the lace undergarments laid out on top of the dresser. A sheer, white bustier and matching string thong. I motion to them with my chin. "No garters?"

I'm not the biggest fan of lingerie, but if you're going to wear it, garters are always a nice touch.

Kate pulls her hair free from its bun and shakes it out. Shiny dark strands fall down around her, making her look bed-rolling wild and accentuating the refined beauty of her dark eyes, pert nose, and sweetly kissable lips.

She answers, "No, no garters. You'll understand why when you see the dress—" She stops, her expression panicked. She glances toward the garment bag hanging next to the bed. "You didn't look at my dress, did you?"

I'm still distracted by Kate's disheveled hair. I imagine running my hands through its soft waves then wrapping it around my fingers for a tug while I'm buried deep inside her.

That's why my voice sounds less than convincing when I answer, "No, I didn't look."

Kate points her finger at me, like a teacher reprimanding a student. "Tell the truth, Drew."

"What am I? Ten years old?"

"Emotionally? Sometimes. But that's beside the point. Did you peek at my dress?"

I reach around her waist and press our lower halves together. "No, baby, I didn't look at your dress."

Kate settles into my embrace, toying with the neck of my T-shirt as she explains, "I'm glad you didn't look, because I want you to be surprised. You're going to lose it when you see me in it. It'll be your new favorite dress."

I kiss her forehead and work my way down over her temple, across her cheek. "My favorite dress of yours will always be . . . the one on the floor."

I nip at her lower lip as my hands skim the silk from her shoulders. "Like this robe." Kate lowers her arms, allowing me to slide it off her completely until it pools around her feet. "It's my fucking favorite."

Then I cup her jaw in one hand and kiss her fully. Deeply. I waste no time in sliding my tongue against hers, which eagerly joins mine in the sensuous give and take.

Between kisses I whisper, "You taste like champagne."

She giggles as I move to her shoulder, scraping it with my teeth and then soothing the love bite with my lips.

"It's a mimosa. I had a few with breakfast and some more in the bath."

I push her knees open with my leg and caress the firm flesh of her ass before dragging her up onto my thigh. The friction makes her moan. She pulls my head back down to her lips for another mimosa-flavored kiss.

Holding her steady, I move us back to the bed. I slide her down my leg and lay her in the middle of the rumpled sheets. Then I pull my T-shirt over my head and push my gym shorts to the floor.

My ever-enthusiastic dick stands hard and thick. Kate leans up on her elbows, devouring me with her eyes. Her cheeks are tinged pink with desire, her lips are parted, and her thighs rub together in anticipation. *Fucking stunning.* With a needy lick of her lips, her gaze settles on my cock as she waits for me to make the next move.

And I think about how hot it'd be to see Kate touch herself. Maybe she needs the "I show you mine, you show me yours" approach? I take my dick in my hand and stroke it up and down. Kate follows my every move, mesmerized. After a few more slow pumps I say, "You know, I've never really liked champagne. But maybe I've just been drinking it from the wrong glass. We should test that theory."

I pick up Kate's glass from the bedside table and sit beside her on the bed. She reaches out and replaces my hand with her own, stroking me expertly, caressing the tip with her thumb.

And I can't help but groan.

I raise the glass over her, tip it slightly, and pour the cold liquid between her breasts. She gasps and her hand tightens around me in the most fantastic way.

Then I lean forward, lapping at the champagne-infused juice. Over her sternum, around the supple base of her perfect frigging tits, I lick every drop, tasting the drink—and her. It's a heady combination.

"Mmm . . . good stuff."

And as much as I love the feel of her hand on me, I take Kate's wrists and bring both hands over her head so she's lying flat on her back. Kneeling on the bed, I lean over her and dribble more of the mimosa onto the peaks of her breasts and suckle hard, flicking at the nipple with my tongue—first one, then the other.

She writhes on the bed and moans, a needy, desperate sound that spurs me on.

A few more drops are poured on her stomach. Kate tenses reflexively, but she relaxes again when my warm mouth glides across her skin, following the path of the sweet liquid.

Her moans turn to gasps as I lick and suck my way around her adorable belly button, then down to her thighs. And her gasps turn to high-pitched whimpers as I nibble on the flesh of her thighs, inching ever higher.

Kate likes to get creative with the pussy grooming. Today it's a barely there landing strip, which has me practically shaking to sink my face into it.

I don't make myself wait long.

I hold the glass above her and pour the rest of the liquid between her spread thighs. Then I cover her with my mouth, sucking and licking, lapping up every trickle like an alcoholic consuming his last indulgence before going cold turkey.

I feel light-headed from the taste, the fragrance, the smooth, slick feel of her pussy against my tongue. I moan against her flesh and Kate cries out in carnal fucking joy.

I bring two fingers to her clit and rub it in firm, quick circles. Kate's hips rise and push instinctively as she gets closer, in time with my tongue as it pushes in and out.

Her thighs squeeze my head and I grip her hips hard, lifting her against my mouth. She stiffens as one last, long, serrated moan escapes her lips.

Then she goes slack in my hands. Spent and satisfied.

And it still gets me. The undiluted gratification of going down on her. Of giving her bliss.

But as happy as I am that I made her come, my own hedonistic craving pushes at me, driving me like the roar of a crowd at a college football game.

Go, go, go!

I rise to my knees and hook my arms under Kate's calves, spreading her wide. Then I bury myself fully in one powerful push.

There's nothing better than this—nothing on earth that feels this perfect. That first thrust, when my cock is enveloped by Kate's tight, wet, warmth—it's rapture so intense, it borders on pain.

My head rolls back on my neck as I savor the feeling. Then I pull my hips back, sliding against her grip, and drive back in.

Using her legs for leverage, I fuck her hard, but slow. When I'm buried to the hilt I rock my hips side to side, rubbing my pelvis against Kate's sweet spot, until she's recovered from her first orgasm and climbing toward number two.

With each move of my hips, Kate cries out in harsh breaths.

"Yes!"

"Drew!"

"More!"

The pleasure tingles and builds, gathering low in my stomach. And when Kate arches her back and clamps down around me, I push forward a final time and pulse inside her as I groan and curse.

Out of breath, I collapse on top of her, and she presses her lips to mine in an openmouthed, chest-heaving kiss. Afterward, I turn my head and pant against her neck.

With a small laugh she says, "Wow. So I guess you really missed me last night, huh?"

I smile. "What gave me away?"

I roll to the side and Kate snuggles against me. Once her heartbeat slows, she complains, "Now I have to take another bath. You made me sweaty."

I run my fingers through her hair. "I like you sweaty. You should stay like this."

Her nose wrinkles. "I smell."

I press my face against her neck and inhale dramatically. "You smell like sweat and sex . . . and me. It's hot. Eau de Cum kicks Chanel Number Five's ass."

For a guy, there's something primordial about a woman covered in your scent—it's the most primitive way of staking your claim. Of showing every other peckerhead that a woman is very much taken. It's animalistic, sure, but that doesn't make it any less arousing.

"That's gross. I'm taking another bath."

I chuckle. "Whatever makes you happy."

Plus, it'll give me a reason to make her sweaty again. *Another* reason.

After five minutes of customary cuddling, Kate lifts her head from the pillow of my chest and orders, "You have to get the hell out of here."

My brow furrows. "Kicking me out already? I feel so used."

She laughs.

I say, "I see how it is. You only want me for my body."

Mimicking my earlier tone, Kate replies, "Well . . . yeah. Although your mind can be mildly entertaining."

I smack her ass with an open palm.

Slap.

She squeaks and jumps out of bed, out of my reach.

"Get dressed." My clothes are thrown at my head as Kate slips into her robe and tiptoes out the door to check if the coast is clear.

I'm dressed by the time she comes back in.

She holds out her hand. "Come on, Dee's in her room. You're good to go."

I pull on her hand until she crashes against me. "I don't wanna go. I want to defile the prestigious Plaza Hotel by having you ride me like a slutty mermaid in the bathtub."

Kate shakes her head. "Not today. I'll see you in a few hours."

I sigh. "Fine." I brush my lips against hers quickly. "I'll be counting the minutes."

Kate pinches me, because she knows I'm being sarcastic. "I'll see you downstairs."

"There's going to be a lot of people downstairs. How am I going to find you?"

She smiles. "You won't be able to miss me. I'll be the one walking down the aisle to you. Wearing . . . silver."

Chapter 2

Marriage.

The final frontier.

Steven went first. He was kind of our test subject. Like those monkeys that NASA sent off into space in the fifties, knowing they'd never make it back alive.

And now Matthew is following in his footsteps.

What? You didn't think *I* was getting married today, did you?

No frigging way. I've barely got the boyfriend thing down. I'm not ready to tackle the title of husband. Don't want to bite off more than I can chew. Matthew, on the other hand, is just crazy enough to give it a try.

And the proposal—now, there's a fucking story. Matthew had this whole romantic thing going. Rented out an entire restaurant for just Delores and him. He even had a string quartet playing music in the background. But when the big moment came? He was so nervous, he hyperventilated.

And then he passed the fuck out.

Nailing his head on the table on the way down.

Delores freaked—Kate said she was never good with blood. She called 911. And even though he swore up and down that he was fine, she made him go to the hospital in the ambulance.

That's when things got interesting.

Because hospitals have certain protocols they have to follow. One of them involves hospital gowns. So when they wheeled Matthew in, a bloody bandage on his head, they started to cut his clothes off. Then they put all of his belonging in a big plastic bag—including the two hundred thousand dollar diamond ring he'd purchased for the occasion.

The idea of losing that ring cured Matthew of his cold feet real frigging quick. So he hops off the gurney, grabs the ring, runs out into the ER, and drops to his knees in front of Delores. And that's how he popped the question.

In the middle of the goddamn emergency room with his ass hanging out the back of a hospital gown, as bare as the day he was born.

Naturally, Delores said yes. And two days later, the four of us jetted to Vegas for the Elvis Chapel Special.

Crazy? Sure. But it kind of fits, don't you think?

Anyway, we come back to the city, where Matthew announces to his parents that he's a married man. I've never seen Estelle Fisher so animated in my life. She started bawling her eyes out, sobbing about how she missed her only child's wedding.

I felt bad, so I can only imagine how shitty Matthew felt. Making your mother cry? That guilt is like the sixth circle of hell.

Frank, being a man of few words, just looked at his son and said, "Fix this."

But his eyes said so much more. They said, "You may be

thirty-one years old, but I will still kick your ass up and down Park Avenue if you don't make this right real motherfucking quick."

And so here we are.

At Matthew and Delores's grand New York City wedding reception, courtesy of Frank and Estelle. No expense was spared—*very* New York high society. It's supposed to be elegant. Classy. And it is.

Except for Delores's dress, of course. Have you ever seen Madonna's "Like a Virgin" video?

Perfect—then you know just what Delores looks like.

Cocktail hour—hands down, it's the best part of a wedding. Exceeded only by that garter thing. I've always been an excellent garter catcher, and there's no better way to get to know a chick than by sticking your hands up her dress as high as you can go.

But that was then. My now is much better.

Because I've got the hottest girl in the room sitting next to me—and I can stick my hands up her dress anytime I want.

Now that Kate is wearing her dress, I understand why she said garters wouldn't work. It's silver and short. I'm talking micro-mini. And strapless. Every time I look at her, I can't help but think about how easy it will be to get it off. And her shoes? You remember my thing for shoes, right? They're very high, very strappy, open-toed and . . .

Amelia Warren, Delores's mother, stands up from the table. She's thin, with shoulder-length, feathered '80s style strawberry-blond hair. And like her daughter after her—she's nuts. When I say nuts, I mean that in the most literal way possible.

For Kate's birthday, Amelia sent her a huge, heavy, natural crystal necklace harvested from the caves of Périgord, because she believes they'll protect Kate's lungs from the city air pollution.

It's a shame how stringent the involuntary commitment protocols in this country have become.

Oh—and Amelia doesn't like me at all. Don't know why. I only met her once before this blessed event, and we didn't speak more than five words to each other. I wonder if the withering glares she throws my way have anything to do with her nephew.

"Oh look—Billy's here! He made it!"

Speak of the Devil and he doth appear. I glance over to the doorway where, sure enough, the ball-licker just waltzed in.

Yep, still hate him. He's like genital herpes—he just won't go the fuck away.

He's been living in LA for the last eight months, and much to my displeasure, he and Kate still talk. She says they're just—say it with me—"*friends*"—but I don't buy it. I mean, sure, for Kate, they're just friends. That I believe. But for a guy? No way.

The "friend" card is one of the oldest hook-up tricks in the book. Right up there with "I think I might be gay." He's just biding his time—waiting for me to screw up so he can be the shoulder Kate cries on. Then when she's all vulnerable and weak, he'll stick his tongue down her throat.

Not gonna happen. Not on my fucking watch.

He makes his way over to our table and Kate goes up to him. They hug, and I grind my teeth together.

"Hi, Katie."

"Hey, Billy."

Pardon me while I swallow the vomit that just surged into my mouth.

"Dee-Dee's going to be so excited to see you. I thought you had a show?"

His smile is smug. Slick. Like a used-car salesman. "I had my agent move some things around." Then he looks Kate over, from head to toe.

And I want to simultaneously cover her with a tablecloth and scoop his eyeballs out with a coffee spoon.

"You look amazing."

She tilts her head to the side with a smile. "Aww. You're so sweet. You look great too."

She's actually stomaching this bullshit? Are you fucking kidding me?

I clear my throat and stand up behind her. "Warren."

"Evans."

Our eyes clash—like a lion staring down a hyena—and Kate is the fresh kill we're both looking to eat.

That's when my mom comes over. "Kate, could you be a dear and help me find your mother? The photographer would like to take a few more family shots outside before the sun goes down."

Kate's dark eyes cloud over with concern. They dart between the two of us nervously. "Ah . . . sure, Anne. No problem."

"Thank you, sweetheart."

Kate looks at each of us pointedly. "I'll be right back." As she turns to go, she stops at my shoulder and whispers, "Be good, Drew."

I smirk. "That's not what you wanted this morning."

Her smile's tight and there's warning in her eyes. "It's what I want now."

I tuck a piece of her hair back behind her ear. "I'm always good, baby."

She walks away, leaving me alone with my arch nemesis. This should be interesting.

He jumps right in with both feet. "So, I left Kate a couple voice mails last week. Apparently she didn't get them." His tone is accusing. Rightly so.

"Maybe she just didn't want to talk to you."

He snorts—as pigs tend to do. "Or maybe you deleted them."

I take a step closer, making him back up. "Maybe you shouldn't be calling my apartment."

"I called to talk to Kate."

"Right—Kate, who's living in *my* apartment."

"You can't fucking tell her who she can talk to. Who the hell do you think you are?"

"Her boyfriend. Which means—yeah—I can. And I don't think that includes you anymore."

"You know something, Evans? I see right through you. You come off all arrogant and full of yourself, but deep down? You're shitting your pants. 'Cause you know it's just a matter of time before Kate is done with you."

My brow furrows in mock confusion. "I'm sorry—I don't speak vagina. Just what the hell is that supposed to mean?"

He moves forward, so we're nose to nose, like boxers before the bell. "It means newsflash, dickhead—you're the rebound guy. A distraction. Kate will have her fun, and then she'll move on to more permanent prospects."

I laugh. "Like you?"

"I do have the whole rock star thing going for me, don't I?"

Kate said he signed a record deal a few months back, and I've heard a few of his songs on the radio. But I don't care how many records he sells—he'll always be a douche bag to me. Though he's got a point about the rock star thing. It's a powerful force. Guys who look like Mick Jagger or Steven Tyler wouldn't have a shot in hell at getting laid without it, and they've spent decades shoulder deep in pussy.

"But no, not me," he says. "Kate and I are in the past. That doesn't mean she's sticking with you, though. How long have you known her, Evans? Eight months? I dated her for eleven years and I was her friend for nine before that. I think I'm a lot more qualified to predict what Kate will or won't do."

Okay—that one hit a little too close to home. It's one of the reasons I hate the fact that Kate still talks to him. Because he had her before I did. I don't mean the sex; I could deal with that. I'm talking about the fact that she loved him, came close to marrying him. So no matter what I do—no matter how good Kate and I are—I'll never be her first where it counts. And that sucks. Second place is just first loser.

But I'll eat my own tongue before I admit that to fuck-face.

"You're talking out your ass. I know Kate. I—"

He cuts me off with a shoulder nudge. "You know what Kate *lets* you know. I had a front-row seat to every significant moment in her life, asshole. Twenty years worth of memories will *always* mean more to her than *you* ever—"

Not to go all Popeye on you? But that's all I can stand and . . . well . . . you know the fucking rest.

I pull back and punch him right in the jaw. Iron Mike's got nothing on me right now, and it feels great. I should've done this months ago.

Warren staggers back. I expect him to come back swinging and I'm ready for the block. What I don't expect is for him to tackle me low in the waist with the skill of a NY Giants linebacker.

We fall back in a heap, taking out the pasta station behind

us with a crowd-drawing crash. Marinara sauce flies everywhere, raining down on unsuspecting heads and spattering people's clothes. Kind of looks like the pigs' blood scene in *Carrie,* doesn't it?

Now, contrary to popular belief, these kinds of things don't go down like they do in the movies. Those fights are planned out. Choreographed. Real-life guy fights involve more rolling around on the ground, cursing and grunting, while getting in the occasional punch or kick between the verbal jabs.

Watch.

We roll over till we're side by side. I straight-arm him, holding on to the front of his shirt. I get in a nice right hook to his chin, drawing first blood. With a growl he flips over so he's on top, straddling my waist. He nails me in the eye from the left.

I shake it off and grind out, "My sister hits harder than that. Pussy."

He grits his teeth, holding me down at the chest. "Suck my dick."

I bring my leg up and knee him in the back. "You'd like that, wouldn't you? Oh, no, that's right—*you* wouldn't. Kate sucks fantastic cock, by the way. You don't know what you were missing all those years, you fucking idiot."

Yeah—I know.

I can't believe I just said that either. In front of a room full of people. In front of Kate's *mother.*

And if the horrified gasp that sounds suspiciously like my girlfriend's voice is any indication? There's an excellent chance I'll go the rest of my life without ever getting head again.

Still, it was a great comeback, wasn't it?

Without warning, the scent of coffee fills the air. And a second later my legs are burning. It's scorching, like the boiling oil castle guards used to pour down on the invaders in Medieval times.

"Ahh! Christ!"

Instantly, Warren and I forget about knocking each other's teeth out. We're too busy trying to get away from the sizzling liquid that's being poured on us.

I look up into the diabolical eyes of Amelia Warren, who's proudly holding two stainless steel carafes that used to be filled with coffee. And now aren't.

She reaches down and grabs my ear with one hand and Warren's with the other. And we're immobilized. Immediately. Amelia Warren—pain in the ass by day, ninja warrior by night.

She drags us out of the room by our respective ears, not unlike Sister Beatrice would have in the good old days. But we don't go quietly.

"Ow . . . fuck . . . oooowwww!"

"Aunt Amelia, let go! I'm a musician, I need my ear!"

"Stop your whining! Beethoven was deaf and he did just fine."

We're dragged toward an adjoining room. Out of the corner of my eye I see Kate tagging along. Arms folded, back stiff—not a good sign for me. She opens the door and the four of us walk in.

And we all stop dead in our tracks.

Because there, on an empty table, is none other than Kate's mother, Carol, and Steven's father—good old quiet, number-crunching George Reinhart—going at it hot and heavy like two teenagers in the backseat at a drive-in movie theater.

I shit you not.

Kate's mouth opens wide, disbelief clear in her exclamation. "*Mom?*"

I raise my brows. "Wow. Go, George."

Have I mentioned that Kate's mom is smokin' hot? She is. Very.

She's in her fifties, with wavy russet hair, familiar dark eyes with the barest of wrinkles, and a warm smile. Her body's softly rounded with age, but still petite. The best way to tell how a woman's going to look in her later years is to look at her mother. If I didn't know I was a lucky son of a bitch before? The moment I laid eyes on Carol Brooks, I was sure of it.

Carol and George bust apart like they're on fire, sputtering embarrassed apologies as they readjust their clothing. Carol's face reminds me of that pink dog on *Blue's Clues*. Guess that's where Kate gets the blushing thing from. George straightens his tie, trying his best to look dignified—like he wasn't just caught with his hands on Carol's fun bags.

He nods in our direction. "Boys. Kate."

I wave.

Then Kate sputters, "Mom, the photographer needs you." Carol seems relieved to have an exit strategy, and they scurry out the door. Amelia-san releases her kung fu grip on my lobe and turns on her heels like a drill sergeant.

I try to lighten the mood. "Boy . . . didn't see that one coming, huh?"

Kate frowns. And Amelia pokes me in the chest. "Even though you are not my responsibility, if I ever hear such profane filth out of your mouth again, I will hog-tie you, hold your nose, and pour dish detergent down your throat like your mother should have a long time ago! Am I clear, mister?"

Her wrath turns to Warren. "And you—for God's sake, act like you have some sense! If you think you're too old for me to take the belt to, you are sorely mistaken, young man. I raised you better than this."

He looks down. "Yes, ma'am."

"I expect you boys to stay on opposite sides of the room the rest of the evening. Any more trouble from either of you, and I'll have you thrown out on your asses." In a huff she walks out of the room, with Warren trailing behind her like a stray puppy.

Leaving Kate and me alone.

Chapter 3

The silence is heavy. Awkward. Kate paces angrily, her movements sharp. She finally comes to a stop in front of me. "I don't even know what to say to you."

I squirm—just a little. "He started it."

Her eyes narrow. "Are you serious?"

I think about it for a minute. "Kind of."

Kate shakes her head. And her chocolate eyes turn wounded. "Do my feelings mean so little to you, Drew?"

I groan. "Come on, Kate. Don't do that."

"Do what?"

"Make this into some big thing about me not respecting you, or caring about you enough. It's really not that complicated. I hate him. I hate that he's here. I hate that you fucking talk to him."

She folds her arms over her chest. "We've been over this—Billy was my friend long before you and I got involved. We grew up together. Like you and Matthew and Steven. You know what that's like."

I do. There's nothing on earth more valuable than an old friend. Someone who understands you, knows why you are who you are, why you do what you do. No explanations needed.

"Matthew and Steven haven't seen me naked." And if they have, they certainly haven't enjoyed it.

"Half the city has seen you naked, Drew."

"Nameless women who mean—"

"Women who we run into every time we step outside the door!"

My voice rises. "I can't help that!"

Hers rises more. "I never asked you to!"

"Then why the fuck are you bringing it up?"

I can feel the discussion spiraling, gaining momentum like a tornado about to touch down. I push a hand through my hair and force my voice to level out. Not exactly calm, but reasonable.

"What if I told you it was him or me—that you couldn't have us both in your life? What would you say?"

Kate stutters, "Are you . . . are you giving me an ultimatum?"

"No. Just a hypothetical. If I told you that, who would you pick?"

Her eyes stare past me, thinking it over. The fact that she even needs to think about it bothers me more than I can put into words.

Then she looks back at my face. "I'd pick you. Billy's my past and I care about him very much. But you're my future."

I let out a relieved breath. Too soon, it turns out, because then she adds, "But I'd resent you for it, Drew. It would hurt me . . . hurt us."

I know I should tell her that she doesn't have to choose. That just knowing she'd pick me is enough. I should—but I don't.

And a second later she's making a beeline for the door. "I have to go help Delores."

I follow behind her. "Hey, we're not finished here."

Her hand's on the doorknob. "Yes, I realize that, but I can't deal with this at the moment, okay? Just . . . stay away from Billy and we'll talk later."

And in a whirl of shiny hair, she's gone.

I walk back into the main ballroom and lean up against the wall, watching the middle-aged, half-gagged, designer-clad guests trying to get their groove on.

My sister Alexandra walks up and leans back against the wall beside me. "Interesting show. Much better than anything WWE's come out with recently."

I scowl. "Not now, Lex."

She shrugs. "Okay. Just happened to see you floating up shit's creek and thought I'd throw you a paddle. But if you're not interested . . ."

She lets the offer hang.

Until I turn my attention to her. "What?"

She sighs. "You're new to this whole thing, so I'm going to give you some advice. Relationships only work when both parties put the other person's feelings before their own. Without that? Things tend to implode rather quickly. Let's take Matthew and Delores, for instance. It's obvious she doesn't like you very much, but she doesn't let that come between them. How do you think he would feel if she told Matthew she didn't want him talking to you anymore?"

I'm already shaking my head. "It's not the same thing."

"Not to you. But to Kate, it's exactly the same thing."

I clench my fists, frustrated. "So what are you saying? I have to invite the guy over to my place for a freaking slumber party? Do each other's nails?"

She rolls her eyes. "No, you don't have to be friends with him. You just have to suck it up and accept the fact that Kate is."

I fold my arms and look around the room, purposely not acknowledging her counsel.

She shrugs. "Or don't. Ignore everything I'm saying, let your insecurities get the better of you, and completely disregard Kate's feelings on the matter." She pats my shoulder.

"Let me know how that works out for you."

Then she walks away. While I stand there. Pouting—yes, I'm aware.

I scan the room and find Kate, talking to Delores. She smiles at something her friend says, but her eyes don't. It's fake. A cover.

Fuck.

And then I spot Warren, sitting at the bar. I look back and forth between the two.

Then I let out a big breath and walk over. I nod to the bartender. "Whiskey. Double."

Eating shit? Doesn't taste very good. I'm going to need something to wash it down.

An hour later, I've learned three things about Billy Warren:

1) He loves music.

2) He's really into his new truck.

3) He can't hold his liquor for shit.

Douche Bag is a total lightweight. Which, for me, is a good thing—a drunk guy is usually an honest guy.

". . . custom leather seats as soft as a baby's ass . . ."

Blah blah blah. I've tuned him out for a while now. It's the only way I've been able to stop myself from getting as trashed as he is. But warm-up time is over now. Might as well get right to the point.

"So listen, Billy, I need you to level with me—man to man. You looking to hook up with Kate again, or what?"

His face wrinkles. "Nah, man . . . me and Kate . . . that's like so yesterday. We were done way before we were done. Water over the bridge."

"Under."

"Exactly. Started too young. I mean, I love the girl, always will. Not like . . . in a sister kind of way exactly, 'cause we've done it . . ."

So don't need to hear this right now.

". . . but almost. Her and Delores, they're like my inner sanctum. For a long time it was just the three of us against the world, you know what I'm sayin'?"

I digest this information while he takes a drag of his beer.

Then he leans forward and his voice drops low, like he's got a secret to tell. "She's happy, you know. Kate. These last few months, she's sounded really happy. More than she ever was with me, that's for damn sure. Dee-Dee says so, too."

He fingers the label on his beer bottle. "But you know how it is—the higher you climb, the farther you fall—and it's not like you're the sticking type. So when I think about how bad you're gonna hurt her? Pretty much makes me want to put a fucking bullet between your eyes."

Now *that*, I can respect.

I slap him on the back. Maybe a little harder than I needed to. "Tell you what, Billy—the day I hurt her? I'll buy you the gun."

His drunken eyes regard me suspiciously. Then he holds out his hand. And I shake it firmly.

Why are you so surprised? I can be mature. Sometimes. Besides, just because I've decided not to punch him in the face the next time I see him doesn't mean I'm going to give Kate all of his goddamn messages.

What do I look like? A saint?

Out of nowhere the lovely woman in question appears beside me, standing between our bar stools. "What's going on? What is this?"

I open my mouth to explain, but Warren beats me to it. "Relax, Katie. Me and Evans . . . just buryin' the old hammer."

"Hatchet."

"That too."

Her eyes flicker back and forth between us. I smile calmly. Reassuringly.

She's not convinced. "So, what? You two get into a fight, have a few beers, and now you're all buddy-buddy? You gonna go outside and pee on the wall together too?"

Warren holds up his hand. "Let's not get crazy. It's not like we're gonna hang out and play foosball or something. But if Evans here ever needs an extra hand with an assisted suicide?" He taps his chest. "I'm your guy."

I raise my glass. "Well said."

He downs a shot and stands up. "And on that note, I'm

gonna head over to that little hottie on the dance floor who's been givin' me the eye all night. Tell Aunt Amelia not to wait up. And hey, Evans—you should watch your back. This shindig is my cousin's deal, and we messed it up. Dee-Dee's not gonna let that slide."

I nod. "Thanks for the warning."

After he's gone, there's a moment of silence. And Kate looks sideways at me. "What's your game, Drew?"

I look surprised. Innocent. "Game? *Me*? No game. I just . . . like you more than I hate him. Simple, really."

She nods slowly, the corners of her mouth turning up in a half smile. "And you couldn't have had this little revelation before you announced my talent for fellatio to our family and friends?"

That probably would have been better.

"Yeah. Sorry about that. Got caught up in the moment. Although it was the truth and nothing but the truth, so help me God."

She snorts, shaking her head. "Jerk."

And with that, I know I'm in the clear. My hands circle her waist and pull her between my legs as I change the subject. "Have I told you how cock-stiffeningly gorgeous you look tonight?"

Kate smiles as she rests her forearms on my shoulders. "Not in the last few hours."

"Consider yourself told."

She leans in and lays her head against my chest.

And all is right with the world.

"Thank you, Drew."

And I know she means for more than just the compliment. I brush my face against her hair, inhaling the scent that still captivates me.

"Anytime, Kate. Anything."

Over her head, I spot Warren—and more important, the woman he's hitting on. And I start to laugh.

Kate's head pops up. "What?"

I motion with my chin. "Warren's talking to Christina Berman—a distant cousin of Matthew's."

She looks toward them. "And that's funny because . . . ?"

"Because up until a year ago, her dick was bigger than mine. She used to be a guy."

Kate's eyes bug out of her head. "Wow. You'd never know it, looking at her."

"Nope."

Then her gaze falls on me. Thoughtfully.

And I ask, "What?"

Her eyes shine. At me. For me. "Nothing. I just . . . I love you, you know."

I shrug. "I'm a lovable guy."

She laughs. And brings her palm to my cheek, smacking it softly. "And slappable—definitely a slappable guy."

"Kinky. We should explore that further, later on."

She chuckles again and kisses me softly. Then she pulls back and hooks her thumb toward the dance floor. "You want to dance?"

I'm almost offended. "'The Electric Slide'? I don't think so." Not that I have anything against dancing. Some guys will tell you it's effeminate, but I'm not one of them. Today's dancing is practically sex with your clothes on, dry humping in a room full of people. And I'm definitely into that.

"What? Too cool for the 'Electric Slide'?"

"Yes, I am. Besides, Steven has the monopoly on group

dances." I point over to where my brother-in-law is burning up the dance floor, at the head of the pack with Mackenzie at his side. "He also does a mean 'Funky Chicken.'"

Kate cracks up.

◈

A few hours later, we're all walking out to the private parking garage together. My tie's gone, the top three buttons of my shirt open. I'm holding Kate's hand, which is lost in the arm of my tuxedo jacket that she's wearing like a teenage girl after the prom. Steven carries a sleeping Mackenzie on his shoulder, while Alexandra adjusts her dress with one hand and holds her shoes in the other. Matthew and Delores are already outside, saying their final good-byes to the departing guests.

When he spots us, Matthew comes jogging up. His face is nervous—and remorseful.

"Drew . . . I didn't know, man. I'm really sorry."

"What are you talking about?"

He rubs the back of his neck and his eyes slide to my car, parked a few feet away at ground level, clearly visible under the garage light.

And that's when I see it. Or more to the point—that's when I see the words that have been carved into her hood.

GROW UP

"No, no, no, no, no . . ."

I stumble forward and fall to my knees beside my baby. I rub over the words, trying to erase the gouges with my hand. Then I yell over my shoulder at Delores, "You heartless monster! How could you?"

I turn back to my car and whisper soothingly, "It'll be okay. I'll get the best body guy in the city. It'll be like it never happened. No one will ever know you were scarred."

From the upper level I hear Billy Warren's wail of anguish, and I know Delores got to his new truck, too.

I feel your pain, Douche Bag.

Leisurely, Delores strolls over. She looks down at me, eyes mocking, one fingerless lace-gloved hand on her hip. "Pull any shit like that again and I'll carve it into your fucking forehead."

Then she smiles cheerily. "Night, everyone. Thank you for being a part of our special day."

And she disappears into the shadows.

I feel bad for Matthew's Guardian Angel. He's going to be working overtime.

'Cause I'm pretty sure my best friend just married a demon.

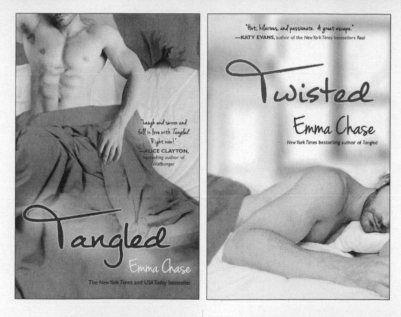